*Chasing Hindy*
by Darin Gibby

This is a work of fiction. The characters are both actual and fictitious. With the exception of verified historical events and persons, all incidents, descriptions, dialogue and opinions expressed are the products of the author's imagination and are not to be construed as real.

Published by

◤ köehlerbooks ™

210 60th Street
Virginia Beach, VA 23451
800-435-4811
www.koehlerbooks.com

# CHASING HINDY

## A NOVEL INVENTION

## DARIN GIBBY

*To my wife, Robin, for her patience in enduring
the fifteen years it took me to write this book.*

# 1

ADDY FELT LIKE jumping out of her car and doing a quick happy dance in the middle of stalled traffic. Her excitement at becoming the newest—and youngest—partner at the intellectual property law firm of Wyckoff & Schechter was nearly overwhelming.

She grinned at the shadow on the hood of Hindy, her treasured retrofitted cherry red Shelby Mustang. The shadow was created by a barrel-sized, hydrogen-filled balloon that floated above the Mustang's roof. Gawkers pointed and laughed as the Shelby eased down El Camino pulling the tethered balloon as if in a Macy's Thanksgiving Day parade. The balloon—which on one side sported her law firm's logo, and on the other *Hindy* in giant cursive script—was just an advertising gimmick to show her passion for alternative energies. It was only strapped to the roof on calm, sunny days when she was travelling at slow speeds using routes that avoided overpasses. The retrofitted Mustang was really powered by four electric motors using electricity produced by solar panels and a conventional fuel cell.

At first, the Wyckoff partners questioned Addy's prudence in strapping a floating balloon to the roof of any vehicle, but they'd come to admire the effectiveness of her marketing innovations. They even lifted their champagne glasses at the end of her mentor's welcome speech acknowledging that her Shelby was responsible for bringing in increasing numbers of the "green" companies sprouting like weeds all over the Silicon Valley— inventive, entrepreneurial companies in need of legal advice and support for their patents.

While the traffic inched forward, Addy chuckled with excitement. "Hindy, ol' pal," she said, patting the dashboard, "you and I are going places now! Next time some overzealous cops accuse you of being a traffic hazard, I'll stare them down and inform them they're messing with the partner of a highly prestigious law firm."

Traffic momentarily loosened and Addy eased Hindy forward, careful not to snap the lines tethering the egg-shaped balloon. Addy sang along with Zissy Spaeth, pop rock's newest and most flashy star, as Zissy belted out her latest hit, *Light in Your Eyes*, over the radio. In the corner of her eye she noticed a blaze of neon orange.

Her heart stopped. In the car next to her someone was pointing a bazooka-sized gizmo at her balloon. She blinked, trying to clear her vision.

A flare shot out, aimed straight at her floating ball of hydrogen.

Even in the late afternoon sunlight, it was impossible to miss the explosion. The dirigible burst into a giant fireball, then slowly deflated and floated down toward the Shelby's crimson hood.

Addy stomped on her brakes, hoping the balloon's momentum would shoot the flaming mass forward. The fireball, safely secured by its fluorescent yellow nylon tethers, crashed down onto the windshield, blocking Addy's view. She screeched to a halt, slammed her shoulder into the door, flung it open, and darted out, catching the heel of her pump on the doorjamb, which sent her sprawling headlong onto the pavement.

She heard tires squeal and at least a half dozen blaring horns. Stinging pain shot up from her elbow and knees. Thank goodness traffic had been just inching along.

Ignoring the pain, she bolted forward, arms raised, ready

to yank the still-burning fabric off the windshield. Before she got close enough to grab it, the sweltering heat from the flames scorched her cheeks, and she shielded her eyes with her forearm. Just when she reached the hood, a breeze lifted the infernal blob and propelled it directly at her, the nylon cords now seared through.

She braced herself for the fireball when she felt arms wrap around her chest and yank her back, barely in time to avoid the searing molten mass of goo about to descend on her head, threatening to fry her face and melt her hair.

"Are you crazy? What are you thinking?" a deep voice bellowed in her ear, still holding her tight.

Together they watched what was left of the blimp float like a falling leaf onto the grassy shoulder, just like the Hindenburg did almost eighty years ago.

"Someone clearly doesn't like you, short stuff," her rescuer said, now standing next to her stroking his goatee, his face hidden behind dark sunglasses and a low-riding Dodgers cap. "More like out to get you. That was some kind of flare the driver shot at your blimp. I tried to spot his license plate, but it was covered up. Snapped a picture with my phone, though," the man said fishing it from his pocket. "You can kind of see a tattoo on his forearm. The police will love this."

Before she could thank him, someone cried out, "Call a fire truck! The grass!"

Brush fires in California were no joking matter. Addy could smell the smoldering grasses. A strong breeze fanned the flames, pushing the fire toward a row of redwood trees.

Then she heard a whiny voice coming from the milling crowd of stranded passengers who'd gathered to find out what was holding up their homeward commute. "I've seen that blimp before. I knew it was trouble," the whiner complained.

"Yeah, but at least she's part of the solution," said someone else. "Her car doesn't use gasoline. Look at what you're driving," he said, sneering at the whiny woman's crossover SUV.

Addy's knees buckled, her head spinning. She plopped down onto the pavement and hugged her bare legs. This couldn't be happening.

Why would someone try to destroy her car? Hindy, her

beloved Mustang, was just a marketing ploy, no worse than a billboard. Hindy's fuel cell and solar panels were just two modern technologies that Addy hoped someday would become mainstream to the automotive industry. And her purpose was noble. Her "green" car told the world of inventors that she was one of them, that she would secure their patents and protect their investments. Now her expensive marketing project was in jeopardy.

Soon, swarms of firefighters were scrambling around dousing the flames, while police officers attempted to reroute traffic. A well-built bald man flipped out a paper pad and scribbled a few notes. After removing his sunglasses, he swapped the pad for a pocket camera and snapped random shots of the avid crowd.

All four local networks had sent news crews, and Addy knew two of the reporters. They had already run stories about Hindy, praising Addy's creative marketing, which one reporter said was a refreshing change from the barrage of personal injury commercials littering daytime television.

As Addy told the reporter during her interview, Silicon Valley was going to be known, not just for starting the computer revolution and launching the social networking scene, but now for making the world green. And Addy was their lawyer.

Reality burst her daydream bubble when she was whisked aside by a team of Sunnyvale police officers. She told them what had transpired, hoping it would help them find the sniper. And she pointed out her rescuer, who was showing another pair of police officers the photo on his phone.

At the end of the interview, one of the officers handed her a ticket. "You were carrying a flammable substance without a permit. You'll need to make a court appearance."

Addy gasped. "But they shot at me."

"And we're not taking it lightly. There's been a serious crime committed here, but that doesn't mean you can break the law. If you hadn't been toting that blimp, none of this would have happened."

Addy's eyes narrowed. "Am I free to go?" she said, snatching the paperwork and turning toward Hindy.

"Yes," the officer said, "but we're going to need to impound your vehicle."

Addy halted. "Hindy? You can't."

The other officer beckoned with both hands, big gestures, as if directing an airplane to the gate. A tow truck wedged its way through the onlookers and began backing up in front of Hindy.

"But Hindy works perfectly fine," Addy protested. "The balloon, that was all for show. The hydrogen for the fuel cell is where the gas tank used to be."

The officer shook her head. "We need your car for evidence. As I said, a serious crime has just been committed, and we need to take the vehicle to the station for a thorough evaluation."

"But I need to get home, and get to work tomorrow."

"There's always Uber," said the officer with a shrug.

# 2

THE OFFICES OF Wyckoff & Schechter were located at the intersection of Lytton and Waverly. It was a coveted corner in the heart of Palo Alto, in large part because of its proximity to an assortment of eclectic shops and quaint restaurants serving nearly every kind of ethnic cuisine.

Addy crept off the elevator and sidled down the hall to her office, shoulders hunched and collar covering her face. It was bad enough she was still freaked out about being shot at, but, honestly, the prospect of the partners' collective frown was worse.

The television perched in front of a leather couch was running a story about oil production, with a tickertape of stock prices scrolling along the bottom of the screen. Addy paused to see if the Hindy story was still on the news. She had already seen news coverage last night. The demise of Hindy's balloon had gone viral before she even had time to wonder whether that kind of attention would be a boon or a detriment to her career.

At least she'd been able to spend the evening figuring out what to say to the partners so they wouldn't summarily demote—or worse—fire her. She was toying with the idea of disappearing into her office until she'd sent out a partner email summarizing everything that had happened. Or maybe she'd do a mass voicemail.

Hector, the receptionist, looked over his bifocals and pointed his pen behind his head in the direction of her mentor's office.

*Well, scratch that plan.* "Perry wants to see me already?" she asked Hector.

Hindy wasn't just about her legal practice. Like most patent attorneys, she had a secret dream that someday a client with a world-changing invention would walk into her office and offer her part of the company if she'd help them secure their patents. It did happen, but not often. When it did, those patent attorneys were set for life. For Addy, though, being a patent attorney was all about discovering a new energy source. She wanted her name in the history books next to Edison, Bell, or Philo T. Farnsworth. What just happened to Hindy's balloon might, ironically, help her cause. But was being shot at worth it?

Toting her briefcase, she strode around behind the reception desk, placing her hand on the door handle. She hesitated and took a deep breath, expecting the worst. Addy swung the door open.

Perry Tomkins, her mentor, was seated behind his desk. He stood and pushed one of his unbuttoned white shirtsleeves up above his elbow, his lavender satin silk tie swaying. Dressing up was a habit the old partners just couldn't seem to shake.

His wry smile contrasted with the bags under his eyes and deep creases in his forehead. His mane of thick black hair was both sprinkled with silver and graying around the ears. Addy gulped, hoping she hadn't compounded his troubles with yesterday's spectacle.

The past month had not been kind to Perry. Normally, this senior patent attorney was the life of the office, but Keri, his wife of nearly a quarter century, had passed away after a long fight with breast cancer.

With no children of their own, the older couple had made Addy somewhat of a goddaughter, and Addy welcomed the family connection. She, too, had felt the pain with Keri's passing. And she couldn't bear the thought of disappointing Perry, especially not now.

He gave her a warm smile and gestured her to one of the armchairs in a corner of the office.

"Perry, I—," she began.

"Nothing's changed, Addy," he said. "So stop fidgeting. In fact, the partners—I mean *the rest* of the partners—consulted, and we're cautiously pleased about the news coverage. Two of them even called you a crusading green lawyer.

"I'm sorry there wasn't time to explain this last night," Perry continued, "because I'm sure you were up half the night worrying, but the partners see the green practice as the next big thing, and you were promoted to partner so you can run the new green division. So many of our practice groups are struggling with languishing client bases, so the firm needs a new source of work.

"And that's you, Addy. We've tried to teach partners how to make their mark in the community, how to reach out and connect with clients, but they just can't seem to do it. The days of hanging out at the country club to get new clients are over. What you're doing with Hindy, with your commitment to a better future, that's what the new generation of clients wants to see in their lawyers. The partners not only want you to head up the green practice, but we need you to teach us old fogeys how to re-energize and reinvent our practices."

Addy sat back, stunned. Yes, she'd worked hard and had gained a reputation for getting patents on green technologies, ideas like more efficient solar panels, LED lights, and wind turbines, but did that warrant making her a partner two years early?

Perhaps it was because she was a woman, because her birth parents were Vietnamese, and the firm was under pressure to diversify its partnership. Or was it really because of her congeniality, for her unique way of attracting clients, for her business savvy, as Perry had just said? Did they really want her to change the conservative culture of Wyckoff & Schechter?

"You could start with a new wardrobe," she joked, leaning closer to tug on Perry's lavender tie.

An uneasy silence settled over the room, and she carefully smoothed down the bright satin tie. Last time she'd teased him about the way he dressed, he'd made a joke about her wearing jeans to work, so this silence unnerved her.

Perry stood and walked her to the door. "Oh, one more thing," he said. "You know your car made the national news, right? Is there anything the partnership should be worried about?"

"No, not at all. It was no big deal. I mean it was a big deal getting shot at and seeing my blimp go up in flames, but it was just a random act of violence. The police said so, too. It will all blow over."

Perry smiled. "For now, what we need is to have you out there taking advantage of the publicity, and showing us old folks how to make a dent in the new markets. I'm very proud of you, Addy. Now get to work and make us even more famous so you can pour even more pots of money into our coffers."

# 3

STANDING IN FRONT of his closet, Agent Jesse Long strapped on his holster and pulled his argyle sweater over his shoulders, which had grown broad from throwing hay bales as a teenager. Now, they were mostly used as a pillow for his infant son.

He looked down at the empty bed. All the covers were pulled to his side, because the other side had been empty for at least half the night.

A cry, almost a squeak, came from the baby's room down the hall. Jesse hurried toward the garage, hoping not to awaken his exhausted wife. As he passed the second bedroom, he cocked his ear and listened to the stirring of his wife of just over a year.

"Goodbye honey," she whispered through the door. "Don't forget to comb your hair."

"Got it," he said.

It was a joke between them. At forty-nine, he was prematurely bald, and he shaved off the small bit of hair above his ears to keep him from looking a decade older.

Long had started his family late in life. He'd grown up on a cattle ranch in Wyoming and thought riding the rodeo circuit was going to be his career. But that dream ended when a bull crushed his right shoulder. He attended the University of Wyoming in Laramie. After that, he joined the FBI, hoping it would take him far away from the windswept plains to see the world.

That he'd done, tracking terrorists in places like Afghanistan, Columbia, and Thailand. He met Laura at a grocery store in San Francisco when stocking up after a two-month training stint in Washington, D.C. She was forty and had also never been married, and they both felt it was time to settle down.

She desperately wanted a family, and since her biological clock was ticking down toward its expiration date, they didn't wait. She was pregnant six weeks after their honeymoon. They pooled their life savings and purchased a two-bedroom home in Brisbane with a large mortgage. They'd wanted to live in the city, but skyrocketing real estate prices in San Francisco made that option a non-starter.

Now they had a baby boy just shy of four weeks old.

He cracked the garage door, squeezed through, and switched his phone back on. He received a notification that his office had a text containing a photo.

He studied the image on his cell phone while he opened the door to his Buick. It showed a photo of a man pointing a flare gun—and it revealed the fuzzy image of a tattoo on the man's forearm. It looked Arabic, but it could just have easily been Greek. The accompanying message indicated that the photo was submitted anonymously.

*ID?* Jesse texted back.

*Nothing yet, can't even figure out what it says*, came the answer.

*Going to forensics lab*, Jesse typed back, then plopped himself in his car and activated the garage door opener.

*Hindy*, he thought. *Funny name. Why would this guy shoot a toy blimp?* He was going to find out.

# 4

BY THE NEXT day, Addy had learned that getting to work without a car was a painful lesson in green austerity.

By the time she arrived, she'd missed two scheduled phone calls, one with a patent examiner, and another with an inventor trying to patent a new type of ceramic specially designed for a hydrogen fuel cell. And the emails were piling up. Addy hung up the phone just as Perry sauntered in and closed the door. He collapsed in the sole chair in front of her desk.

"Got a minute?"

"No, but I suppose we should talk. Have a seat."

He smiled and straightened his tie, then gazed out the window at the neighboring Indian restaurant. In the courtyard, a couple was sipping coffee, enjoying the morning sunshine. Perry linked his hands behind his head and stretched out.

Addy bit her lower lip and tried to calm herself. She worried that this would be a long conversation.

"I've seen a lot over the last three decades. Semiconductors booming, then busting, Apple rising from the dust, ten thousand internet companies coming and going, the dominance of Google and Facebook."

"Silicon Valley is the place to be if you want to be a successful inventor," Addy said.

Perry stood and went to the window. Addy looked up to the ceiling and told herself to relax.

"And the best thing that happened to me over those fast-paced years," Perry's breath hitched, "was Keri."

His head dropped forward, his shoulders heaving slightly. She couldn't decide whether to go comfort him or pretend it wasn't happening. Any display of emotion was completely out of character for him. Perry, the highest-paid partner in the firm, was all about business. His world revolved around himself and his clients.

"I'm so sorry," she said when she realized he truly was on the ragged edge emotionally.

Perry stood and tried to compose himself. He kept his back to her while he spoke.

"I had no idea I would miss her this much. Perry and Keri, people often joked about how we were such a good match." Perry turned to face her, his eyes moist. "We tried to have children, but it never worked out. Keri could never get pregnant. We tried every test, went to see every fertility specialist. We never adopted because we both believed one day it would magically happen. But it never did. You should know that Keri was so happy when she first met you. You were like the daughter she never had."

Addy felt sorry for Perry's loss and appreciated what he'd done to make her partner, but she also wondered if Keri was the real reason behind the special treatment. She wanted no part of nepotism. She wanted to earn her success. Still, his story resonated.

"I guess we both know what it's like to be alone in the world," she said.

Perry nodded. Over dinner one night, she'd shared her story with him, about being born in Vietnam, then put up for adoption by her birth parents. She was adopted by an American couple living in Cyprus, California, but their fairy-tale family never worked out. Addy grew up with the understanding that her adoptive father had fallen out of love with his wife two years after the adoption. After that, he completely disappeared from Addy's life.

Her adoptive mother had been unable to deal with the divorce, which led to alcohol addiction, then pot, then meth. Addy fended for herself by hanging out at friends' houses, devouring whatever she was offered from their refrigerators, and sometimes even sleeping on their couches. Through high school, Addy clung to the belief that the only things she could trust in life were getting good grades, making a life for herself, and being on her own.

Along the way, she also fell in love with science. *Science never lets you down,* she often thought. It was the one thing she could fully trust. Her hard work paid off when she was accepted to MIT, funded almost completely by the university's scholarship fund for the underprivileged.

Addy sometimes wondered whether Perry even remembered the story of her traumatic upbringing. Even if he did, had he ever realized the significance of what she told him? Did Perry even care about her life? Did he have any compassion in his soul? Did he realize what it was like to grow up alone? Now that he'd lost Keri, perhaps a few of the scales covering his hardened heart were ready to fall.

"I didn't come here to feel sorry for myself," he said, quickly returning to the business at hand. "I need a favor. I have your first assignment as a partner."

Addy perked up. This was the Perry she knew, barking out orders.

"With Keri's passing, there are a thousand loose ends I need to tie up. I'm supposed to attend the Asian patent conference next week in Hanoi, but I just can't make it. I need you to go in my place."

Addy's eyes widened. She had a passion for travel, but she'd never been outside the United States as an adult.

Every year a large part of the Asian patent profession met in a different city to discuss the latest patent trends, and, more importantly, to do business with each other. Every country had its own patent laws, which meant that in order to patent a product globally, a separate patent application had to be lodged in every target country. Because every foreign jurisdiction had its own rules about what was and wasn't patentable, it was necessary to retain local patent attorneys in each country. The

annual gathering was where those filings could be coordinated—
and new business secured.

"You've got a great jump start on your client base, but you're
going to need more to move up the partner ranks. You've got
the perfect background for this conference, being from Vietnam
and all."

Addy bristled, straightening her spine. She'd always sensed
his lack of enthusiasm for any firm program with even a hint
of diversity. Sure, he said all the right words at firm events, but
deep down she questioned his commitment to helping anyone
who wasn't white.

"Perry, need I remind you that I don't speak Vietnamese, or
Japanese, or Korean, just a little bit of Spanish that I learned in
my *American* high school."

"I didn't mean it that way," he responded quickly. "I just
meant that . . . Well, forget what I said. What I mean is that
over the years I've developed a large network of international
patent attorneys, and they feed the firm millions of dollars. I
think you're the right person to take over for me, and now is the
perfect time, regardless of where you were born."

Addy nodded. Blunder or not, she was thrilled. Not only
would she get to visit her birthplace but there was a vast, new
market for her to tap into. She'd go the first year, learn the
ropes, soak up the etiquette and protocols, then be prepared the
following year with a strategy.

"I'll go," she said. "It sounds like a great opportunity. Thanks
for thinking of me."

"I'll email you the details and the itinerary. You're going to be
extremely busy, because I already have about twenty meetings
set up. Be prepared for jet lag, and try not to get too frustrated
if you can't understand broken English. You're going to hear a
lot of it. Why don't you connect with Janice to see if she can
handle your docket while you're away? With the time difference,
it is next to impossible to keep up with day-to-day matters while
you're overseas."

She smiled. Perry did love to hover. "I'll manage."

# 5

THE THIRTY-MINUTE CAB ride from the Hanoi airport to the conference hotel was one of contrasts. Modern electronics plants made up of campuses dotted with an assortment of factories, office buildings, and stacked parking garages, intermingled with ramshackle huts similar to the favelas in Rio or the cardboard shacks of Tijuana.

When her taxi exited the three-lane freeway it was immediately surrounded by bicycles, rickshaws, and motorbikes, which altogether outnumbered the automobiles five to one. Still, the traffic was fluid, with the small vehicles weaving around the automobiles like water flowing around boulders in a stream.

The streets were lined with cheaply-built storefronts enabling Vietnamese shop owners to hustle potential buyers inside for some inexpensive silk scarves or local Vietnamese cuisine. Her hotel, the new five-star JW Marriott, was shaped like a dragon and looked out over miles of sheet-metal shacks, where wood stove pipes spewed smoke into the air when the poverty-stricken residents cooked their meals.

After being shown her room, Addy changed into business attire, collected her conference materials, and dashed off to the welcome reception at the conference center. It was so humid, her back was covered with sweat by the time she slipped into her seat and clipped on her official badge, one that had Perry's name crossed out and her own handwritten beneath it.

By the time she was seated, the opening ceremony had already droned on for about an hour, with obligatory speeches given by elderly Asian men in broken English, the official language of the conference. Next, the entertainment featured local Vietnamese folk dancers in brightly colored costumes. While they whirled and danced, Addy slipped out her phone, checked a few emails, and waited for the meeting to end.

A formal reception followed, with catered hors d'oeuvres. Addy didn't recognize anyone among the sea of brown faces, mostly older men with gray hair. Her stomach growled, and she snatched up the first morsel offered, a piece of coconut shrimp, then stood behind a table half concealed by a large plant, strategizing various ways to drum up new business.

Still hungry, and feeling awkward standing alone, she loaded up a plate at the buffet and returned to the small table, fishing out her phone, and pulling up her calendar so she would look busy. She had an early morning breakfast meeting with three Japanese attorneys whose firm name she recognized from some of the cases they were handling for her own firm.

"Mind if I join you?

Addy looked up, then fumbled her phone, sending it skidding across the table. Her visitor's hand shot out and snatched it before it hit the floor. Her gaze followed his sleeve up to his broad shoulders, which were draped with a hand-stitched collar. She could feel the heat in her cheeks and wondered if he noticed her blush. His clean-shaven face was vaguely familiar, as was the sound of his resonant, baritone voice.

"That would have been a disaster," she said.

"We've all done it," he said with a beaming smile, revealing a set of large, extra-white teeth. He handed back the phone. "I'm Quinn Moon."

"Addy," she said, taking back her phone.

"Formerly Perry."

Her mouth twisted until Quinn pointed to her badge, where her mentor's name was still visible through the strike-through.

"Last minute substitution. Perry's one of the partners at our firm. He couldn't make it, some family business. I'm his proxy."

"Then this is your first time at the conference?"

"Yes, and I feel totally lost. All these people I don't know, speaking in languages that make my head spin."

"You're American?"

"What makes you guess that?"

"Your accent, and your firm name. Wyckoff. I've known them for years. They have a stellar reputation."

Addy studied Quinn's tag. Unlike all the other name badges, she didn't see a law firm associated with his name.

"Your English is nearly perfect. But you're not American."

"No, don't I look like it?"

"No more than I do. I was actually born in Vietnam but raised in the States. But don't expect me to speak Vietnamese."

"Fair enough. Tell me a little about yourself."

Addy gave him a quick précis of her background.

"Didn't go to Stanford?"

"I wish. Couldn't get accepted. I'm not a good test taker. The LSAT wasn't kind to me."

"Looks like it all turned out. Partner, I assume?"

She studied his dark brown eyes, his muscular shoulders and neck, and strong cheekbones. His build was anything but slight. "Just made partner last week, but enough about me. Tell me about yourself."

"Well, congratulations," he said, ignoring her request. "Not easy today to make partner, especially with a firm like Wyckoff. You must be good."

"I can't read the name of your firm," she said, cutting him off.

He raised his badge. "Missing, isn't it? My secretary was late filling out the registration form. I'm associated with a small Korean firm. Hey, by the way, if you know anything about clean tech, I may have a client you'd be interested in."

She straightened and pushed away her plate. "Very interested."

Quinn raised his hand and beckoned a passing waiter toting a silver tray with an assortment of wines. "We'll take two of the reds."

The woman's white-gloved hand swiftly slid a pair of wine glasses onto their small table.

"Here's to your first time in Vietnam," Quinn said raising his glass.

Addy's glass remained on the table. "I'm afraid I should have asked for a soda," she said. "I don't drink."

"Really? Not just a little wine every now and then?"

"No, not ever. Sorry to ruin your toast."

"What?" Quinn probed. "Something religious? Training for a marathon or something like that?"

"I wish it were that easy. It's more like alcohol hasn't been a friend to my family. It's best if I just avoid it entirely."

Quinn frowned. "I'm so sorry. I totally understand family drama. Why don't we talk about something more cheerful? What do you know about fuel cells?"

Addy perked up. "My car's got one under the hood. Well, until—" she stopped herself. Quinn didn't need to know about her recent run-in with the law. "I'd love to see the day when the gasoline engine is a relic."

"Might happen sooner than you think."

"What makes you say that?"

"Lots of people are working on a solution."

"Including you?"

Quinn took a small sip from his glass. "We should talk once you're settled in."

Addy's phone beeped, and she dove to snatch it off the table. Janice, her paralegal, had sent her a text. Addy plucked it up before he could read the message.

*Hindy's going to stay impounded. Call Perry ASAP*, the text read. Addy bit her lower lip.

Quinn raised his eyebrows. "Problem at home?"

"Something's come up at the office. I've got to run. Can we talk later?"

Quinn slipped his fingers into his shirt pocket and handed her a business card. "Send me a text before you leave. I'll treat you to a soda," he said with a wink.

The walk from the convention center to the hotel was short, but meandered through a dimly lit, rickety neighborhood. Addy had been assured that in Communist Vietnam crime wasn't a problem. If a nationalist ever attacked a tourist, the consequences were so severe, execution wasn't out of the question.

Patent attorneys who'd had their fill of small talk straggled out of the convention center in small groups, bound for their hotels. Addy joined a small group, mostly attorneys from Singapore, who were going in her direction. After a few blocks, they passed a small boutique hotel, and her companions excused themselves, leaving her alone. Luckily, her towering hotel was within sight. Addy picked up her pace and avoided any shadows while she scurried along the dirt sidewalk and passed corrugated metal shutters covering the now-closed shops.

As she sidestepped a deserted food stand, a man leapt out of a darkened alley. His thin leather sandals skated silently over the pavement. Addy stepped aside to avoid him, but he was coming too fast. She could see his coarse black whiskers dance when he smiled, revealing a mouthful of brown teeth.

"You look beautiful in that skirt. You know, I could make one for you."

Addy put her hand over her chest and took a deep breath the moment she realized this was a tailor trying to peddle his wares, not some maniac.

"I'm late for a phone call, and I need to get back to my hotel right now. Maybe tomorrow I can come see you."

Addy's mind raced. *What if he attacks? What should I do?* A female in a communist country, alone. She shook her head. No, nothing like that would ever happen. Perry assured her that she would be safe, that tourists were worshiped.

"Come on in, come in, let me show you," he said waving his hand toward the alley.

Addy slowly took a few steps back. "I'm okay."

He waved again, this time swinging his shoulder. "You really need to come inside. Now," he snapped.

*Someone help me,* she prayed. *I don't even know where to find the American Embassy.*

From behind, she heard more scuffles. Footsteps. Someone else was behind her. She was boxed in with nowhere to run. She slowly twisted her head, like an owl looking for prey. Behind her was a man with a dark complexion dressed in a black button-down shirt with the sleeves rolled up and a dark splotch on one arm.

Addy decided to do nothing other than stand erect and confident. If they wanted her in the shop, they would have to drag her kicking and screaming.

The man in front of her continued in his thick Vietnamese accent. "You should go back to America. Now, before anything happens."

"You must have the wrong person," Addy responded. "I am a patent attorney, here at a conference. You've seen us in your store."

She realized he couldn't possibly understand what she was saying. She pointed to the only building that rose above the shacks. "My hotel."

The man took a small step toward her, and Addy contemplated crashing an elbow into his nose. Realizing the odds were against her, Addy turned to run. But as she did, her heel caught the edge of a cobblestone and she tripped, sending her sprawling onto the pavement where her forehead struck the ground. Immediately, a pair of muscular arms wrapped about her, hefting her upright. Her nose burned with the smell of a strange liquor. She felt a stinging sensation above her left eye.

Her initial assailant lunged forward, craning his head toward her face. "Go home to where you belong. No talking to anyone. Vietnam doesn't want you. And, trust me, you don't want to talk to anyone here at the conference. Nobody. Mind your own business. If anyone approaches you to talk about some invention, you leave it alone. Just leave it alone." He stepped closer, their noses nearly touching. "Understand?"

Addy nodded slowly.

The strong, ruthless arms of the person behind her shoved her forward, toward her hotel, snapping her head back.

She mustered her courage and turned to face the man who had shoved her. "You must have the wrong person. This is a mistake."

He shook his head. "We know you've spoken to a Korean named Quinn. Twice. Once in America, now here."

Addy gaped at him. Yes, she'd just had a conversation with such a person, but not in America. And this man spoke perfect English. She tried to see his face, but his baseball cap was pulled low, casting a dark shadow across his face. "But—" she protested.

"Your car, the one with the blimp. He was right behind you. We saw him pull you from the wreckage."

Addy jerked and paled. "You!" she spat out. "*You* shot my car. It was you."

"As a warning. Don't get involved with that Korean."

She heard the distant voices of other conference attendees making their way back to their hotels. The man with the baseball cap turned and looked up the street. The chatter grew louder. He swooshed his hand in the direction of her hotel.

"Go! And don't come back."

\* \* \*

Addy hurried through the revolving doors of the hotel and rushed to her room where she fumbled her key card twice trying to insert it into the slot. Safely inside her room, she collapsed onto the desk chair and tried to collect herself, her eyes fixed on the ceiling. What should she do? She was more furious than scared, though there was plenty of scared, too, especially since the stinging sensation above her eye persisted.

Hindy had been impounded, and now someone had given her a stern warning, all because of this Quinn character. Who was he, and why had he been following her? More important, what did he have that someone didn't want her to know about?

She decided to make a cup of tea, and sipped the warm beverage while she tried to sort through what had just happened. She chewed her lower lip. What would happen if she did stay? Her anger swung to fear. She was now terrified.

Yet this might be part of her destiny—her belief that she was going to find a world-changing technology. Perhaps she'd just stumbled on it. Why else was Hindy's balloon torched? Why had Quinn wanted to talk to her about fuel cells? The two events had to be related.

She rolled her cup in her hands. Terrified or not, she couldn't leave yet, not until she had some more answers, not until she discovered the source of these bizarre events. Some kind of new technology was at the core of these events, and she was determined to find out what it was. It was time to confront Quinn.

She set down her cup and squeezed her temples in a feeble attempt to get rid of an excruciating headache. She blinked and then widened her eyes a few times, hoping the double images would somehow come back into focus. Hopefully, whatever was ailing her was nothing more than a serious case of jet lag.

In her bathroom she tapped out a few painkillers, gulped them down, and cleaned and treated the abrasion above her left eye. After taking a closer look, she decided it was small enough that a heavy dose of makeup could cover it.

With her phone tethered to one hand, Addy kicked off her shoes, tugged back the duvet with the other hand, and collapsed onto her plush bed. Sinking into luxury, she could feel herself fading away.

But not yet. She needed to call Perry, and jerked herself awake to dial the office. She rehearsed what she was going to say, and how she would avoid any mention of the attack. Perry wanted to talk to her about Hindy, and Addy wanted to know why the police had decided to keep the Shelby Mustang under lock and key.

If Perry was upset, his mild answer didn't reveal it. Although they were separated by the Pacific Ocean, Perry's voice was as clear as if he were there in her dimly-lit hotel room.

"Look, I'm really sorry about Hindy," she began.

Perry cut her off. "No need to apologize. I'm taking care of it. I just want you to worry about getting some more clients."

"So you know about my citation?"

"For not having a hydrogen permit? Yes, it's all in the notice. Totally bogus. They just want to keep the car until they can confirm this wasn't some act of terrorism. We can go to the hearing together and let them have their say then. Like I said, this is all going to be fine."

Addy sat up and tucked her hair behind her ear. Perry was always controlling. While she appreciated his help, sometimes she wanted to handle her own issues without his interference.

"Could have been worse," she said trying to lighten the conversation. "I could have been hiding drugs."

"Not funny. I know you too well."

Perry was right. She'd never felt the slightest temptation to take any illegal substance. "This is my problem, you don't need to—"

"That's where you're wrong. Now that you're part of the partnership, things are different. We look out for each other. And before you say anything else, I need to tell you that I'm really sorry about what I said before you left—that bit about you being Vietnamese. Please don't think for a minute that I sent you to the conference because of your ethnicity. You're there because you're good at landing clients. Really good."

Addy rolled her eyes. While Perry had apparently recognized his blunder and tried to smooth over an apology, she didn't believe it was real. That was Perry—always finding a way out of his slip-ups.

It wasn't like Perry was unfamiliar with her past. She'd told her story to her coworkers at least a dozen times. On one occasion, she even revealed that after her single mother turned to drugs, Addy sometimes wished that she'd never been adopted and hauled off to America. Vietnam sounded like a better place. She actually packed a duffle bag after her two best friends copied her answers on a test and she was the one accused of cheating. She had nowhere to turn and was ready to run away and find passage on a boat to Vietnam.

Now that she was in Vietnam, she realized how foolish she'd been.

"No need to apologize. Let's put it behind us," Addy said, knowing it was pointless to dwell on the issue.

"Good, tell me about the conference."

Addy smiled. Perry would always be Perry.

She enthused about the Asian culture, then went on to tell Perry about her new lead, carefully avoiding any mention of the attack.

"Be careful," he said. "Nearly everyone there will tell you they have a client for you. Remember that US law firms generate most of the work for foreign law firms, and they'll do just about anything to tap into the firm's US clients. You'll need to vet them and make sure you're getting someone who can really deliver."

# 6

THE PHONE ALARM buzzing on the nightstand startled Addy out of a sound sleep. She tugged her eyelids, but they were too heavy to pry apart. She slapped her hand on the nightstand and fumbled with her phone until the annoying racket was silenced.

Her mouth was pasty, and her tongue thick, like she'd had too much to drink. So this was the glamorous life of international travel. Addy sat up and rubbed the sleep out of her eyes, then skimmed her fingers above her brow, feeling the roughened skin. If she had to, she could explain it away as an errant step into the bathroom door.

She stumbled over to the corner table, switched on the desk lamp, and shuffled through her registration materials. Today was "excursion day," and the attendees were encouraged to select one of a few dozen activities designed to help the attorneys mingle business with pleasure. At least she'd be with a large group of attendees all day, so she'd be safe.

Activities ranged from trips to museums, cultural events, and golf. She was probably stuck with whatever Perry chose when he submitted his registration. She ran her finger down the page until she came to Group H, some kind of fundraiser described as a reverse treasure hunt. It was designed to let the conference delegates see a bit of the city while also raising money for several local charities.

Addy shrugged. *It could be worse.* If Perry had chosen golf, the day would likely have been a disaster. She'd only golfed once, and after taking more than a hundred shots on four holes, she'd called it quits. Addy slid her finger further down, searching for the most crucial piece of information—what to wear. Perry had warned her that Asians tended to show up in suit and tie, even if jeans were appropriate. It was then she noticed that her bus was leaving the hotel lobby in fifteen minutes. There was no time to vacillate about what to wear.

To be safe, Addy slipped on a skirt and casual blouse with some low-heeled pumps, hoping that they wouldn't be doing too much walking. A touch of lipstick added some color to her face, and she applied some concealer above her left eye. With her hair pulled back into a ponytail, she could easily pass for a local. She threw a round piece of pink fruit that she'd never seen before into her purse and hustled down to the lobby.

Three buses were already lined up in front of the Marriott. She found the one labeled Group H, skipped up the stairs, and plopped down into the first available seat. She'd barely tugged her purse open when another conference delegate slipped into the empty seat beside her. His cologne smelled familiar.

She worked her eyes upward. Instead of a dark suit, her seatmate was dressed in jeans and a tight-fitting shirt, revealing a toned, fit body.

It was the stranger from last night—Quinn.

Her first instinct was to blurt out a demand for an explanation. But she kept her cool. For all she knew, the bus could be loaded with spies wanting to eavesdrop.

"I see you're on the same tour," he said. "Do you know what we're doing today? Addy, isn't it?" he said holding out his hand.

She played coy, nonchalantly sliding her eyes down to his name tag. "That's right, Quinn."

"I hope you got everything ironed out. You left in such a rush."

"Yes, all taken care of. Ready for a day of helping out a few charities."

Their conversation was interrupted by a squawk from ceiling speakers. In broken English, their Vietnamese guide began informing them of the day's events. Addy could barely see him over the seats in front of her. Half the passengers kept talking, busily engaged in business conversations. Addy strained to hear his announcement.

"I hope you are ready for a fun day," their guide began. "My name is Tran, and we go to the Old Quarter, named Paris of the East, to treasure hunt."

The bus jerked, the air conditioning began blasting, and they bolted off. Despite the lack of attention, Tran continued his spiel.

While the bus wound its way through the narrow streets, Tran pointed out the historic sites, beginning with the Ho Chi Minh Complex that boasted Ho Chi Minh's mausoleum, his former stilt-house residence, and the Presidential Palace. Then they moved on to the Hoa Lo Prison, and finally to their destination in the Old Quarter, bordered by Hoan Kiem Lake.

Addy watched modern cars, Mercedes and BMWs, weave around bicycles and rickshaws, as she calculated her next move. How was she going to find out why Quinn was so interested in her, and why had she been forbidden to speak to him?

The sidewalks were busy, with restaurant owners squatting and cutting their vegetables on the bare cement. She decided to wait until they were off the bus, perhaps in front of one of these shops, before confronting Quinn.

The bus parked in front of a yellow stone building built in the French colonial style, with green awnings and shutters.

"Everyone look at this," Tran said. "If you are lost, come here. This famous building is the Green Tangerine restaurant, and serves most delicious food in North Vietnam."

The hot sun was already beating down, the temperature seeming even hotter thanks to the chill from the bus's air conditioning. Tran moved them under the shade of a Bael tree.

"Who knows about geocaching?" Tran asked.

A blond Australian wearing aviator Ray Bans stepped forward with his hand raised. "Do it almost every weekend."

"Good! Please describe it for your fellow passengers."

"Right," said the Aussie, folding his arms and pushing out his chest. Addy noticed he was the only one wearing shorts. "It's pretty simple. Several years ago some guy came up with the idea of hiding a treasure and then using the internet to challenge people to find it. The word cache just means to hide. The old trappers in Canada coined the name when they stashed their furs until they were ready to haul them to market."

"How does it work?" Tran said, trying to move the Aussie along.

"Right. Each cache is identified by geographic coordinates that you download to your GPS device. Something like north at a certain degree and west at another degree. The GPS tells you where to go. It's really cool. Down Under, we hide stuff on the beach, in the Outback, even in the Sydney harbor."

"What do people hide?" a Japanese lawyer asked.

"Oh yeah, I forgot. Each cache has lots of stuff, usually little trinkets like an old watch, a piece of jewelry, or real cheap stuff like a pack of gum. When you open the cache, you sign your name on the register, and if you take anything, you need to replace it with something better, kind of like trading down."

"Sounds fun," Addy said to Quinn, sensing her moment of opportunity drawing near.

"I'm up for it," he said.

Their guide raised his hand to regain their attention. "Good, good, but this time is little bit different. Each treasure site has a box where you make a donation to a local charity. We make it easy. With these gift cards you can leave in the boxes. Cards can be used to buy at local stores here in Hanoi. The gifts for victims of land mines, adoption agencies, schoolteachers, and many others. You deposit gift card that is good for that charity, then take out your little prize, a souvenir or memento of your visit to lovely Hanoi.

"The treasure sites are hidden all over the Old Quarter to also make it a tour of this famous place." He swept his arm in front of him. "So you don't get lost in the narrow alleys, called the thirty-six streets, you have your own rickshaw with driver. Maybe doesn't speak English, but he does know his way around. You go in teams of two, and here is a GPS unit for each team."

Addy's bleary eyes gleamed. "This could be fun. I love this kind of stuff," she said, hoping to hide her anxiety about being alone with Quinn. She was leery of being lured into another dark alley.

"I know," Quinn said.

Addy gave him a once-over. "You do?"

"Don't think I'm some kind of creepster, but I Googled you last night. I see you really like adventure."

"Sounds like creeping to me."

Quinn pointed to a three-wheeled rickshaw that was being pedaled by a spindly Vietnamese man wearing torn leather flip-flops and calf-length pants. A wide-brimmed bamboo hat protected him from the burning, ever-present sun. "I think this is ours. Hop in and I'll explain."

Vietnam had two kinds of rickshaws, also known as *tuk-tuks*—ones with motors, and ones with pedals. For Vietnam, like many other third world countries, this was an important means of transportation.

Their driver smiled while they settled into the cloth seats, revealing a near toothless grin. Addy tucked her skirt under her legs, watching Quinn's eyes slip down for a glance.

"So, you were stalking me?"

"Nothing like that. Well, kind of. I just planned to look up your background on your firm's website, but your name popped up all over the place. Looks like you're some kind of local celebrity. Sorry about your car. Hindy, wasn't it? I love the idea, but it kills me you castrated a Shelby. Why couldn't it have been a VW bug?"

"What do you know about muscle cars?"

"Enough. Still, your idea is very clever. Tell me more about how it runs. Fuel cell, I presume. But why the hydrogen balloon? You couldn't have used that to supply hydrogen to the fuel cell."

"I replaced the gas tank with a canister filled with compressed hydrogen. Pretty standard stuff. The blimp was my nonconventional way to promote my patent practice." Addy tugged her phone out of her purse, pulled up her browser. "Spell your last name."

Quinn paused.

"No, it's only fair. Spit it out."

As Quinn answered, she tapped in the letters, wondering what she was about to discover. She clicked on a few links while he hovered over her.

"Isn't that interesting? It looks like you are a talented fencer.

An Olympic hopeful at one point."

"Put that away," Quinn said, reaching for her phone. "Those days are over. I get your point. No more creeping on you. I promise."

The driver stopped. "Where now, Mr. Quinn?"

Addy's eyebrows raised, and Quinn gave the driver a stern look. Addy didn't recall telling the driver their names.

Quinn quickly cleared his throat, and the man shrugged his shoulders and jabbered something in Vietnamese. The rickshaw didn't budge.

Addy wondered what was going on. Quinn obviously knew something she didn't. She cut the tension by nudging Quinn's round bicep. "I think he wants you to quit paying so much attention to me and tell him where to go."

Quinn fumbled with his GPS device and punched a few keys. "Okay, so I have the coordinates. Now what?" He looked into her brown eyes. "I seem to recall you don't speak Vietnamese?"

Addy gritted her teeth. "Correct. How about pointing where you want him to go?"

Their driver gave them another toothless grin. "I speak little bit English. Was just kidding with you."

Quinn directed him down a side street, and Addy wondered whether they were really going to the geocache. She thrust her hand into her purse and slipped out her makeup kit. "Forgot my makeup," she said, flipping the case open. She pretended to blot on some blush while studying the mirror. Behind them, she could see a man in tattered clothes dashing between buildings, trying to remain incognito.

Addy swung around violently just as the man darted across the street. "There is a man following us," she snapped.

Quinn nodded to the driver, and they took a quick right into another narrow alley, passing several silk stores where women in brightly colored silk dresses tried to wave them inside for a high-pressure sale. He looked over his shoulder. "I can't see anything."

"But a man was sprinting after us," Addy insisted.

"Could you blame him? You're probably the most beautiful woman he's seen in years. Nothing to worry about. Just enjoy the ride."

Addy again looked behind her but saw nothing. She exhaled and forced herself to lean back into her seat, still tense with apprehension. She took another deep, calming breath and smelled the sweet spices from restaurants preparing for lunch.

"Since you know all about me, how about sharing something about you, Quinn?" she tried again.

"Fair enough. Even though I don't look American, I feel like one. I went to high school in Colorado. I loved math and science, so I went to Colorado School of Mines to get my Chem E degree. That wasn't painful enough, so I got my master's degree at Purdue, then a PhD at Caltech. After graduation, I wanted to see a bit of the world, so I took an engineering job in Korea with a company that has some prolific inventors. And that's why I'm here at the conference. I need to recruit an attorney to help our company with its patent strategy."

"And what about the dream of becoming an Olympian?"

"That's a long story that's best saved for another day."

Then Addy sprang it on him. "What were you doing in Sunnyvale earlier this week?"

Quinn jerked to attention, then relaxed. "Sunnyvale?" he said with one eyebrow raised.

"You know, when my car exploded? You were wearing sunglasses and a goatee."

He stroked his face, just as he'd done a few days before.

"And you were doing that same scratchy thing with your chin."

Quinn froze, then shoved the offending hand is his pocket.

"We're not going anywhere until you're totally straight with me."

Quinn remained silent.

"You know I'm onto you. C'mon now, out with it. What in the hell is going on here?"

Quinn exhaled and looked up to the sky. "Okay, you got me, but it's not what you think."

Addy folded her arms. "Lay it on me."

"Yes, I admit I was at the scene of the incident with your car, but I wasn't stalking you."

"Then what would you call it?"

"I think the term you lawyers use is 'due diligence.' "

"You're pathetic," Addy growled.

"No, let me explain. I need a US patent attorney—a really good one—who I can trust. I was in the States working on a marketing initiative for my new invention and interviewing potential candidates at the same time. You were the top one on my list. I was going to set up an appointment to formally introduce myself, but you high-tailed it to Vietnam. So I had to follow you here."

Addy scrunched her nose. "Is it really so important that you had to come halfway around the world? It couldn't have waited?"

Quinn rolled his eyes. "Time is of the essence. Look, we really should get going and get to the geolocation. I can explain more later."

"I think we have all day," Addy said, arms still folded.

Quinn sighed. "As I said, my company needs a really good patent attorney. We generate tons of US filings, and we've tried out several of the best firms, but it hasn't really worked out. We don't think they understand our business."

"Which is?" Addy asked.

"Let's put it this way; we know a lot about hydrogen and fuel cells."

This time it was Addy who raised her brows. She turned and rested her hand on Quinn's forearm. "Really?"

"I'm convinced you're a perfect fit."

Addy turned to fully face him, her knees touching his. "I guess that kind of changes things . . . But there's this little issue about somebody wanting to hurt me if I speak to you, or don't you know yet about the incident last night?" She ran her finger over the fading abrasion above her eye.

Quinn grasped her shoulders and pulled her forward while he inspected the wound. "What happened?"

Addy shrugged, waiting for more of a reaction.

Quinn leaned down closer to examine the wound. When he was satisfied, he looked into her eyes. "Tell me what happened."

"Just a few thugs inviting me to fly back home to the States."

"They hit you?"

"They didn't need to. I tripped trying to escape and took a spill. My forehead broke the fall."

"I'm sorry. I didn't know."

"Well you do now. I was warned not to speak to you, or else—" Addy pointed to her forehead.

Quinn pounded his fist on his knee. "Damn!"

"An explanation would be nice. Have you ever felt someone twice your size putting the squeeze on you? Makes having hemorrhoids seem like getting a massage."

The corners of Quinn's mouth curved up. "At least you have a sense of humor."

"There are people who don't want my technology to reach the market." Quinn paused and inspected the street. "Let's leave it at that for now. We really should get going. You'll understand a bit more when we're alone and I can explain my invention. Since you're in Hanoi, I can arrange for you to meet with a few of my colleagues from Korea. And I'll make sure you're completely safe."

"I guess that would be okay," she said, still leery about whether he could, or would, keep his word. "I'll need to check my schedule, but I'm sure I can fit you in sometime."

"Let me know, and I will make the arrangements. I'm certain they will be impressed when they see how clever you've been to use a car named Hindy to market your practice."

"A castrated Mustang?" she said with a grin. "How do you know it doesn't really run on water?"

"Because that would violate the laws of thermodynamics, and I know you're smarter than that."

"Maybe today," she said. "But tomorrow? It's possible."

Quinn raised his eyebrows and slipped on his sunglasses. "I'm looking forward to our meeting."

Quinn tapped on the screen of the GPS unit and nodded to the driver, who immediately began churning his pedals.

"Up a block and turn right," he said.

The driver swerved around a roadside food stand and down a narrow street lined with stores advertising foot massages. One had a fish tank filled with what looked like minnows darting through the blue water.

"You've got to be kidding me," Addy said. "Our first stop is a masseuse?"

"Foot massage," the driver corrected. "You dip your tired feet into the water and those little fish eat away all the dead skin."

"A real pedicure," she said. "I wonder if it tickles."

They hopped out of the rickshaw and skipped up onto the bamboo floor.

"Welcome," said a woman holding a laminated brochure listing prices for foot massages.

Quinn held up his GPS unit. "No time for a massage. We need your geocache."

The shop owner smiled and pointed at a square metal box in the corner.

"You first," Quinn said gesturing to the back of the room.

Addy leaned over and lifted the latch gingerly, half expecting the box to explode. She pulled out a clipboard with a tethered pen. "It's for a home for the blind. I'm going to put in my gift card for the electronics store. Maybe they can purchase a music player and some headphones. It will be perfect." Addy signed her name, dropped in the card and fished out a T-shirt from the bottom of the box. She shook it out and held it over her chest.

"Welcome to Hanoi!" Quinn said reading the pastel letters. "I guess we're off to the next cache."

Rather than taking care of his own donation and souvenir, he turned his back and stared intently at their driver, who was sitting on his rickshaw, nervously flashing hand signals.

Another rickshaw appeared at the storefront with two more conference attendees, both Asian males with graying hair, who hopped out of their rickshaw and bolted into the store. Both had conference badges dangling from their necks. Addy couldn't recognize what language they were speaking. The moment they saw Addy, they switched to English.

"I see we made it to the right place," the first man said.

Addy pointed to the box. "Help yourself." She studied his badge in an attempt to determine his name and nationality. In bold letters, she saw "South Korea."

Before she could say something, the other man addressed Quinn in Korean.

"I'm glad there is such a beautiful lady to show me how this works," the first man said, taking Addy by the arm.

Addy bristled, but didn't want to cause a scene. "There's nothing to it. Just reach in and take out one of the prizes, then replace it with one of your cards."

The Korean smiled and leaned toward her, his lips nearly reaching her ear. "You don't want to get involved. If Quinn tells you his secret, we will get it from you. The choice is yours. Understand?"

Addy folded up her T-shirt and tucked it under her arm. "It was so nice to meet you, but we need to get going."

With that, Addy turned and stormed out, hauling Quinn behind her. "You Koreans need to learn some manners," she said while they tumbled out into the street. "I think I've had enough excitement for today. Why don't you call me a cab?"

Quinn didn't bother asking what the man said, as if he already knew. He quickly flagged down a cab and insisted on escorting her back to the hotel. They rode in silence, with Addy staring out the window, struggling to process everything that had happened. *What's Quinn's invention?*

When they reached the Marriott, Quinn held out his hand. "I hope we did a little bit of good today. I'm sorry it ended on a sour note. I really would like to meet again and explain why you're getting so much unwanted attention."

Addy gave him a narrow smile, then placed her hand in his meaty palm. She wondered whether muscles made for a good fencer, and what was it that made him give up the chance to be an Olympic contender. "Of course we did."

"Let me know your schedule, and we'll set up a time to talk."

"I'm thinking about it," she said, even though she already knew she had to know more.

# 7

AGENT JESSE LONG jerked himself awake in his Buick sedan—an old man's car. It was a perfect fit, according to his colleagues back at the office. Long rarely spent any time in his cubicle. After a quarter century with the agency, he had no desire to compete with the millennials who thought the sexy way to follow terrorists was using the latest high-tech equipment. That was fine with him. Instead of being proficient at shooting electrons, he was as good as any gunslinger from his hometown of Cody, Wyoming, at putting a slug in a sniper.

And he preferred to stake out his suspects the old-fashioned way, which was why he found himself perched on Lytton Street in Palo Alto, directly across from the offices of Wyckoff & Schechter.

Long rubbed his eyes. He loved being a father, but was still adapting to everything that came with it. He now knew what it was like to work after no sleep and a shrieking, colicky baby. He calculated that he'd slept a total of two hours that night.

As he watched a pair of Wyckoff attorneys cross the street for the coffee shop, Long tried to sort through the facts of his latest assignment from the Department of Justice: After receiving his PhD at Caltech, Quinn Moon interned with an American company, HydroGen, Inc., which had won a contract with the Department of Energy to find a way to economically produce hydrogen fuel. After six months, HydroGen's president, Jerry Wilcox, filed a complaint alleging that Quinn had recently left for Korea to start his own company, WTG, after stealing HydroGen's intellectual property. Long had been tracking Quinn's visit to the States over the past year. This stopover, however, was different from the others. Quinn was involved in his own stakeout, following a patent attorney named Addeline Verges. Which was fine, except Quinn just happened to be following her when Addy's hydrogen blimp went up in flames.

Why?

Long was familiar with cases involving the theft of trade secrets. Hackers from Eastern Europe to China constantly broke into the databases of US companies, but this case was different. Here, a Korean national had worked for a US company with strict national security requirements, then left the country with a head full of technical data. Still, Long knew he couldn't arrest Quinn for being competitive. He needed a smoking gun, and the DOJ insisted he find it.

Long pulled out his phone and studied the photo of the man with the tattoo who'd shot the flare. Initial assessments were that he was Middle Eastern.

The Bureau was working to improve the photo's resolution to sharpen the tattoo, but had nothing yet, other than it appeared to be some kind of Arabic writing. The most logical conclusion was that the man was part of a radical terrorist group like ISIS, which was committed to blocking technology that might reduce dependence on Middle Eastern oil. *But how did they know about Quinn? Had they tapped into his computer network in Korea? Heaven knows, the FBI had tried to hack the WTG files without luck.*

Long wasn't in Palo Alto to observe Addy. He already knew she was in Vietnam with Quinn. The moment US Customs scanned her passport, he'd been notified.

He needed some paid time off, self-imposed paternity leave, so he'd told his office that he was getting a feel for the neighborhood, trying to find a good place to spy on Addy when she returned.

# 8

AT ADDY'S REQUEST, Quinn arranged for dinner the following evening at the Green Tangerine, the one their tour guide, Tran, had touted as being world famous. She was ready to hear what Quinn wanted to tell her, in detail.

The hostess greeted her by name when she walked in through marble pillars framing the open courtyard. "Your guests are waiting," she said, turning and shuffling in her tight skirt through a series of open-air tables. "You'll be in our alfresco dining area this evening."

The restored edifice was constructed in 1928 as a French villa. Addy felt a sense of nostalgia as she left the bustling streets of Hanoi behind and entered the ambiance of a bygone era. The architecture was a blend of French and Vietnamese, as was the cuisine.

They traveled over a cobblestone floor and passed through an open courtyard laced with lush green plants, where a Vietnamese musician was playing blues on his guitar.

The moment she emerged through a pair of green French doors, Quinn jumped up to greet her. Two other men, also Korean, rose to their feet and buttoned their blazers. Behind them was a woman with high cheekbones and American-looking eyes, no doubt the result of the latest in vogue surgery.

Addy felt outnumbered. She exhaled with a whoosh and unclenched her fists. *Stay calm, even if you're not,* she told herself.

"We're so glad you made it," Quinn began. "I brought a few guests—Yun Lee, our chief technical officer, and Jeyhu Mock, vice president of green technologies." Addy shook their hands. She'd been expecting a gray-haired crowd, but she was mistaken. Yun and Jeyhu looked about her age. Both were wearing thick-framed square glasses and had close-cropped hair. They were almost bouncing with energy.

"And this is Kin Sumi, our office administrator." Addy took her for the token female. Kin's cocktail dress, form-fitting and low cut, could have come straight from Paris.

Their hostess pulled out Addy's chair and Quinn gestured for her to sit.

"I hope you don't mind, but the chef has already prepared his special sampler menu. It's French-Vietnamese fusion. We won't have to worry about ordering, so we can spend time getting to know each other a bit better. Do you have any food allergies?" Quinn asked.

"No, I'm fine. This is a great idea. I love trying new places, new foods. I hate being stuck in a rut."

"You're just like us," the CTO, Yun, said with a mild Korean accent. "We're always inventing, always looking for a way to improve our world."

Addy browsed the sampler menu, salivating at the offerings: spring rolls, soy-soaked duck with pomegranate, Ca qua fish in tamarind sauce, succulent quail and, for dessert, chocolate truffle fritters perfumed with tamarind and a red fruit flower sauce.

Their waiter served the appetizers while Quinn explained that Jeyhu and Yun were both chemical engineers, and Jeyhu had also gone to business school at Drexel in Philadelphia.

"What's your company's name?" Addy said after the first course.

"WTG Company," Quinn said.

"That's not a very sexy name," Addy said bluntly. "Nothing like Apple or Google, more like IBM."

"We like to keep a low profile—at least for now," Jeyhu explained.

"An acronym?" Addy said.

"Possibly. Do you want to venture a guess?"

Addy tapped her chin with her index finger. "The *We're The Good* company?"

They all burst out laughing. "You'll figure it out eventually," Quinn said. "But I guess I should quit dancing around the edges and tell you why we've asked you here."

"By all means," she said.

"Okay, here's the deal," Quinn began. "As I mentioned yesterday, we at WTG do a lot of inventing. Our company's intellectual property is the key to our success. If we can protect it, we'll be another Apple. If we can't, life will be difficult. Our investors have insisted that we do everything possible to make sure our patents are solid. And because America is our most important market, we're interviewing US patent attorneys to see who can best protect our ideas."

"I'm happy to help out," Addy said.

"That's music to our ears," Jeyhu said. "We haven't had much success with big US firms, and so we're looking for a different model. The reason we like you so much is that you 'get it.' I can't tell you how much we envy your marketing savvy. Hindy is brilliant. When our technology hits the market, we could use a fleet of a hundred Hindys. We're going to be the green of all green companies, and we want you on board to guide us through."

Addy wondered when the probing questions were going to start. Didn't they want to know about her experience? About her clean-tech clients? How much she knew about hydrogen? Her outrageous billing rate of six hundred an hour? That was usually the first question any potential client asked.

"I've worked extensively on several fuel cell portfolios," Addy broke in.

"Yes, we know," Quinn said. "We did a search of the Patent Office database. We've looked at every patent application you've ever touched. You do great work. That's a given."

Addy scrunched her nose. "Then?"

"There's a little twist," Quinn said.

Addy sighed. So it was too good to be true. Her assailants weren't just handing out empty threats.

"We need an independent law firm, one devoted just to our matters."

"My firm couldn't commit to that," Addy said.

"We had something different in mind. We want to set you up with your own law firm," Quinn quickly responded. "That way there would never be any conflict issues with other clients. We'd give you all our US work and, trust me, you'd have more than enough to keep you busy."

Addy set down her fork and folded her arms. If this offer had come four years ago, she would have seriously entertained the idea. She'd always wanted her own law firm. But now it was too late. She'd made a giant personal investment with Wyckoff & Schechter, and she couldn't jump ship for such a risky venture. The only way she could possibly walk away from Wyckoff would be if Quinn had a technology so important that it would change the future of humanity. Hadn't that been her dream all along? Perhaps, but now the stakes were much higher. It was one thing to join forces with a start-up company as a first-year associate, completely another after making partner.

"You should know that I just made partner the day before I came to Vietnam," she said.

Quinn scooted his chair closer.

"Hear me out. I know that becoming a partner at a major law firm is a huge deal, but what we're offering can't compare. It will be more than worth your while to start your own firm and join with us."

"More like a once-in-a-lifetime opportunity," Jeyhu chimed in.

"And you'll love our new office space," Kin added.

Quinn leaned in closer, until his elbows were resting on his knees. "I'm sorry for being so evasive yesterday, but once you hear what we've discovered, I know you won't turn us down. I know you're a dreamer, because you're just like me."

The vice president stood and made his way around the table, going down to one knee on the other side of Addy. "We love you as a lawyer, and even more for the concept of Hindy. You have this sense of excitement about using hydrogen to fuel a car that we haven't found in anyone else. You've created the perfect platform to advertise the importance of green technologies."

Addy looked up to the ceiling, struggling with what to say. During her first few years at Wyckoff, her dream had been to find just this kind of opportunity. That was exactly why she put up with the inconvenience of a hydrogen balloon tethered to her car. It was why she held her annual high school inventor competition to crown the best young inventor in the state. It was why she spent hours updating her blog on current issues facing fledgling inventors.

And now, right when her opportunity was staring her in the face, she had been resigning herself to the belief that being a partner at Wyckoff was the wisest career choice.

"Aren't you all just a little bit worried about my safety? Because I certainly am. You personally observed what happened to Hindy, and then, the first day of the conference a strange man warns me to stay away from you."

The men in the room sat erect. Quinn looked deep into her eyes. "WTG takes security issues very seriously. We're looking into what happened with Hindy, as well as what's been going on here in Hanoi. We'll make sure you're protected, even if that means I am personally assigned as your bodyguard."

Addy bit her lower lip, trying not to smile. "I don't think that will be necessary."

"Then you're ready to sign up?" Quinn persisted.

"I just don't know. The timing of this whole thing is all wrong."

Quinn smiled. "Remember, this is the chance of a lifetime."

"Maybe, but I've already committed to my firm. Are you sure Wyckoff can't take you on as a client?"

They nodded in unison, faces intent.

Addy leaned back, trying to distance herself from Quinn to separate herself from his engrossing charm.

She noticed the half-eaten quail on their plates. Such a lovely dinner, ruined.

Her life lessons had come with a heavy price. Trust. It was always the issue. Her gut told her she couldn't trust them. And the two threats were striking evidence that this wasn't about fun and games. Risking her career was one thing; risking her life was quite another. Addy knew she couldn't accept Quinn's offer. It was time to go back to America, where she'd be safe, where she could go to Wyckoff and do what she'd always done.

"I'm afraid I'll have to decline, then. Being a partner at Wyckoff has also been a dream of mine. And they've been so good to me. I can't simply walk away."

"Can we go for a walk?" Quinn said after an uneasy silence.

Addy scooted back her chair and gently laid her napkin over her half-finished entrée. Quinn escorted her out into the empty street.

Addy scanned the shadows.

"We're safe," Quinn assured her.

Addy hesitated. Quinn took her hand and led her onto the cobblestone sidewalk. She felt her resolve fade and ventured after him.

The warm, moist air was so different from the cool evenings of the South Bay. They walked several blocks in silence. When they reached the lake, Quinn slipped off his jacket and slung it over his shoulder.

"Aren't you at least curious to know what we've invented?"

She spun to face him. "Of course, but can't you understand? This is all so odd. The day after I realize my dream of becoming partner, I'm shooed off to some strange place with a culture I barely understand, and in the middle of all this, some really good-looking guy, who just happens to be a world-class athlete, starts creeping on me and says he has an offer I can't refuse. And my life is threatened—"

Quinn studied the gravel walkway. "Yes, I can see your point. I suppose I'd feel the same way. I should apologize. I get so excited; I just assumed you'd see everything through my eyes. In so many ways, I feel we're very much alike."

"This has taken me by complete surprise. I need some time to process what is happening. Besides the punches I took at my MMA gym while in college, I've never had someone try to attack me."

"Fair enough." He looked into her eyes. "I admit I was a bit presumptuous, but there is a good reason. As an attorney, you'll understand. We've invented something that is earth-shattering; I liken it to the discovery of atomic energy. We've got to move quickly to protect our rights. I can't trust a big law firm. Yes, we did some diligence on you, but we had to find someone we could trust to protect our interests. I'll make sure nothing happens to you."

*Trust.* There was that word again. Addy bit her lip, the way she always did when she was uncomfortable.

"I'll let you in on my secret—at least at a high enough level that you can understand the stakes, and why people want to stop me. I've invented a technology that will allow a car to run on water. Not like Hindy. Real water. I can convert water on demand into hydrogen. You can literally fill your gas tank with water and run it through the fuel cell. And I want you to be the one to clear the legal hurdles so everyone can have a water-fueled car."

Addy could feel her smile begin, in spite of her best efforts to maintain a neutral face. "Should I remind you that a water car would violate the laws of thermodynamics?"

Quinn kicked the dirt. "You're good. But you're wrong. And I was wrong. I thought the same thing, but I've found a way to do it."

Addy's smile grew. For decades, novice inventors had claimed to be able to economically extract hydrogen from water, but none of their claims had turned out to be true. It took so much energy to break the hydrogen-oxygen bond that formed the water molecule that it wasn't worth using hydrogen as an energy source. You might as well pump oil out of the ground— it was much cheaper. That's why nearly everyone still drove gasoline-powered vehicles.

"No, I'm not kidding. This isn't like one of the cold fusion scams. I'm an engineer, a scientist, and I know what I'm talking about. This is for real."

Grin intact, Addy shook her head.

"It's for real," Quinn insisted. "Ever heard of the Manhattan project?"

"Come on. This is nothing like developing the atomic bomb. That took billions of dollars and a world war as the catalyst."

"We've got some wealthy backers. This isn't some idea scratched on the back of a napkin. We have real scientists who have been working on it for years. You should see our facilities."

Addy nodded. "Okay, now you've piqued my curiosity. How

did you do it?"

This time Quinn shook his head and waved his finger. "Nope, I can only tell you that after you commit. I need you all in. And you'll be required to keep everything in the strictest confidence. All information will be communicated to you personally. Nothing goes over the internet, not even if it is encrypted."

Addy noticed she was chewing on her lip again. *What if Quinn is right? What if he really has invented what he claimed? It was a technology that could change the course of the world. It was an invention that people would kill to acquire—or to make disappear.*

"The clock is ticking," Quinn continued. "We need to act quickly to secure our rights. I know we're putting an immense amount of pressure on you, but if you want in, we need to have your answer before you leave Vietnam."

Addy gasped. "That's tomorrow."

"I'm sorry, but it's a race to the patent office, and it's a race we can't afford to lose. We have too much invested."

This time Addy studied the gravel path. What if Quinn was telling the truth? Would she leave Wyckoff for that? Would she risk her life?

"I don't know," she said, shaking her head. "I've got so much invested in my law firm. What would I do with all of my clients? They're almost like family."

"I understand. If it makes your decision any easier, we could let you bring on your existing clients after you've secured our first round of patents. It's just that for the first few months, we need you totally dedicated to WTG's patents."

Addy sighed. "Tell me more. I need to know more details about the arrangement. I've never run my own firm. I'd need office space, secretaries, paralegals, computers. You don't just set up an office in a day." She began rambling. "And my clients. And how could I possibly keep this a secret? I mean my secretary would see all the documents. And how would we handle security?"

Quinn reached out and rested his hand on her shoulder. "Easy. We've thought all this through. We'll take care of all those details. All you'll need to do is concentrate on protecting our ideas."

Addy moved enough that his hand slipped off her shoulder

before sauntering down the path around the lake, watching the reflected light from the lamps shimmer off the still water. "I've got a loyal secretary and a loyal, skillful paralegal. I couldn't just leave them. And Perry's been so good to me."

Quinn followed behind, careful to give her space. "You'll be a part of the most significant technology breakthrough in the last century. And did I mention that there will be stock options?"

She walked in silence, listening to his feet crunch along the gravel path. She didn't go into law for money, but her mind raced with how much a company like this could be worth. It would dwarf Microsoft, even in its heyday. But would she live long enough to see that kind of money? For all she knew, she might never make it back to America.

"We'll also give you a bonus for each patent you can secure, and that amount goes up exponentially, based on how fast you can push them through the patent offices. And we will even help you fix Hindy, make her so she can run on water."

Addy spun around, her ponytail whipping over her shoulder. "You're not going to give up easily, are you?"

"We'll even let you use Hindy to make our grand announcement—after we've secured our patents."

He knew how to tempt her. "And my safety?" she asked.

"Nobody's going to touch you. If you want a bodyguard, just say the word."

Quinn seemed to have an answer for everything.

He held out his hand. "Let's go back and finish that dinner with my colleagues.

# 9

STILL IN HER nightshirt, Addy chomped a bite of an Asian pear, savoring the sweet, white flesh. It was about the only breakfast she could stomach after a late night dinner with far too many courses.

In spite of the tensions and emotional highs and lows of yesterday, she'd been so exhausted that eight hours of sound sleep came easily. She should have felt refreshed, but her mind felt cluttered and her chest was tight. She reflected on the previous night's events, trying to feel confident that she'd made the right decision. She couldn't give up her career on a mere whim. She congratulated herself that her will was strong enough to overcome Quinn's charisma.

Addy tried to convince herself she was ready to take on the rest of the conference, the real reason she'd come halfway across the world. The day's agenda included meetings with two more Japanese firms, an Australian associate of Perry's, two attorneys from New Zealand, and dinner with a British colleague.

She sighed. Once the focus of her foray to Vietnam, these stuffy interviews now seemed meaningless. Once again she second-guessed her decision. Maybe she would enjoy working with Quinn. She looked down again at her agenda. If she left her legal practice, none of this business development would matter.

She looked into the mirror. Her eyes looked worried, and her mouth drooped. Nearly every meeting came with a drink or an appetizer, or both. With no exercise and a continuous smorgasbord of finger foods, she felt like she'd already gained ten pounds. The pear would be more than enough for breakfast.

She scooted her chair up to the mahogany writing desk and powered up her laptop. While she'd been asleep, her US clients had been busy at work. She watched as the emails loaded up, a continuous stream of dozens of messages. The scrolling stopped after 249 messages. She breathed deeply. She had a decent legal practice. No, a superb practice, one that 95 percent of attorneys could only dream about. For most lawyers, the practice of law wasn't glamorous. Work was hard to come by, as evidenced by the hordes of annoying legal commercials on daytime TV.

Addy had more work than she could do by herself, and clients who paid her full billing rate. That almost never happened for the rest of the legal profession.

And now she had been asked to give it all up for something she'd always believed was impossible. Since last evening, she'd told herself a hundred times that she couldn't walk away from her practice. Everything in her life, from a missing father to a drug-dependent mother, had been so unstable. With partnership in hand, she'd finally felt secure. She'd even mused about a future relationship. Marriage was still too painful to contemplate, but was she ready to take the first step toward a close relationship with a man?

Quinn's ultimatum less than twelve hours ago had thrown all that into a tailspin. *Why do I have to decide before I leave Vietnam?* She felt more hounded and pressured than she had when she decided to buy a used car years ago.

She needed to talk this through. But with whom? She'd kept her distance from close personal relationships to protect herself. Now she wished she had a confidante. Most people had a mother or father they could run to for advice.

Addy felt her pent-up anger beginning to swell. Her mother was probably passed out on her latest boyfriend's filthy floor. Her estranged father died last year after a short bout with cancer. Addy had protected her heart ever since middle school.

The one time she'd let herself down was in high school, when Seth Montgomery asked her out to prom, only to discover it was a practical joke, a dare from his football teammates.

There was Perry, but that was pretty much a non-starter. He might listen for a few minutes, but then he'd start into a lecture on why leaving Wyckoff would be a terrible mistake. And if he knew she'd been threatened, he'd be on a plane to personally bring her home. There was no way he'd approve.

Even asking him about it would be a slap in his face after he'd secured her partnership with the firm. Addy played out the conversion with her mentor: *Thank you for making me partner and sending me on an exotic venture, and I did just what you asked. I found a great new potential client. The only problem is that they want me to start my own firm.* She couldn't do that to Perry.

Still, if anyone could give her advice about whether to trust an elusive start-up company, especially when it involved giving up a lucrative legal practice, it would be Perry. She reached for her phone, then stopped herself. Running the scenario again through her mind, she realized the situation was ludicrous. Perry's questions would be like the cross-examination from hell. She knew nothing about Quinn's company—WTG. What kind of name was that? She thought for a few seconds. *Water-to-gas?* *That's it!* She had to admit, the jingle had a nice ring to it.

She typed the acronym into her computer. Up popped a list of possibilities, including the phrase *way to go*, and a telecommunications company in Maryland. Nothing related to running a car on water.

Red flags sprang everywhere. Here was a company that nobody had ever heard of, but yet had secured millions, maybe even billions, in investment dollars. The technology was touted by Quinn's team as being more significant than atomic energy, yet she had not even a scintilla of proof of its existence. Even worse, such an invention did appear to violate the laws of thermodynamics because the amount of energy needed to remove the hydrogen from water appeared to be greater than what could be generated by running the hydrogen through a fuel cell. Quinn was claiming just the opposite, that he could extract hydrogen from water using less energy than he could produce using the hydrogen as fuel source.

Yet the problem was that she, too, had dreamed of this kind of discovery. That's what Hindy was all about. While Hindy required a tank filled with compressed hydrogen to run the fuel cell and produce the electricity needed to operate the motors, the whole idea behind Hindy was to attract some promising start-up company that might be able to deliver on the concept of hydrogen that could be produced on-demand, thus eliminating the need for a tank of compressed hydrogen and an array of solar panels. Was Quinn trying to tell her she could make her dream come true? The fact that she'd been threatened meant there had to be something to Quinn's claim.

Janice, Addy's paralegal, was probably her closest friend, if she could even call it a friendship. Addy wondered if Janice's loyalty was nothing more than a vain hope on Janice's part that Addy could mentor her into law school. Addy knew if she asked Janice for advice, her offer from WTG would soon get back to Perry and the other partners.

Then there was Quinn. What was it about him that made her want to give up her all-too-secure life? Was it him, or his dream, or her dream?

Her biggest concern was why Quinn wanted her to form her own firm. It would be so simple to make WTG a client of Wyckoff & Schechter. They had the resources to take WTG where it needed to go. Something didn't ring true. Why would any company make such a huge legal investment, setting her up with a brand new, fully-staffed law firm? The offer bordered on the bizarre.

Everything told her to run far away from Quinn and WTG, if the company even existed.

Still, she'd always believed someday, somebody would find a way to get hydrogen out of water economically. If Quinn really had discovered a way, it could be worth billions. Paying for the creation of a law firm to protect that idea would seem like a pittance.

*But why me?*

Addy noted the time stamped on the lower corner of her computer screen. It was the middle of the night in California. Janice would be in bed.

Okay, enough back and forth. *What would I do if this were the usual new client? I'd have Janice check them out,* Addy thought. If there was a paralegal who knew how to dig into the technology sector, it was Janice. More important, Janice had access to proprietary databases and knew how to quickly eliminate superfluous information. Addy quickly tapped out an email, along with a plea that Janice keep the request confidential. In just a few hours she'd have every publicly available document on Quinn and his baby, WTG.

# 10

ADDY WAS SCURRYING through the hotel lobby, late for a meeting with her Japanese colleagues, when she caught a glimpse of Quinn's familiar athletic figure approaching.

"You have a minute?" Quinn asked.

"You've been waiting for me."

"Yes, but I'm not stalking you."

"First the internet, now in my hotel lobby. What's the logical conclusion?"

"It's nothing like that."

"It's not? What is it like, then?"

"Can we take a walk?"

"I've got a meeting with some Japanese attorneys."

"When?"

"In thirty minutes at the Conference Center."

"Good, I'll drive you there. We can talk on the way."

Addy relaxed her arms. "I'd better not be late."

Quinn motioned to the window and snapped his fingers. A black limousine appeared on the street, and Quinn escorted her inside. The leather seats were immediately cool to the touch, and goose bumps popped up on Addy's bare arms.

"You can turn down the air conditioning," Quinn told the driver, taking off his suit jacket and draping it around Addy's shoulders. He loosened his tie and undid his top button. "I'm not into this formal stuff."

They drove through the side streets near the hotel, winding through the rows of corrugated steel hovels where the vast majority of the city's population lived.

"I still don't understand why you can't use Wyckoff," Addy said before Quinn could even begin. "I'd keep everything confidential. And if you're talking about filing all over the world, you are going to need a big firm. A small shop just can't meet your needs."

Quinn rolled up his sleeves. "Hear me out. I'm going to tell you what we've invented, then you'll understand. But before I do, you've got to promise me you won't tell a soul, even if you decide not to join us. Do I have your word?"

"Of course. The rules of legal ethics require me to keep everything confidential between us, even if I don't take you on as a client."

"Good. So we were talking about the Manhattan project at dinner."

Addy nodded.

"This is kind of like that. No, we haven't built another Oakville, Tennessee, but the idea is the same. Even the Germans knew about enriching uranium to build an atomic bomb, but nobody was able to do it until FDR channeled the resources to actually do it."

"But we're not talking atomic energy here."

"No, but extracting hydrogen from water is nothing new. The concept has been around for a long time. It's all about how to do it economically. If it takes more energy to get the hydrogen out of water than you can get putting the hydrogen through a fuel cell, why bother?"

"Exactly."

"What I've discovered is a catalyst that reduces the amount of energy needed to break the hydrogen-oxygen bond. With this catalyst, you save so much energy in the disassociation process that it is now economical to take ordinary water, remove the hydrogen, and run it through a fuel cell to power your car, or any other small energy need."

Addy raised her eyebrows. People had been searching for this type of catalyst for a long time. "Is there a catch?"

"Yes and no."

"What do you mean?"

"It's wicked hard to make the catalyst."

"Like how hard? Like enriching uranium was in 1945?"

"Sort of. Yes, it has taken us hundreds of millions of dollars to produce just a small amount of this catalyst, but now that we've figured it out, we're confident we can reduce our costs."

"What, from a hundred million dollars a gallon to a million a gallon? That still makes the current cost of gasoline quite the bargain."

"I like your sarcasm," Quinn said. "We have the catalyst. We know how to make it. It's just a matter of time before the price is comparable with gasoline. Who knows, it may even be less expensive. Pick up a packet of catalyst in the grocery store, fill your tank with distilled water and pour in the powder. No more combustion engines. Nor more drilling for oil. No more pollution. No more greenhouse gases. No more interest in the Middle East. Addy, we're going to change the world. The world culture as we know it won't exist a decade from now."

The goose bumps again rushed down Addy's arms, but it wasn't from the temperature. The ramifications of eliminating fossil fuels were almost unfathomable.

"Do you have to mine the catalyst?" Addy probed.

"Yes, there is some mining, and a refinement process."

"And where are the mines?"

"That I can't tell you."

"But aren't you just moving the problem from one location to another. I mean are you going to blow up a mountain instead of sucking oil out of the ground? And aren't we going to be fighting over the mines, just like we do with barren sand in Saudi Arabia?"

"Yes and no."

"There you go again."

"The mineral we use is typically found in mountainous regions, but it's everywhere. There is more than enough in the States alone to power cars for centuries."

"Greenpeace?"

"They'll throw a fit, but there is a way to mine the stuff without disturbing the environment."

"Like strip mining for coal?"

"Nothing like that. And some of the mountain ranges aren't too appealing anyway."

"Beauty is in the eye of the beholder."

"It's land nobody wants, for the most part. We've already secured leases and the mineral rights. We're set for large-scale production."

"Harmful byproducts from the reaction in the fuel cell?" Addy asked.

"Perfectly safe, and even if there are any emissions, they are an order of magnitude less than with a combustion engine."

Addy's right leg was bouncing. She steadied herself.

"That still doesn't say why you need me instead of Wyckoff."

"Two reasons. Like I said, we don't want the secret out until our patent applications are published, which would be eighteen months from filing, if I have my facts straight."

"That's right. Every patent office in the world will post your application online a year and a half after you file."

"Until then, we need to keep down the number of people who know about the catalyst and the process for refining it. The biggest problem with large law firms is it's impossible for them to keep a secret. We have reason to believe that big oil already knows about our operations. Do you know how much they would pay to bribe one of your paralegals or secretaries to steal documents?"

"But even if I went with you, I'd need to bring my paralegal. She does all my filings."

"We'd need to change that. You'll need to be the one to process all the documents."

"I'm sure you could find other people as qualified as I am to do an electronic filing."

"Perhaps, but that leads to my second reason for needing you. I'm about the most paranoid person in the world."

"No you're not. Every inventor thinks the world is out to steal his idea."

"That's because they're right. I filed a few test cases,

applications with bogus technology, just to see what would happen. I used two of the most prestigious law firms in the US"

"And?"

"The US government slapped them both with secrecy orders."

Addy flipped Quinn's jacket off her shoulders. "What?"

It had actually happened to her once. She filed for a ceramic-based material that arguably could be used for body armor. The Department of Defense screened the case and handed down a secrecy order, requiring the information contained in the patent application remain secret until cleared by the DOE. It took her two years and a call to her senator's office to get it removed.

"I need a creative patent attorney to figure out how to get my applications through the Patent Office without the Defense Department meddling with them. Investors don't like it when the US government tries to suppress their patent applications."

"If they take your idea, they have to pay you for it. It's in our Constitution."

"Perhaps, but I'm not a US citizen. And just the idea that the government is on the verge of taking such a course of action is enough for my investors to get skittish and walk."

"I understand."

"You're creative. We know that. I figure you can find a strategy to get them through the Patent Office unscathed. By using an unknown law firm, we figure our chances are better. And there won't be any conflict issues in case one of your firm's big clients claims to have invented the same thing."

Addy sighed. Quinn was right on all fronts. He was far more savvy about legal matters than she had surmised. And on the technology side—if what he said was true—he was an absolute mastermind. Somehow, he inherently knew how to push her buttons. Beside him, she could feel his body heat, and she felt herself sinking into his side.

Quinn took up his jacket and motioned the driver. They turned the corner and pulled in front of the Conference Center.

"I really do need to have an answer by the end of the banquet tomorrow evening. I can't wait any longer to get my applications filed."

Addy turned to face him. "I still have so many questions."

"But I just told you my secret. What else is there to tell?"

"The most important thing. I don't know about you, about how you got involved in this. Why did you give up your dream to be an Olympian?"

"Oh, that wasn't my dream. It was my father's dream. I didn't want any part of it."

Addy folded her arms and sank back into the plush seat. "Explain."

"Did I like fencing? I'd say it was just okay, but it wasn't my passion. I know so many kids grow up with a dream of being a famous athlete, and for a while, so did I. But as the years wore on, the glamour wore off. I didn't have any kind of life. I'd get up at four in the morning, go to practice and sweat for three hours. From there, we'd go straight to school, then back to the gym again for workouts after school. Every weekend I was on a plane or in a car traveling to some match."

"I suppose that's what it takes to be the best in the world," Addy said.

"Don't think I'm a quitter. I would have kept up with it if that had been my dream, but it wasn't. My father was a famous fencer. He's now a referee for most of the big matches. I finally realized I was doing it for him, but I didn't really enjoy it. When high school was over, I had scholarships to all kinds of universities in Korea, but I wanted to go to school in America. I'd been there many times for fencing meets and loved everything about it. I loved the culture, the food, the entertainment. And I loved chemistry, so I decided that I wanted to give up fencing and get a chemistry degree in the States. Eventually I want to become an American citizen."

"And your father, what does he think of all this?"

"You need to understand Korean tradition. To disobey my father's wishes was to dishonor the family. When I told him, he said our family would be disgraced if I quit fencing, and if that was my decision, I was not welcome in his home."

"But you quit anyway."

"I did. Believe it or not, I got an academic scholarship to the School of Mines in Colorado. But even with the scholarship, I had to take a job on the campus grounds crew, shoveling snow at five in the morning, to make it through."

"That's impressive. Did your father ever have a change of heart?"

"No, not a chance. I've been on my own since high school. I guess you could say my invention is an attempt to redeem myself."

"You don't owe them anything."

"In Korea, it's not that easy. Besides, I want to prove I can really do it. And when I do, when we make our grand announcement, I'm confident I can restore my family's honor. And what about you? Does your father approve of you trotting around in a car that sports a hydrogen-filled balloon?"

Addy looked out the window. She didn't want to discuss her family situation, although she suspected Quinn probably knew about the divorce, since it was public record.

"My father passed away last year, but we hadn't spoken for over a decade. He wasn't my real father anyway. You probably already know I was born here in Vietnam and was brought to America by an adoption agency. When I was only two, my father left the family, and my mother struggled to raise me."

"I'm sorry," he said. "This I didn't know. Are you close to your mother?"

Addy bit her lip while wondering how much she should reveal about her dysfunctional family. "My mother had a breakdown when my father abandoned her. She turned to drugs, and has had an addiction problem ever since. I've pretty much been on my own since day one. Let's just leave it at that."

Quinn smiled softly. "I'm sorry. I guess we're more alike than either of us wants to admit. We both have fathers who have abandoned us, and in our own way, we're trying to prove them wrong, prove we can really make something of ourselves without them. We're both thinking this is going to take away the pain, but we both know that somehow it won't."

Addy reached for the door. "I think we should get going. I'll have an answer for you before I leave."

# 11

HINDY AND THE seared balloon were housed in the vehicular forensics lab, a building akin to an oversized garage that housed a bullet-ridden 4x4 and a Lamborghini confiscated during a drug raid. Agent Long was leaning over a lab table, studying the ballistics report. Speckled on the seared balloon, they found trace chemicals from the flare: potassium nitrate, charcoal, and sulfur. It was too generic to tie to a specific flare gun or even a manufacturer.

"Fred," Long said to an investigator dressed in a lab coat. "Any theories on why this guy took out the blimp?"

"It's a giant mystery. At first we thought this Addy person was driving some kind of top secret car that some Muslim faction didn't want to interfere with oil consumption, but that's clearly not to the case."

"What do you mean? It looks terrorist-driven to me."

"Perhaps, but this car is nothing special. The blimp was all for show. The car's got a set of off-the-shelf electric motors and a fuel cell you can purchase from half a dozen companies. Runs on compressed hydrogen. Pretty standard stuff."

"Nothing more on the photo?"

"Maybe. We think we've deciphered the Arabic characters."

"And?"

"This guy isn't the sharpest tool in the shed. We think he intended it to say *Bad Ass*, but the way it translates into English, it really means *Asshole*."

"So this guy doesn't speak Arabic."

"I doubt he's even Muslim. Shariah Law prohibits tattoos."

"So he's not from the Middle East?"

"Doesn't appear to be, but I'm not sure whether that's a good thing or a bad thing. Anyway, I think we can go ahead and release the car."

Long held up his hand. "Not so fast. Let's keep it a bit longer. I may need it as leverage."

"For?"

"To find out what Quinn's been telling Addy. They're together in Vietnam."

"Fine, but you can't store it here."

"Put it in the impound lot."

"Isn't she going to ask for it? We have no reason to keep it. When's the hearing?"

"I'll find an excuse."

"Blame it on Homeland Security."

"Good idea."

# 12

ADDY HAD JUST slipped into her evening gown and was struggling with her zipper when an email notification popped up on her computer screen that Janice had sent her a batch of daily reminders. Janice's third email indicated she had some information about Addy's "diligence project." That was one reason Addy knew she couldn't work without Janice. She was discreet and professional. She knew better than to put any name in an email, and certainly not WTG.

She latched the clasp on her dress, pulled her hair back and dialed her mobile phone. As usual, Janice's voice conveyed the bright, energetic attitude of a true morning person.

"How's Vietnam?" Janice said.

"I think the food is getting to me. My stomach feels like it has an angry kitten inside."

"You're not getting any sympathy from me. I'd trade places with you in a heartbeat."

Even with flaming intestines and the stress imposed by Quinn's demands, Addy had to admit that, aside from having her life threatened, there was something exciting about international travel. It might be fun to have more of that in her future.

"Tell me what you've got," Addy said.

"Not a whole lot. WTG has one pending trademark application, two patent applications on some kind of fuel cell, and an article in a Korean journal on WTG's focus on alternative energy."

Addy wondered if those were the patents Quinn had mentioned. Probably decoys or test cases filed with the US patent system.

"The only really interesting piece of information I found was a blog about a giant industrial park being built about an hour outside of Seoul. The blogger was whining about some big tax break a company called WTG had gotten when nobody has any idea what they're doing there. Looks like some real money is behind them."

"Anything else?"

"Just the obligatory social media sites, but I'm assuming you've already looked at those."

"Roger that," Addy said.

Addy had found Quinn on LinkedIn and confirmed his educational background, including his PhD from Caltech, but his current position mentioned only that he was a research scientist without listing an organization.

"That's about it," Janet concluded. "Like I said, I couldn't find much. If you're wondering whether they would pay their bills if we took over their work, I think we'd be fine. Besides, they only have two patent applications, not enough to worry about."

Addy couldn't tell Janice that she had no intention of making WTG one of Wyckoff's clients. The more interesting discussion would be whether Janice would join her if she went with Quinn. Janice had a six-year-old daughter with a history of severe asthma, and health care would be a deciding factor. Just mulling over the question meant it was time for Addy to face the fact that she was seriously considering a divorce from Wyckoff.

"Okay. Look, I've got to run to dinner. I'll read your emails later tonight. Thanks for looking into it for me."

Addy set down her phone and stared out the window, musing over the sea of tin-roofed shacks spread out on the horizon. Hundreds of hand-built fires were being stoked to warm these peasants' evening meals, sending up a skyline full of gray plumes. They were modern hunter-gatherers. In some parts of the world, life hadn't evolved much over the past ten thousand years.

Addy stood and glanced at the clock on the nightstand. The closing reception would be starting in ten minutes, and there was no more time to vacillate. Quinn would want an answer right after the banquet.

If she stayed with Wyckoff, she'd always regret not taking a chance. But if she left and Quinn turned out to be a fraud, it could take another decade or more to rebuild her career, if it was even possible.

She struggled to find a definitive answer. What really matters? What's my passion? What gets me up in the morning?

Addy knew her drive to be someone different, someone who stood out, was the real reason behind Hindy. She wanted to make a name for herself, to show her adoptive mother that she could not only make it on her own, but change the world in the process. In that sense, she *was* just like Quinn.

If Addy and Quinn could get their names up in lights, they both believed, somehow their pain would go away. She'd always secretly dreamed of being famous, of traveling the talk show circuit, explaining how she'd solved the world's energy problems, how she'd found a way to curb climate change, maybe even be on a reality television show. With these thoughts, the fear created by the threats of the previous days seemed to melt away.

This seemed worth the risk, and the inevitable battles.

*But should I make a decision based on such a selfish motive?*

Addy returned her gaze to the smoke plumes wafting up to the heavens like burning incense.

Could she honestly say her decision was based on creating a world that would be so much better off if it had this technology? *Yes,* she thought. If ordinary water could be used as an energy source, would there be any more poverty? The vast scene of suffering spread out before her—could it change in her lifetime? Could all these people someday be able to drive cars of their own? Wasn't this what her decision was all about?

Yes, but only if it was true, only if Quinn really had invented what he claimed.

Addy hurried to finish applying her makeup, threw a few

extra business cards into her purse, clipped on her name badge and slipped out into the darkness of the evening.

\* \* \*

During dinner Addy sat at a table hosted by a group of Indian attorneys with accents so thick she could only understand every third word. It didn't matter, though. She wasn't listening anyway. She followed the conversation with her eyes without actually seeing them, nodding her head every few sentences to make them think she was engaged. Between bites of rubber chicken, she mentally tossed around her options.

*Can I trust Quinn?* The question rolled over and over in her head. *What if this is nothing more than a harebrained scheme?*

Her waitress reached over her shoulder with a bottle of red wine. Addy looked up into her face. The girl smiled, and Addy noticed an array of crooked teeth, one of which was half yellow, half brown. Her bony shoulders made Addy wonder what she was going to eat when she went home. *How many people live like this?* she wondered.

While they finished dessert, she saw a tuxedo-clad Quinn get up and excuse himself. She looked at the time on her phone. The moment had arrived. She had an appointment with Quinn back at her hotel. The time for waffling was over.

She watched while he worked his way to the back of the room, weaving through the tables and guests adorned in gaudy cocktail dresses and ill-fitting tuxedos. His figure was striking. He was so purposeful, so alluring. If his claims were true, he might well be the world's most brilliant scientist, one who had discovered a technology that would rank him with Alexander Graham Bell or the Wright Brothers.

A chill shot down her spine. She couldn't let this opportunity slip away.

Too many lives were at stake for her to worry about getting hurt one more time; too many people had no idea where they would find their next meal. Had she ever experienced such misery? Not even close. Yes, she never felt the arms of a loving father or mother around her and she'd lived off the charity of others, but she'd always had food, there were always clothes in her closet, and she'd received about the best education America could offer. To imagine she understood what peasants endured was almost laughable. If anything could drive her past her own fears, it was the thought of giving this waitress, this skeleton of a figure, a chance for a better life.

Addy excused herself, and the Indian men stood in their white suits and wished her safe travels back to the States. She shook their hands and hurried after Quinn.

\* \* \*

They had decided to meet at the pool deck on the top floor of the Marriott, a secluded venue where they could view the city lights while they discussed their future plans. Quinn was already there, standing with his arms folded. The city lights were glittering behind him, and his face reflected the constantly changing color of the pool lights. It reminded Addy of a scene from *The Bachelor* reality show, where the only remaining contestant came to accept the final rose. They were only missing the flaming tiki lights.

"So," he said as Addy approached. "I've given you a lot to think about. Have you decided?"

"What kind of package are you offering? We haven't even discussed the terms of my employment."

"Twenty percent more than you're making now, plus stock options. And, like I said, there will be bonuses for every patent you get us. A year from now, you'll have more money than you could ever spend."

"That's quite generous."

"We want you on board."

She stood facing him, gazing into his sparkling eyes. He couldn't possibly be deceiving her, not with that kind of reflection.

"Just one question," she said.

His lips parted and his large white teeth sparkled. "Why did

I suspect this was coming?"

"Because with me nothing is easy."

"As I said, I don't want a pushover. I don't need an attorney who tells me what I want to hear. I need someone I can confide in, a partner who can help me make this happen. With what is at stake here, you know this isn't going to be easy."

Addy nodded, wondering if he was testing her resolve. "Of course."

"Well then, ask away."

She stood erect and reached out for his arm, feeling his steady influence. "If I join, and I'm not saying yet whether I will—" Addy paused.

"Yes?"

"If I tell you that I'll give up everything I've worked for, give up my partnership, risk my career for you—" Addy studied his eyes, but Quinn's countenance remained stoic, unmoved. "If I take a position with WTG, will I really be the one to stand next to Hindy and tell the press about what you've invented?"

Quinn threw his arms around her. "Is that it? Of course! I never go back on my word. You and me both, for the world to see. Then you're in?"

Addy felt the security of his solid figure surrounding her. "I'd love to join you."

Her tension evaporated miraculously, and she savored the moment while Quinn hugged her tighter.

"You are going to be a major part of my company, not just my patent lawyer," he said holding her apart from him and staring deeply into her eyes.

She sighed. "There's so much to do." Already she was creating a mental list of what lay ahead: resigning her partnership, telling her clients, cleaning out her office, saying her goodbyes, trying to convince Quinn to let Janice join her. Then there was learning a new technology, planning her legal strategy. And finding the skeletons. Lawyers knew skeletons always came with every deal.

"Don't worry about logistics," Quinn said. "We're taking care of all that so you can get right to work. We already have office space in Mountain View, and you'll be up and running in less than a week."

"I'll need to give at least a month's notice."

"See if you can negotiate it down. Since you aren't taking any of the firm's clients, I can't see that your partners will mind."

It seemed like the honeymoon was over even before it got started. She hated facing reality.

"I'm coming to the Bay Area next week," he continued, "and we can go over the technology together. I want the patent applications drafted as soon as possible."

"I'll need Janice."

Quinn raised his eyebrows.

"My paralegal. I can't function without her. She's like my right arm."

A frown crept on his face. "There are only a handful of people who know about the catalyst. The board has only approved one other, and that is you."

"Janice is an English major. She wouldn't know a catalyst from a Cadillac."

His scowl changed to a grin. "Quick-witted as well. Is there any way we could wall her off so she could never have access to any of the science?"

"Maybe, but she'd need to teach me all of the details of electronic filing if she can't see the paperwork."

"All right, I'll consider it, but the board is going to have to approve. No exceptions."

She leaned over and kissed him on the cheek.

"One more thing," he said. "I told you that we take security seriously. We'll take you to the airport. You should be much safer in the States, but we're still going to watch out for you."

"Are you sure?"

"They'll stay back. You won't notice them."

"Okay, thank you. And I'll be careful. I promise."

# 13

ADDY PRODDED THE squishy rubber tire with her finger. It had been more than three months since she'd ridden her bicycle. With Hindy impounded, she needed either a cab, a rental car, or the bike, and she'd had enough of strange drivers. Besides, after a week of constant eating, the exercise was welcome.

Her level of physical fitness had slipped in recent years as her caseload at Wyckoff increased. In high school, she ran cross country, and when she went to college a classmate introduced her to a grungy MMA gym a few blocks from their dormitory. The kickboxing regimen was a welcome relief from her studies. By her junior year she was invited to enter a tournament, but after her first opponent landed a stiff roundhouse to her ribs, she decided to keep to recreational training.

She found the pump leaning against the wall, hooked it up to the inner tube, and began pressing and lifting. With every cycle, she rehearsed how she would begin her resignation speech. As she twisted the valve cap back on, she noticed her hand was shaking. Nothing she rehearsed sounded credible. She'd never seen the technology that would supposedly revolutionize the energy industry, done almost no diligence on WTG, and was trusting the word of an unseasoned inventor who dressed like he should be on the cover of *GQ*.

The morning was cool, and the breeze flowing over her tightly-clipped hair seemed to clear her mind. By the time Addy reached the office, she was emboldened to make her announcement. She found Perry with his phone tucked between his neck and shoulder while he frantically typed out an email. He was the king of multitasking. As soon as he saw Addy, he motioned her inside and pointed to one of the two leather chairs facing his desk. Perry ended the call and sat erect.

"So tell me about Vietnam."

"It was nice," was all she could muster.

"Nice, that's it? I've heard the food is excellent. What did you think?"

Addy shrugged. "Some of it was good, but I got sick. That part wasn't so much fun."

"Tell me about your meetings."

Addy could feel her heart racing. She put her hand over her chest and breathed deeply. "That's what I need to talk to you about," she managed.

"Did something happen?"

"Do you remember that new lead I talked to you about?"

Perry pinched his chin, his eyes reflective. "The first evening?"

"Yes, that's the one. Oh, I don't want to drag this out. I've decided to resign from the firm. I've been given an offer to start my own firm to support this truly remarkable company."

Perry fell back against his chair, frowning. "Truly remarkable? Are you out of your mind? What kind of fraud has you under his spell?" He slapped his hand down on the table. Addy jumped. "Tell me about this so-called remarkable company."

"I'm sorry," Addy fought back, "but I can't give you any details. I'm under an NDA."

Perry rolled his eyes. "That's what I figured. Then tell me what I need to know."

Addy danced around the edges of what Quinn had revealed to her, mentioning only that it was an energy company that could allow a car to run on water.

"Hydrogen production—from water! Don't tell me you fell

for some sweet-talking dreamer. We all know it takes more energy to get hydrogen out of water than you'll ever get out of the hydrogen."

Addy wished her mentor hadn't been so quick to drill down to the real issue.

"That's the discovery," she said.

Perry stared at the ceiling, then slowly lowered his head. He began tapping his finger on the desk, softly at first, then coming to a crescendo. He abruptly pounded his fist.

"What discovery! Sounds like a perpetual motion machine. Addy, you can't defy the laws of thermodynamics. Trust me on this one. I'm looking out for your best interests. I don't want to see you get hurt. Why would you do this? You've worked so hard to be Wyckoff's youngest partner. The sky's the limit. If you want energy clients, I have three I'm ready to turn over right now. Not to mention you're already doing work for one of the country's most promising fuel cell companies."

"I'm sorry, but I can't tell you any more than that. This is just something I need to do. It is an opportunity I simply can't pass up."

Perry flew out of his chair, sending it crashing into his credenza. "This is such a bad idea. Trust me, I've been around the block enough times to know that this is totally crazy. This is some kind of scam."

"No, I can feel it in my bones. This is my chance to really make a difference in the world."

Perry folded his arms and strode to the window. After a few moments he spun around. "I'm sorry for my outburst. It's just that you took me by surprise, and I'm having a hard time processing what you've said. I understand your desire to make an impact, but I've got clients in the same space. What about ChargeIt? Their next generation batteries will let a car go nearly eight hundred miles on a single charge. I was planning to introduce you to their patent counsel next week, telling them that we'd just made you our youngest ever partner."

Addy lowered her head. If there was one person in the world who had looked out for her, it was Perry. He was almost like the father she'd never had. Maybe he was right. Should she trust him and tell Quinn that she'd changed her mind? She didn't want to let him down.

"This is so hard," she finally said. "You've done so much for me, and I don't want to seem ungrateful."

"Then stay at Wyckoff. When you get to be my age, you'll understand. Nearly every young patent attorney goes through this phase. The daily grind of churning out patent applications sets in, and there's this allure of joining a promising new start-up touting a groundbreaking technology, and lots of stock options. I'll bet more than 80 percent of the associates we hire jump ship in the first five years. A few of them make it big, but most don't. Plenty come crawling back, tails between their legs, asking for their jobs back. We tell most of them no."

Addy wondered if he'd read her mind. The security of getting her old job back had helped make her decision easier. Now Perry was telling her not to count on that option.

"If I never take a chance," she said panning the room with her hand, "this could be my life." She stopped herself. "I didn't mean it that way. You've had a great career with Wyckoff. I just don't want to reach your age and wish I'd taken a chance to make a real difference."

"What about your high school invention competition? Isn't that making a difference? And we have a great pro bono program. You can help out a lot of indigent people in our own community. If you want to make a difference, why don't you volunteer to give legal advice to families of domestic violence? And we're donating a significant amount of the profits from your practice to new green-friendly start-ups. What more could you want?"

Addy clasped her hands in her lap and bowed her head. She'd forgotten about that perk. Wyckoff was on the cutting edge in the area of giving back some of its profits to the community.

"Why don't you give it some more time? Take the day off, get over your jet lag, and we can talk tomorrow. If you still feel the same, I'll give you my blessing."

Addy looked up. "I wish I could, but I've already committed. The ball is already in play. My office is being set up, and they want me to start as soon as I can. I'm here to ask if the thirty-day notice requirement can be waived."

Perry shook his head. "I really can't believe this. You're

making a giant mistake. Who is this new client, some Asian company, I presume?"

"Korean," she said. "His name is Quinn Moon and he was educated in the States."

"Of course he was; it's just like them. They come to America, take up all the spots in the good schools so the Americans can't get in, then take all the jobs. You know how it is. Just look at the Patent Office. Half of the examiners can't even speak English, just some gobbledygook that nobody can understand. And you can't trust them, those Asians are all alike."

"What about me?" Addy interrupted. "Are you forgetting that I'm one of them?"

"No you're not. You're an American. You don't even have an accent."

Addy's brows drew together and she gritted her teeth. "You're a racist, plain and simple."

Perry shook his head. "No, I am not a racist. I totally adore you, and you're from Vietnam. That's not being a racist. I'm just making a point that you need to treat other cultures differently. The Chinese steal, that's just how they are. You just need to expect that they are going to steal you blind every chance you get. And the Koreans want to outdo you. They'll do anything to make it happen, just like this Quinn fellow."

"You're wrong. That's racism. You can't categorically say that an entire culture is bad or immoral. Yes, they may be different, what drives them might be different, but that doesn't make you any better."

"Fine, if that's how you want to put it, we'll leave it at that. But I'm warning you about this Quinn person. It's only going to lead to heartbreak. Then you'll see I'm telling you the truth, hard as it may be to take right now. I'm just being upfront with you, because I'm worried that you're going to get hurt.

"Now, isn't there anything I can do to make you reconsider?"

Only Perry could accost her, then pretend it never happened. She refused to look him in the eye.

"I'm not taking my secretary, but I'd like to see if Janice will join me. We work well together, and I'm going to need an experienced paralegal."

"Taking any clients as well?"

"No, no clients, at least in the beginning. I'll have more work than I can do with this one. I'd like to start next week. I can work late to make sure everything on my docket is up to date before I leave."

"So I guess your mind is made up?"

"I'm afraid so. I hope this doesn't come between us. I'm hoping we can stay friends."

Perry shook his head. "Sure. The executive committee will need to approve your early departure. I'll ask Pingree to rush through the request."

Addy stood and held out her hand. "Thanks for everything you've done for me."

Perry stood to face her. "You're forgetting something. You've got a little problem with Hindy. Remember?"

Her bike ride into work put that issue front and center, but in working through the logistics of leaving Wyckoff, she'd completely forgotten that Perry had been negotiating Hindy's release.

Addy bit her lip.

"I've already filed papers with the court to act as your attorney, and the judge wants a hearing before he will release the car. The Department of Homeland Security wants an investigation into whether the sabotage was a terrorist act. DHS wants to throw some questions at you during your appearance before the judge."

Addy threw down her arms. "What? That's not fair. I was the one who was attacked."

"Fair? As a lawyer, you should know better than to think the law is fair."

Addy knew he was right. But this was ridiculous. This wasn't an act of terrorism. She was just being harassed. But why?

"Don't you think it is just a little bit suspicious that Hindy gets blown up, and then you immediately get an offer from some unknown company with a promise to roll out a technology that defies the laws of physics? Addy, I'm worried about what is happening to you."

In her zeal, Addy had suppressed all thoughts about threats on her life. Now she reconsidered. This wasn't some kind of game she was playing. She'd been warned to keep out of the energy space, and now she was ignoring certain danger.

"Okay, I could use your help with Hindy. You can make me a client. I'll pay my bills."

Perry smoothed his dark, gray-speckled hair. "I'm not going to charge you. I'll see if I can get Hindy back, but I want you to reconsider."

# 14

ADDY HAD TOUCHED up her lipstick and snapped her purse shut when an email notification popped up on her computer screen. The email address was unfamiliar, but the subject line caught her attention.

*Will you forgive me?* it read.

Addy thought it was spam and was poised to hit the delete button on her keyboard. But then she wondered who might be asking for forgiveness. She studied the Gmail account associated with the message. It contained a form of her last name, and the initial *L*. Her stepmother's first name was Lynda. That, along with the subject line, was too irresistible. She at least needed to peek.

As she read, she gasped, sat bolt upright, and smacked her hand over her open mouth. She quickly scanned the short letter, eyes flashing back and forth along the lines. It was an admission from her stepmother and a plea for reconciliation.

Addy felt her throat tighten as she continued to stare at the screen, her mind unable to focus.

"You ready?" came a voice from behind her.

It was Janice. Addy clicked the email closed, tucked her

hair behind her ear, and breathed deeply. Maintaining an expressionless face, she said, "Perfect timing. Let's go."

Janice drove with Addy to Oren's Hummus Shop, a new restaurant serving Israeli cuisine. It was far enough away from Wyckoff's offices that they wouldn't run into any Wyckoff partners. They were escorted to a sunny courtyard, partially shaded by redwood trees.

"You were staring at your computer screen pretty intently," Janice said while they waited for their server.

Addy preferred keeping her past private, but with everything that was happening in her life, she was ready to explode. She needed somebody to understand her life.

"It was from my stepmother," Addy said.

Janice's eyebrows shot up. Addy had previously shared the details of her father's passing and subsequent funeral with her.

"This is the woman who conveniently didn't tell you your father had passed away from cancer until the funeral was over. Correct?"

Addy nodded. The episode of her father's passing brought back all her painful childhood memories.

"Yes, the same woman," Addy said. "She said that after a year of feeling bitter, her feelings have mellowed, and she wants to apologize. She said it was wrong not to tell me about the funeral. She told me I have a stepbrother in the eleventh grade. Evidently, he's the star of a boys' soccer team, and she would love for me to meet him, maybe even watch one of his games. She says he has all kinds of questions about college he wants to ask me. And, I found out my stepsister is expecting her first child. I could be an aunt pretty soon."

"Sounds like great news to me. Are you going to accept the offer? You'd be crazy not to. You need a family."

"I'm thinking about it," Addy said. "I've just got a few things to work out."

"Like leaving Wyckoff."

Addy nodded.

"News travels fast," Janice said shaking out her napkin. "I already heard."

"I'm sorry, I was hoping I could break the news," Addy replied, while the waiter filled their glasses with water and handed them each a menu.

"All I can say is that it must be some kind of incredible deal for you to give up becoming a partner. It's all anyone can talk about."

"What else are they saying?"

"You really want to know?"

Addy nodded.

"They say you stabbed Perry in the back, especially after he went out on a limb to make you partner early."

"I was afraid of that. Perry is the last person I wanted to hurt."

"I hate to be frank, but I kind of agree. Why are you doing this?"

Addy explained about the opportunity, and how this wasn't about the money, but about a chance to be a part of something that would be in the history books for centuries.

"This is for that company you asked me to research? WTG, wasn't it?"

"Yeah."

"But I didn't really find anything. Are you sure about this? When you say things like 'changing history,' it seems a little farfetched."

"I know it's risky, but I have such a strong, positive feeling about it. I've got to go with my gut. This is my dream. I can't pass it up."

"You know what I think? I think you're emotionally caught up in this and there's more than you're telling me."

"Not at all."

"Well, I don't get it, then. Why leave Wyckoff when you've worked so hard for this partnership? I thought that was your dream. Something is making you not think with that brain God gave you," Janice said as she tapped her forehead.

The waiter returned and they placed their orders. Addy worried. She needed Janice to leave Wyckoff and follow her to WTG. Without her, Addy couldn't file the applications or even handle most of the back-and-forth correspondence with the Patent Office. Addy had assumed Janice would come with her. Now she was not so sure.

"I asked you out to lunch to see if you'd join me at WTG."

Janice rolled her eyes. "What, are you crazy? You have lost your mind."

Addy scooted forward. "Look, I know this must seem really weird, maybe crazy, but we're talking about a technology that can change the world. Before your daughter gets to college, I'll bet you won't be driving the same kind of car. You're going to want to be part of this."

"That's great for you," Janice said, "because you're an engineer and a lawyer, and that's all you ever think about. That's your dream, not mine."

"It was your dream," Addy reminded her.

"To be a lawyer, yes. But that's not going to happen. I've accepted my lot in life. Right now, I've got a six-year-old with severe asthma. That's my life. You know I can't leave, not with my family commitments and insurance."

"I've been authorized to offer you a 25 percent raise, and the insurance package is even better than at Wyckoff. And you'll be working for a start-up. No more policies and procedures. You come to work, get the job done, and nobody cares what time you start the clock or if you have to leave for a doctor appointment."

Janice sipped her tea. "Now I am really skeptical. Why would anyone want to offer me that much?"

"I told you. This is really big. Think of it as a new Google or Facebook. Their patents are critical, and they need someone who won't mess up their filings. I told them you're the only person I trust."

"But you hardly know anything about them. Who is this Quinn fellow you told me about?"

Addy snatched up her phone, swiped the screen and held it up. "That's Quinn in the tux."

Janice sat back and cross her legs. "So now I understand. Is this about his looks or his technology?

"It's nothing like that."

"Well, I wouldn't mind having him for my boss either. Perry can't compare to that."

"Then you'll come?"

"I'll think about it, but no promises."

The waiter returned with their meals and Janice asked about what it was like to be in Vietnam. It didn't take long until the discussion turned back to Wyckoff.

"If I leave Wyckoff, how will I know I'll get paid? You know how these start-ups work. Half of them go bankrupt in the first year and we never get paid a dime."

"They've got lots of wealthy investors," Addy assured her.

"And who would that be? From what I found, they seem to be just a shell company. And, do I get any stock options?"

Addy hesitated. It had been hard enough trying to convince Quinn to let her bring Janice in with such a large raise. "I'll need to check on that."

"And what about your other troubles?"

"Troubles?" Addy asked.

"Yeah, with Hindy. Didn't Perry tell you?"

"He told me that the judge wants a hearing before he will release Hindy, something about an investigation by Homeland Security."

"It's more than just some terrorist threat. Perry found out that the word on the street is that there are dozens of terrorist cells who are worried about the US weaning away from Middle East oil. They are finding ways to discourage alternative technologies. Business is business, no matter what your political or religious affiliation."

"That's crazy. That can't be true."

"You do represent a fuel cell company, and Perry's practice is loaded with them. It's not like you aren't throwing it in everyone's face with that blimp on your car. I don't think you can dismiss it. Homeland Security certainly isn't."

"That's nonsense," Addy said, wondering if her Vietnamese assailant was tied to this group. "Perry is going to go with me to the hearing, everything will be sorted out, and I'll get Hindy back."

"But seriously," Janet said. "Could I end up in some kind of serious trouble, or even danger, if I come with you?"

"Nothing to worry about," Addy assured her, while her insides were churning. She was asking Janice to trust her, when she herself refused to trust anyone. Worse, Addy knew she wasn't being forthright. They were all at risk if they continued with this venture.

Staring across at Janice, she felt a guilty pang. What if the venture with Quinn didn't work out? Was that worth ruining Janice's future, and putting the health of her daughter at risk? If she couldn't even trust her own mother, how could she trust Quinn?

Rehashing the issues was pointless. She'd made her decision, and there was no turning back. "We'd better get back. I've got to pack up my office. I'd love to have you join me. I'll need an answer by tomorrow."

\* \* \*

Addy didn't wait to respond to Lynda's request. She had made that mistake once, and it cost her a final visit with her father. She typed a reply on her phone, telling Lynda that she too thought it was time to forget about the past and move on, and she'd love to visit. Addy further explained that she was leaving her law firm to start her own practice, and that she would send Lynda a note about going to see them as soon as she was settled.

# 15

AGENT LONG SMOOTHED his hand over his shiny head and breathed deeply. He'd been waiting in customs at San Francisco International Airport for over an hour. He knew Quinn's Korean Air flight direct from Seoul took just under eleven hours, but he wasn't taking any chances. Long had met with all the customs agents and instructed them to escort Quinn straight to secondary screening the moment he turned over his passport.

How he interrogated Quinn depended on what he found in his luggage. Long had learned from HydroGen President Jerry Wilcox that Quinn's research there focused on the development of a catalytic reaction that facilitated the separation of hydrogen from oxygen. Wilcox and Quinn had worked side by side for months on the project, although their working relationship was anything but collegial. They constantly disagreed over their research protocols and possible catalytic materials. According to Wilcox, Quinn was so competitive that it was his way or no way. It was as if he'd brought a fencing competition to the research lab. But he put up with Quinn because of his raw talent, or as Long surmised, because Quinn had better ideas than his own.

The reason for Quinn's sudden departure to Korea was still unclear. At first, Wilcox claimed he'd fired Quinn because of an unprofessional working relationship, but he later changed his story, saying Quinn had left in a huff once Wilcox had invented the catalyst and refused to place Quinn's name on the patent application, because Quinn didn't invent anything.

Whatever the reason, being fired or leaving on his own initiative, Quinn's employee agreement required him to assign all of his inventions to HydroGen, who in turn was obligated to assign its rights to the Department of Energy. Even if Quinn was disgruntled because Wilcox wouldn't put his name on the patent application, that was no reason to steal the idea. He didn't own it anyway.

Long's phone beeped, a signal that Quinn was on his way. Long jumped behind the large X-ray machine. While Long was under immense pressure to obtain enough evidence to arrest Quinn for theft of trade secrets, the Justice Department wanted Long to stop Quinn without any publicity.

The official story was that the DOE felt that the technology wasn't fully developed and did not want a premature announcement of any so-called water cars until they were sure it really worked. Being embarrassed on the international stage if they couldn't make good on the outlandish claims was political suicide for anyone at the Energy Department. Long privately surmised it was because of the politics behind protecting a massive investment in US oil production, but that was all way above his pay grade.

From his hiding place, Long observed Quinn being escorted by a single customs agent to the luggage scanner. "Throw all your stuff on the conveyor belt," the agent said placing his hands on his hips, above his holstered handgun.

"I've got computer equipment in there. Can I pull that out?" Quinn said.

"Computer equipment?"

Quinn hesitated. "Couple of flash drives."

"Your data will be safe. If it doesn't go through our scanner, we'll need to download the data. Choice is yours."

Quinn's jaw muscles flexed. Long leaned his ear closer to hear Quinn's response.

"Put 'em through, then."

"And we're going to need to search your person."

"Meaning?"

"We'll start with a pat down."

"And if I refuse?"

"We take your computer equipment and send you back to Korea."

Long peeked around the corner to catch Quinn's reaction. Quinn hesitated, then held up his hands and beamed a smile. "If you put it that way, I'm all yours."

Long pounded his fist against his leg. If Quinn had the catalyst, there was no way he would consent to the search. While Long could run to a judge and try to get a search warrant for the drives, he knew the DOJ wouldn't want that sort of public record. Besides, the drives were probably encrypted at so many levels that he'd never be able to uncover the information in his lifetime.

He knew he had struck out again.

# 16

"THIS WAS A GIANT mistake," Janice said, her feet perched on Addy's desk while she studied her cracking fingernail polish. "I should have never let you talk me into leaving Wyckoff."

"Give it some more time," Addy said.

"More time isn't going to fix the problem. You told me that working for a start-up would be fun. No more policies, as I recall. I now have four different passwords to get my computer to work, my Android doesn't get a signal unless I go outside, and that requires squeezing through a scanner. Before long, one of these Koreans will be patting me down."

"I admit, it's a real pain, but that's only because the technology is so valuable."

"And what technology would that be? We haven't seen anything that resembles a patent application since we walked through those doors. I haven't done a single thing I'm trained to do, unless you consider teaching a bunch of tech geeks about how to use the Patent Office website. These guys can barely speak English."

"I take it you didn't hit it off with Sung-soo?" Addy said, referring to the tech guy that Jeyhu, the VP over green technologies, had sent to the States to set up Addy's computer network.

Janice burst out laughing. "I call him Gawk-soo, because that's all he does—gawk at me."

"You and me both."

Addy had the same concerns about the idleness. She had heard nothing about the catalyst, and received no word from Quinn. He'd told her to expect radio silence, but the lack of activity was nerve-racking. She was accustomed to scrambling nearly all day, billing every possible minute. After setting up her computer, arranging her office, and meeting with the new staff, there was nothing left to do. The most exciting event during the past week was going to lunch with her favorite former client and explaining why she'd left the partnership.

"All I can say is that we're all set to file those applications whenever they come in," Janice said. "We've registered with the Patent Office, even got an account with two hundred grand in it to pay the filing fees."

"Two hundred thousand?" Addy gasped.

"That's how much Gawk, or Sung-threw, or whatever his name is, put into it. Must be planning on a lot of filings."

"Sung-soo," Addy reminded her.

When Janice left, Addy pulled out her cell phone and checked email. Lynda had replied, telling Addy they would love to have her come whenever she had time. She said they had an extra room, and suggested that she stay a weekend. If Billy, her stepbrother, was playing soccer that weekend, they could even see his game. Cassandra, the result of her father's affair, would be there as well.

Addy wondered if she should go this weekend. Heaven knows she had enough free time. But she didn't want to leave before Quinn arrived with the patent applications. She decided to wait before suggesting a date.

The idleness changed later that day when Addy's office door flew open. Janice, half asleep in the guest office chair, startled Addy who nearly jumped to attention. Panting, Quinn barged in and loosened his necktie. He was holding a package like he was carrying a football.

"Good to see you both." Quinn set the package down on Addy's desk and held out his hand as he introduced himself to Janice. After some small talk, he asked if he could be alone with Addy.

Janice huffed, folded her arms and pushed her way past Quinn. "I'll be in my office if you need me."

"Sorry, I'm late," Quinn said when the door clapped shut. "Got delayed at customs."

"For three days?"

"Long story. Anyway," he said as he pointed to the package, "that is the flash drive with all the patent applications. I'm going to have Sung-soo—you've met him, right?" He continued before Addy could answer. "I'm going to have him load all these on your computer. They'll be password-protected, encrypted, and require a biometric scan to gain access."

Addy raised her hand. "Before you go any further, do you mind if we go over a few things?"

"Like?"

"The office. Janice is about ready to walk—either that, or she's going to scratch Sung-soo's eyes out. Nobody here knows anything about running a law firm, much less anything about patent filings."

Quinn rolled his eyes. "What else?"

"All this security stuff. I appreciate your concern, but this is ridiculous. Body scanners. Really?"

"Company policy. I can't change it."

"But you are the company. You can change anything."

Quinn sat on the corner of the desk and swung his leg. "I thought you'd appreciate the safety aspect. And speaking of safety, I understand you've been riding your bike to work."

"My car's in the shop, remember?"

"You told me it was impounded."

"Same thing. I can't use it."

"I'm going to arrange for a driver."

"I'm okay," Addy said. "I need the exercise. Besides that, we're a renewable energy company. Why would I drive a gas guzzler?"

Addy watched Quinn's jaw muscles flex as he gritted his teeth. "The driver will take you in a Tesla."

"Please." Addy knew she was being obstinate, but that was her nature.

Quinn's tense face relaxed and he smiled. He too knew that electric cars relied on fossil fuels to generate their electricity because nearly two-thirds of power plants in America used coal and natural gas to produce electricity used to charge the car batteries. There wasn't much difference between that and a gasoline-powered engine.

"Get Hindy back for me."

"I have a lot of connections, but not that many. I'm afraid I can't impose on the US legal system. I'm Korean, remember?"

"I'm not finished with my demands," Addy said, ignoring him. "We need an office manager. Someone who speaks English without an accent."

"You're changing the subject. I need to have someone look after you. Remember what happened in Vietnam?"

Quinn was right. The threats in Vietnam had terrified her. America had provided her with a false sense of security. The fact that she wasn't driving Hindy was evidence enough that she was vulnerable to anyone who didn't appreciate her "green" activities.

"Really, I'll be okay. I need the exercise, and I do my best thinking when I'm outside. And, it's much safer here. I'll promise you that if I ever suspect anything, I'll let you take over my life. Okay?"

Quinn scooted himself off her desk. "I thought I was the most stubborn person on the planet. This one is non-negotiable. I've got a security detail who is going to escort you, and if the weather's bad, you're in the Tesla."

"Will the driver have a California license?"

"Funny," he said snatching up the package. "You handle the patents, I'll handle security. Trust me on this one."

"Famous last words. And I'm going to hire an office manager. If we can't leave this prison, somebody's got to order lunch. And it's not going to be Sung-soo. We can't live on kimchi."

"I'll give you that one. I'd much rather have a burger. I'll get someone to run this place. And, you'll be glad you had this brief vacation. Tomorrow I'll have you so busy you can't think straight."

\* \* \*

The security guard rushed to the door while Addy struggled to yank it open. With one hand stabilizing her bicycle, she didn't have enough strength to pry it ajar. The Korean man, dressed in a dark blue uniform with a yellow security badge embroidered on the shoulder, swung the door open, grasped the handlebar and chaperoned the bike into the lobby. Addy wiped the sweat from her brow.

"You'll be glad this is the last day you have to help me," she told the guard.

Quinn insisted that they all be in the office by six, which meant the sun was still down and the cool, damp air required her to wear a sweatshirt. After the vigorous ride, she was drenched. Still, the guard asked her to walk through the body scanner while he inspected the bike.

As she passed the conference room, she saw Quinn tapping furiously away at his laptop. He jumped to his feet. "You're punctual."

"Always the dutiful employee."

"Let's meet in your office. I've got everything loaded on your computer."

"Sure. Is Janice here yet?"

"Yes, but I need to meet with you first."

Addy frowned. "She's not going to be happy. And when Janice isn't happy—"

Quinn sighed. "Any suggestions?"

"You've got to do something to make her feel a part of the operation. Somehow get her invested. For starters, how about letting her know what we are trying to accomplish?"

He folded his arms. "All right," he said after a moment of reflection. "Have her come in and I'll give her a primer on hydrogen and fuel cells. It will be a good test. If she can understand my simplification, I know it will work for a patent examiner."

"Just don't tell her that's what you're doing. Talking down to her isn't a good idea."

"Got it." Quinn turned and asked Sung-soo to invite Janice to join them, then made his way to Addy's assigned room, one with four bare walls and no windows.

"It's like a prison in here," Addy said wiping her face with the back of her arm.

Quinn shook his head. "If you're not going to let me drive you, can I at least ride with you? I can get a bike."

Addy tapped her chin. "That I would like to see. Sure, any time."

"Let's get this show on the road," Janice said, interrupting them as she nudged her way through the door while sipping her coffee.

Quinn scooted up a second chair next to the monitor, motioned for Janice to have a seat, and hit the keyboard to illuminate the screen. "I think it's a good idea for all WTG employees to understand how we plan to run a car on water. For that, you need to understand the basics of fuel cells."

Janice put down her cup and scooted her chair closer, scanning the screen over his broad shoulders. "Now we're talking."

Quinn tapped a few keys, and soon they were all staring at *Water to Gold* in bold styled letters. Addy grinned. Now she understood the acronym, WTG. Quinn spun on his chair to face Janice. "I'm going to present a summary of what we tell our investors. If you have any questions, or I'm going too fast, just stop me."

"I will," she said, leaning toward him eagerly.

"All right, water to gold. WTG is all about producing cars that run on water or, more correctly, about making cars that will run on electricity that is generated from hydrogen that we extract from water. Instead of a gasoline engine, our cars will use fuel cells."

Janice nodded. "What's a fuel cell?"

"Fuel cells are similar to biological cells," Quinn continued. "They take in fuel, like hydrogen, and convert the fuel to electricity, which is then used to run the car's motor. But the beauty of a fuel cell is that it uses hydrogen that we get from ordinary tap water—not gasoline. Therefore, you don't have to worry about pollution, greenhouse gases, and all those things."

"But you didn't invent the fuel cell, right?" Janice said.

"No, they've been around for a long time. In fact, a Welch scientist, Sir William Grove, came up with the concept in 1839."

"And he was a patent attorney," Addy added.

"That long ago?"

"Surprising, isn't it? We've come a long way in one hundred and fifty-plus years, haven't we?" Addy said.

"I love your sarcasm," Quinn said.

"So," Janice said, "you put in hydrogen and out comes electricity. How does that work?"

"Let's start from the basics," Quinn continued. "Everyone knows that a water molecule is made up of two hydrogen atoms and one oxygen atom."

This time Janice smiled. "Yes, $H_2O$."

"The simplest way to break apart the water molecule is a process called electrolysis, which involves running an electric current through water. This splits the water into hydrogen and oxygen. That's what Sir William Grove was doing when he made his fuel cell discovery. He wondered what would happen if he reversed the process, and instead of trying to make hydrogen from water, he combined hydrogen and oxygen. Would it produce electricity? He tried the experiment, and it worked."

"What Quinn is saying," Addy said, "is that you take water, or $H_2O$, and do a process to split the water molecule into hydrogen and oxygen. Then, do the reverse process in a fuel cell where you combine the hydrogen with oxygen to get water and electricity. We use this electricity to run the car's motor."

Quinn spun back around and hit another key and a photograph of a sandwich appeared on the screen. "Think of a fuel cell as a ham sandwich—you know, a piece of ham smashed between two pieces of bread. Now let's define some terms. One piece of bread we're going to call a cathode, and the other one we'll call an anode. The slice of ham is the membrane.

"Okay, you already know that to produce electricity we're going to need to combine some hydrogen and oxygen, and that will turn into water and electricity."

"I got that much," Janice said.

"What we need to do is to put some hydrogen in the cathode, and the oxygen in the anode."

"So the piece of ham separates the hydrogen and the oxygen, right?"

"Exactly. But here's where it gets tricky. The hydrogen is really a bunch of positively charged ions, and they want to move through the piece of ham toward the other piece of bread—the one that has the oxygen. When the hydrogen comes into contact with the oxygen, water is produced.

"At the same time, negative ions—or electricity—are produced, and they leave the piece of ham and go into some kind of electrical conductor, like a copper wire. From there, the electricity can go to a motor and then back to the fuel cell. The negative ions—or electricity—that are pumped back into the piece of ham make the hydrogen want to keeping moving through the ham toward the oxygen on the other side. Remember the hydrogen is positively charged, and opposites attract. So, as long as you keep feeding the fuel cell with hydrogen and oxygen, you'll always get electricity to run your motor."

"Believe it or not, I think I've got it."

"Now, to finish things off, you get a whole bunch of ham sandwiches, put them side by side in a bread bag, and run them all at the same time so you get lots of electricity—that's a fuel cell."

"So is that how electric cars work?"

"Unfortunately not. Most of them forgo the fuel cell and simply store electricity in batteries. That's where we are different. We're going to be making electricity on demand—when you press the gas pedal."

"Well, if it's that easy, why don't we all have fuel cell cars?"

"It's a good question. NASA's been using fuel cells in space for over thirty years, so we know they work. The problem is producing the hydrogen from water."

Janice smiled a wry smile. "So that's why you call yourself WTG. You're not turning water into gold, but into hydrogen."

Quinn smiled and held up his finger. "And hydrogen is just like gold when it comes to making electricity. We use the water to get the hydrogen, and that's our big invention."

Janice cocked her head. "Why don't you just have gas stations that sell hydrogen?"

"I wish it were that easy. Producing and storing hydrogen is a big problem. You need a huge tank or some kind of storage mechanism to hold it."

"Think of Hindy," Addy said.

"You used that blimp-like balloon to store the hydrogen?

I can't see how it is practical for cars to drive around pulling blimps," Janice said with a smile.

"You're right," Addy said. "The balloon was just for show to make a point about how difficult it is to store hydrogen. Hindy had a metal tank filled with compressed hydrogen, which has its own set of problems, like how dangerous it can be driving around with a compressed gas."

"That's right," Quinn continued. "Our challenge was to find a way to get the hydrogen atoms out of the water molecule so we can fill the car's tank with a few gallons of water—not hydrogen."

"Is that hard?"

"Not hard, but it takes a lot of energy, and usually a big factory."

"So how are you going to do that underneath the hood of a car?" Janice asked.

"That's where you two come in. We've invented a way to do it, and we need the patents to protect our intellectual property."

Janice nodded. This was familiar territory.

"And the cost?" Janice asked. Addy studied Quinn's reaction.

"If we made millions of fuel cells like we do internal combustion engines, the price will be comparable. Starting off, it will be more. But you could make the same argument about the car versus the horse at the turn of the twentieth century. A new Winton touring car cost twenty-five hundred dollars, and a decent horse went for only eighty."

Janice picked up her cup and took another sip. "I'm on board. Let's hear how you do it. I want to get these patent applications filed."

Quinn hesitated. "Unfortunately, I can't tell you that."

"Why not?" Janice said. "You're doing such a good job. I really want to know what's so secret."

Quinn scowled at Addy.

"She's playing you," Addy said. "I already explained. She can help me with the filings, but only I can read the applications."

"I can take a hint," Janice said pushing her chair back and standing. She turned for the door, then paused. "But thanks for telling me why I'm here."

"That was nice of you," Addy said when she disappeared. "Ready to get down to business?"

"Ready. I've uploaded all the applications on your computer. You'll see we have twenty-two so far. A few cover various improvements to our fuel cells, but most are about how we use the catalyst when producing the hydrogen from water. Without the catalyst, we don't have a business. It's the key to cost-effective production of hydrogen. We've not only described the catalyst, but also our new extraction process, along with how we are going to implement this in a car. There's a lot here. My suggestion is that you spend the rest of the day going through this, then we can talk strategy."

Addy crossed her legs. "So now's when I find out how you aren't violating the laws of thermodynamics?"

"It's all in there. You'll see what we've done. Then you'll understand why you're the only person who can know. And why I'm so anal about security. Remember, nothing leaves this computer. Nobody gets your passwords, and you can't download any files. If you do, Sung-soo will let me know immediately."

Addy frowned. "You don't trust me."

"Don't be offended. I don't trust myself. But I do trust you. I'm trusting you to work your magic and figure out a way to get these patents granted. We've invested hundreds of millions of dollars. I picked the best person in the world to do the job, and now I'm counting on you to deliver."

Addy swallowed. Quinn was right. He was placing a huge load on her shoulders. She looked into his dark eyes. "I'll deliver."

"Good. I'll have Sung-soo come in and show you how to access the files. Unfortunately, there's going to be a retina scan and you'll need your passwords to decrypt the files. If you need to make any modifications to the applications, Sung-soo will show you how to save them as new documents."

"He's not going to be hovering over my shoulder."

"Just by camera," Quinn said nodding to a camera mounted in the ceiling.

# 17

A WALL OF fog from the Pacific Ocean was just rolling over the mountains to the west. The cool breeze flowing over Addy's body helped relax her mind. After twelve hours in her stuffy office, reading dozens of patent applications containing detailed descriptions of WTG's secret technology, the exhilarating, cool breeze on her face as she raced for home was a welcome relief. She peered over her shoulder, noting the ever-present black Audi S4—Quinn's security detail.

She couldn't quit thinking about what she'd just read. For more than a week, she'd fretted over making a giant mistake when she left Wyckoff. Worry that she'd been played for a fool nagged at her constantly.

Now she'd studied the technical details, she was positive Quinn and WTG were for real. The technology was sound. They'd not only discovered a catalyst that would make hydrogen production economically feasible, but they'd invented ways to allow a car owner to fill their car's tank with distilled water to produce the hydrogen. From a marketing perspective, it was brilliant. Television ads could tout that all a person needed to do was to grab a gallon of distilled water from the grocery store and pour it into their car's tank.

When she wasn't gloating about this extraordinary invention, she was combing her brain for strategies to get the Patent Office to give its stamp of approval. If it was true that they had suppressed two of Quinn's earlier applications, it was conceivable that they would slap a secrecy order on these as well. She'd seen it happen before. The Patent Office was only supposed to keep patent applications secret if they potentially impacted national defense or nuclear energy, subject to a release from the Department of Energy.

Quinn's ideas didn't fall into either of these two categories, and Addy wondered why his earlier cases were suppressed. Rumors were always rampant that the federal government routinely perused the Patent Office files to steal ideas that were important to the national interest, but Addy was sure it couldn't be true. Still, small inventors always thought the world was out to steal their ideas. Addy was beginning to wonder if there might be a sliver of truth to it.

She smiled as she pedaled even faster. *Let them try.* She had ways to ensure her patents would be granted without governmental meddling.

Addy made a sharp right turn to cross a set of railroad tracks, passing behind a set of abandoned warehouses that were being remodeled into office space for the ever-growing tech industry in Silicon Valley.

From behind, she heard the revving of a motorcycle engine. Addy veered toward the shoulder to give the motorcyclist more room to pass. The scream of the engine intensified, and she heard the gears shift. When she turned to look, the motorcycle swooped down on her, and a man dressed in black and red riding gear leaned into her. He threw out his forearm, catching her in the chin. With astounding force, he leaned in further, throwing her from her bicycle. She flew headlong into the gravel, then rolled head over heels down the embankment, where her head struck a culvert drain.

Stunned, Addy gazed into the drifting layer of fog spreading across the heavens. She felt a stinging sensation in her right elbow, and her hip felt like it was on fire. But she was more worried about the pinging in her head, just above her eyes. She reached up and felt a goose egg above her right eyebrow.

*Where's my security detail?* Addy wondered. They'd been right behind her the entire way. She worried that if they didn't show up, the rider would come after her—to finish the job. Relief came when headlights from a car beamed down the embankment. It wasn't her escort, but at least there was someone to rescue her, Addy guessed. In the distance, she could hear sirens. A man and a woman skidded down the slope, their arms flailing as they tried to keep their balance. In the brilliant light, she was unable to make out their features.

"Ma'am, are you alright?" a female voice asked. Addy relaxed. With the headlights blazing down, Addy couldn't make out anything but the shape of their bodies.

Addy sat up, and a wave a dizziness crashed over her. "I think so. Not sure if anything is broken or not."

"Here, let me help you up," the woman continued. From behind, she slipped her forearms beneath Addy's armpits and hefted her upright until she was on her feet. The sharp pain in her hip escalated.

"Are you alright?" she asked again.

"I think so," Addy said. "Lots of cuts and bruises, but nothing seems to be broken."

Suddenly, the woman clenched her arms about Addy's chest. Before Addy could resist, her colleague stepped forward, momentarily blocking the beam from the headlights. His dark skin was framed by close-cropped, coarse dark hair that matched his beard. He delivered a swift punch to her abdomen, so hard that it felt like her stomach was forced into her throat. She struggled to breathe. The man's fist crashed into her ribcage on her left side. She felt a rib crack. She tried to scream, but there was no air in her lungs.

The wailing of the police siren was getting louder, and Addy prayed someone would save her. *Where are my bodyguards?*

"We warned you to stay away from Quinn and you wouldn't listen," the man said. "This is your last warning. Next time we'll make sure you never walk again. And if you want to eat, you'll need a set of dentures."

With that, the woman flung her to the ground. And now Addy knew where she'd seen her assailant. He was the man with the tattooed arm, the same thug who'd fired the flare into Hindy's balloon and held her tight while in Vietnam.

Addy screamed as the two dark figures scurried up the embankment and zoomed away in their car. She began sobbing. Every breath brought excruciating pain. She hadn't wept out loud since she was a junior in high school, when she won the award for the best science student in the district and was honored at a special dinner. She was the only student without a parent until her drunken mother, hair ratted and wearing tight jeans and a crop top, sauntered in and plopped herself down beside her.

The police car screeched to a halt and the beam of a spotlight flashed in her eyes. She wiped her nose with the back of her arm.

The next several hours were a blur: a scratchy blanket thrown about her shoulders, an ambulance ride to the hospital, poking and probing by too many nurses and doctors, and finally questions from the two officers who had been called to the scene by an unidentified good samaritan.

They had asked her for details, and she explained that the blow to her head had made everything fuzzy. Still, she'd remembered a motorcycle getting close, then something about her front tire going off the shoulder into the gravel, which made her lose control. She didn't mention the punch to her gut.

It was nearly ten o'clock before the questioning was over and all the medical tests were completed. She'd sustained a concussion, the skin on both her elbow and hip were rubbed raw, and her lower left rib was cracked.

Finally she was moved to her own private room. Addy was quietly resting when Agent Long appeared in the doorway. Although he'd seen her from afar, he'd never formally introduced himself.

Long found her with her head elevated and a heart rate sensor clipped to her index finger. A breathing tube was taped below her nostrils. Her normally clipped-back hair fell limply on her shoulders. Her breathing was labored.

"I'm Agent Jesse Long from the FBI," he said. "You okay to speak?"

At this late hour, Addy was annoyed at the appearance of yet another law enforcement officer. Still, she nodded and adjusted her oxygen tube, but when she tried to speak all that came out was a gasp. She held her hand over her rib.

"I see," Long said. "I understand you already told the officer on scene what happened, and I'll let him debrief me a bit later. For now, I just need a quick description, if you can."

"A man and a woman," Addy breathily replied.

Long scribbled a note.

"Ages, ethnicity, distinguishing features? "

Addy paused. "Pretty sure he was Arabic, heavy dark whiskers. She looked Caucasian."

Long raised his eyebrows. His hunch was right about one of the assailants, but the addition of a white woman threw him. "Seen them before?"

Addy grimaced, and Long wondered whether it was her rib or whether she was hiding something. "He could have been the guy who shot at Hindy," she finally said, "but I can't say for sure."

"Hindy, that's your car, the one with the large balloon?"

Addy nodded.

"What makes you say that?"

This time Addy responded quickly. "He looked at me the same way, this look of hate, both when he shot the balloon on my car, and right before he ran me off the road."

Long wrote another note. "Any tattoos?"

"It was too dark, and I wasn't actually paying attention to his body art." Addy grimaced again.

"Okay. Let's let you get some rest. We can talk more later."

"Thanks," Addy whispered.

Long stood to go, then stopped. "One more question. Why didn't Quinn get you a car? I'm sure he knew something like this could happen."

*How did Long know about Quinn?* Addy wondered. Addy raised up to say something but then clutched her stomach and laid back down. Long left and Addy was furious, but at least she was finally alone. Despite her pain she wanted to speak with Quinn—now. She asked the nurse for her phone, claiming she needed to call her mother. The nurse reluctantly sorted through her clothing and located her phone, handing it over to Addy once she'd extracted a promise to keep it short.

When the nurse left, Addy whipped off a text message. Quinn replied immediately. He was in the lobby, but didn't dare come up. Visiting hours were over except for immediate family.

He asked if she was okay, and said he would spend the night in the waiting room. He would come up as soon as visitors were allowed.

Morning brought another round of tests before the doctors approved her release. Quinn was still on the first floor, patiently waiting to take her home. Addy debated whether that would be wise. If she were seen in his car, who knew what might happen to them both?

She could call Janice, but that was out of the question. Janice would be hysterical and assume the worst, that someone wanting to steal this new technology had attacked Addy. The only other person was Perry, her former partner. Addy dismissed that as well. She couldn't bear yet another lecture right now.

She texted Quinn and asked him if he had an armored vehicle to take her home. Quinn texted back an emoji of a smiling face and said she'd be safe with him.

A nurse wheeled Addy to the front desk, where she was released and escorted to a set of sliding doors. Addy wasn't the least bit surprised when Quinn pulled up in a Range Rover with tinted windows. She suspected it was bulletproof glass. The shock of the fall, the medical testing, and probing by police officers had now sunk in, and Addy was burning to let it all out.

The passenger side door had barely shut when Addy let loose. "What have you gotten me into?" she screamed, shoving his shoulder, and then gasping at the pain in her ribcage. Quinn quickly swung back the wheel before the SUV veered into a parked car. "You did this to me! I had the perfect career, everything I ever wanted, and now this."

Quinn clenched his fingers around the steering wheel, but kept his cool.

"You knew I'd be attacked. You knew what happened to me in Vietnam, and you let this happen. Where in the hell was my bodyguard? I'm done. Do you know what they told me would happen if I don't stop working for you? They said they'd break all my bones and smash in my face. How would you like that on your conscience?"

Quinn waited her out, listening to a five-minute tirade while he headed north along the 101 Freeway, then exited toward Half Moon Bay.

"Are you finished?" he said.

She folded her arms and pursed her lips.

"Need I remind you that you're the one who insisted on riding your bicycle?"

Addy turned and slapped him in the face. "Don't give me that crap. You knew. You could have protected me. Your security guys are incompetent."

"That's not true. We kept our distance so we wouldn't blow our cover. By the time we caught up, the police were arriving. We had to stand back or risk being caught."

"Caught doing what? Trying to protect me? That's bullshit and you know it. Are you saying your guys sat around and watched as I got the crap beat out of me?"

Quinn looked up to the ceiling. "It's extremely complicated. Let's get you home, and I'll explain then."

"Pull over," Addy insisted. "Now. I want an explanation. Your guys don't know what they're doing. Admit it."

When Quinn hesitated, Addy shot her hand out for the wheel. Quinn blocked the attempt, but pulled over anyway.

"Hand me your cell phone," he said.

Addy pursed her lips, but she obeyed the order. As soon as it was in hand, Quinn flipped to her first social media site. It showed a selfie of Addy on her bicycle.

"Not too smart."

Addy shrugged. "Agreed. It's a habit. I can't live without my phone."

"There's more," Quinn growled. He ripped off the case, yanked out the SIM card and bit it between his teeth. "There, at least they can't track us anymore. They've probably been pinging your location for weeks. We can't talk here. We're not safe. I want to get you home."

"My home is the other direction," Addy said. "And you'd better fix my phone. That's non-negotiable."

"You're coming to my house, at least until we can come up with another plan."

"You're sleeping on the couch, because I'm not."

"No. I have an extra bedroom. My place overlooks the ocean. It's easier for our security detail to see who gets close."

Addy grunted and again folded her arms. "You can give me

the full download there, but I want to know who did this to me. Who is following us?"

Quinn shook his head, picked up a shortwave radio and told his detail to hang tight.

"All right, here's what I know. I already told you that the US Department of Energy has tried to stop my patents. The US has invested billions, if not trillions, of dollars to become energy independent, meaning that the US has found ways to get oil from everywhere but the Middle East. A good part of this money has come from private investors. They need to get a return on their investment, and what I've invented could put a real big damper on that. We're pretty sure that's who ran you off the road."

Addy rolled her eyes. "That's baloney and you know it. And I suppose they are also the ones who threatened me in Vietnam."

Quinn stared straight out at the road but remained silent.

"Out with it," Addy said, "or I'm finished. I might be finished anyway, but you still owe me an explanation."

When Quinn didn't respond, she grabbed his shoulder and began shaking him.

"Stop it!" he finally said. "I'll tell you what I know."

"Now!" she yelled.

Quinn refused to look her in the eye. "We're not absolutely certain, mostly because these guys are really good at disguising themselves, but there could be Middle Eastern interests involved as well."

She thought about the man with the tattoo, then about Perry. He'd told her that the Department of Homeland Security suspected a terrorist link to Hindy's sabotage.

"Hindy," she whispered.

"What about Hindy?" Quinn said.

"DHS thinks there is a terrorist cell in the US that doesn't want to see America free of its dependence on Middle Eastern oil."

Quinn nodded. "That's possible, but we just don't know."

"But you do know it's not just these so-called disgruntled investors."

"I can't rule out anything at this point. That's the best I can give you right now."

"So let me see if I understand this. We've got the most

powerful nation in the world, and one of the most radical of terrorist groups, all wanting to make sure that your water car invention doesn't see the light of day."

"Perhaps a little oversimplification, but there are risks. I told you that."

Addy let her head fall into her hands. "I can't believe I let you talk me into this. You can't protect me. Even the FBI is asking questions."

Quinn jerked his head and his mouth fell open. Before he could respond, his radio beeped, and he put the vehicle into gear and merged back onto the highway. "I'm not going to ask you right now whether you want out. I know you probably do, but I want to get you to bed, let you get some rest and have a good meal. Then we can talk. I promise you'll be safe with me."

*I promised myself I'd never trust anyone again. I did, and look where I am.* But she was too sore and exhausted to argue.

# 18

WHEN ADDY AWOKE, she had no idea of the time. She flipped off her blanket and noticed she was still wearing her clothes from the previous day—a sweat suit provided for her at the hospital since her clothing had been cut off.

Addy gently turned the handle and peeked outside. She was greeted by a narrow hallway that led to a small living room with a majestic view of the sun setting over the Pacific Ocean. Quinn was standing by the window with his arms folded, evidently deep in thought. In his tight-fitting T-shirt, Addy could see his well-developed lats and his broad shoulders.

"I'm awake," she said softly. Startled, Quinn spun around. "I didn't mean to scare you. I just woke up, and I'm starving. I think I'll take you up on your offer for a nice meal."

The house was so small that its entire front consisted of the living room and kitchen, but both had floor to ceiling windows and a sliding door leading to a wooden deck that afforded an unobstructed view of the green hills and the shimmering waters of Half Moon Bay.

Quinn smiled and flashed his large white teeth. "I wasn't sure when you would wake up, so I put your supper in the refrigerator. It's barbecue from down the street. I'll warm it up in the microwave."

"Nice view," Addy said while Quinn lifted off the aluminum foil. He was right when he said that she would feel better after getting a good sleep.

"How are the injuries?"

She bent over at the waist and grimaced. "My hip has stiffened up, it hurts to breathe and my elbow still burns, but my headache is gone."

Quinn looked up. "That's great news. I was worried we'd have to take you back in if your concussion was too severe."

Quinn's genuine concern softened her.

"I owe you an apology," Addy said when she had finished a bite of toasted sourdough bread.

"For?" Quinn said.

"Slapping you."

Quinn rubbed his cheek. "I've felt worse."

"I can try harder next time."

"I deserved it. You were right. I should have been up front with you from the start. Will you accept my apology?"

She reached out and took his hands. "Apology accepted. I'm not sure what came over me. Too many changes too fast. I quit my job, I finally heard from my stepmother, and then I was attacked—for the third time."

Quinn pulled her closer. "Wait, you *finally* heard from your stepmother? What do you mean?"

"The same day I quit Wyckoff I got an email from her. She sent an apology for not telling me about my father's death or his funeral." Addy lowered her head.

Quinn quickly reached over and lifted her chin with his finger, searching deeply into her eyes.

"I'm sorry. You want to talk about it?"

"It's a long story. My mother's drug and alcohol addiction nearly drove him crazy. He messed up and had an affair, then left my mother. He said he was sorry for leaving me. That woman was my stepmother. He wanted to tell me all this before he died, you know, to ask for my forgiveness, but I never replied until it was too late. My stepmother was so upset that I didn't come see him that she didn't bother telling me about the funeral. It went downhill from there. Anyway, she now wants to make amends. I have two stepsiblings she wants to be part of my life."

"What are their names?"

"Cassandra and Billy. Cassandra's married with kids, but Billy's still at home."

"Where does she live?"

"In Sacramento. I thought about making a quick trip, but then all this happened."

"Well, you definitely should see her. Everything else can wait. I'll even take you. Let's go see them."

She squeezed his fingers. "Thanks for the offer, but let's get the applications filed first. Then I'll go spend a weekend with them while we wait for the Patent Office to examine the cases."

Addy walked over to the counter and sat down on a leather-covered barstool, then turned to face Quinn. "When was the last time you had a serious conversation with your father?" she said.

"The day I left for America. I handed him my fencing gear and said I wouldn't be needing it. Now I regret that. It was just adding salt to his wounds. If it's the last thing I do, I'm going to make this car work and repair the relationship with my father."

Quinn scooted a barstool next to her. "Your father was a good man. Even if he abandoned his family, he did adopt you and bring you to America. And in the end, he did apologize. My father wouldn't even do that for me."

She smiled and tucked a strand of hair behind her ear. "You should follow your own advice. You know you're going to need to forgive your father, not just show him he was wrong—before it's too late."

Quinn shook his head. "It's not that easy. You don't understand Korean culture. I dishonored him, and if I fail, it will just make matters worse for my family. Korean fathers sacrifice everything for their children, but I chose not to accept his sacrifice. I must make things right by making WTG a success."

"I'm trying my best," Addy said.

Quinn put his arm around her. "I know you are." He left to finish warming up her barbecue.

"What about your mother?" Quinn said.

"She's still a mess. I don't think she'll ever recover. Sometimes I think I was just like you, desperately wanting to prove myself to her. But now I hope I'm past that."

Quinn raised his eyebrows. "Whatever the case, when this is all over, you should get her some help. Never give up on a loved one."

He checked the food in the microwave and returned to her side.

"Well," she said, "I guess you and I are both a lot alike. But enough about that. Since I'm not going to be able to sleep tonight, we might as well get to work."

"Then I take it that you're back in the game?"

"You're out of the doghouse. I'll give you one more chance."

Quinn leaned over and kissed the scrape on her cheek. "I knew you were the one for the job. You've got the fire in you that we're going to need."

Addy felt herself blushing. "Like I said, let's get to work. If the DOE is determined to lambaste your applications, I've got to find a way to outmaneuver them."

"Any ideas?"

"Lots, but I am going to need your help. First, I am going to need you to set up a dozen or so shell companies so we can file the applications under different legal entities. Make them all US companies, even better if they are incorporated in Nebraska."

"Done. We already considered that. What else?"

"My next idea is bordering on the unethical, but the Patent Office isn't playing fair, so I feel justified in bending the rules a bit. Every patent application must be filed in the name of the inventor. But if your name is plastered on the filing documents, they are going to get screened out, guaranteed."

"Any ideas?"

"I suggest we file with variations on your name. Maybe misspell it or use a nickname. That way we can technically skirt the law. We can correct it right before the patent issues."

"I'm fine with that as long as you can get me my patents."

"There's more. The Patent Office will also do subject matter searches. The intake official will do a key word search and immediately recognize that this technology could be problematic to the DOE. That makes things a little more difficult, but not impossible. I'm going to need to use words that disguise what you are really doing. Like, a fuel cell will now become a—" Addy tapped her chin, "an electricity generator, or something like that."

"But if you change them will I still be protected? Can't an energy company design around my patents?"

"Not if I do it correctly. Let me worry about that part. That's why you hired me."

"What about timing?"

"Normally three to five years to get a patent. Sorry about that."

Quinn stood straight, sending his chair crashing to the floor. Addy laughed and shook her finger at him. "That's payback. Relax. I have a way to expedite examination. The Patent Office has a program where you can legally bribe them to move your application to the front of the queue. I do it all the time."

"Is it expensive?"

"A few thousand dollars. Pocket change considering how much you're already spending."

Quinn picked up his chair and sat down again. "Okay, but we're always watching expenses."

Addy rolled her eyes. Companies always did this—spend millions on worthless stuff, then penny-pinch on the legal budget. That explained their dreary offices.

"Save a few dollars for interviews. We'll need to personally visit the examiner in D.C., unless we get lucky and one or two of our cases get assigned to the satellite Patent Office in San Jose."

"That won't be a problem."

"And we should do a demo. Show and tell always works wonders, and in this case it is going to be critical. The examiner is going to think this is a perpetual energy idea. We need to dispel that idea before it takes root. It would be even better if we could use it in Hindy, but that's not going to happen anytime soon."

Quinn sighed. "That could be a problem."

Addy glared. "Come again?"

Quinn raised both hands. "Wait right there. I know what you're thinking. I do have the catalyst, just not any that I can spare right now. Here's what I can do. I can build a model fuel cell to demonstrate how we will use the catalyst."

"But no catalyst."

"I'm afraid I just don't have enough produced yet. It's not that easy."

"It better be that easy, or your little venture is useless. That's going to need to change real quick."

"Once we get the full production lines up and running we can make tons of it, but that will take time."

"How much time?"

Quinn hesitated. "A year or more for decent yields. But don't fret. You've seen the patent applications. The science is sound."

Addy nodded. "Level with me. How much of this catalyst have you produced—since the very beginning?"

"A decent amount. It's just the scientists need every bit right now."

"You'll need to figure it out," Addy said. "The examiner is going to want to see it work. Otherwise, you're not getting a patent. Trust me."

"I'll try my best."

"One more thing. I need my phone back."

"Oh, yeah," he said, tugging it out of his pocket. "Got you a new SIM card, but lay off the social networking for a bit. And keep it off until you absolutely need it."

# 19

QUINN DISAPPEARED FROM the US as suddenly as he'd arrived. Once Addy had filed the applications with the Patent Office, he jetted back to Korea, offering little explanation other than Jeyhu and Yun were having issues with the production line. Boredom once again set in, and so did the bickering. Janice wanted something to do, and insisted she have a personal chauffeur like Addy. To keep the peace, Addy had her driver pick up Janice on the way, never mentioning to Janice that she was commuting all the way from Half Moon Bay.

While they played the waiting game with the Patent Office, Addy figured now would be a good time to meet her father's family. She emailed Lynda, asking if she could come by next weekend for a visit. Lynda agreed immediately. Addy was apprehensive, but ecstatic at the same time. She'd never had a family, and she wasn't sure how she would fit in. Would they accept her? Would they be a permanent part of her life, or just a passing fancy?

Addy had barely started making plans for her weekend in Sacramento when Janice burst into her office with news from the Patent Office. The first of the twenty-seven cases had been preliminarily reviewed. Addy's jaw dropped when she saw the Patent Office correspondence. The office had slapped a secrecy order on the case, despite her attempts to hide the technology and the real name of the inventor. That meant this application wouldn't be examined until the order was removed—which might never happen. The day before she was to leave for Sacramento another case received the same letter. Addy tried to hide it, worried that Quinn would question her legal strategy, but Sung-soo, who monitored every flowing electron, scooped up the notification and told Quinn. Still, Quinn kept radio silence.

She'd borrowed one of Quinn's suitcases and began tossing in her weekend necessities, an extra pair of jeans and a sweatshirt, followed by a few pairs of socks. Part of her wanted to stay glued to her office chair, hoping that she'd get some favorable news from the Patent Office. But she also recognized that a break from WTG would be welcome.

With little to do besides report bad news, it would be good to distance herself, especially from Janice whose frustrations were ready to boil over. Addy's suitcase was half full when she received a text message from Lynda. Her stomach sank. The family had unexpectedly come down with the flu. Lynda apologized but said they were in no condition for a visit. She asked if they could reschedule for the next weekend. Addy was disappointed, but she understood. But if one of Quinn's cases finally reached an examiner, it could make a visit more difficult.

On the other hand, Addy realized that Lynda's suggested date was Super Bowl weekend, and the game was being played in Santa Clara. Addy wasn't much of a football fan and decided it would be nice to be away from all the traffic and hype. She texted back to Lynda that the new date would be fine.

Addy returned to the office, hoping to find favorable news from the Patent Office. She didn't. No correspondence from the Patent Office at all. Addy sauntered into Janice's office to kill time. They passed the rest of the day talking about life at Wyckoff and gossiping about old friends. The next week was more of the same. Nothing from the Patent Office. Janice finally insisted they go to their usual lunch stop so she could have it out, away from Sung-soo's electronic bugs. Addy agreed a good talk was what they needed.

The driver opened her door and as Addy stood to exit her ribs knocked the inside door handle. She winced at the jarring pain but didn't let it show. Janice didn't need to know about her injuries. The bruise on her forehead was hard enough to explain away.

"I think we both made a huge mistake," Janice said the moment they were alone at the table. "Did you hear the latest from Wyckoff?"

Addy shook her head. As Quinn had requested, she hadn't been following the gossip networks.

"They hired Jerry Cochran from over at Bloomberg to take your place. And rumor has it Perry landed an electric motor company as a new client. Don't want to add insult to injury, but thought you should know."

Addy remained stoic, refusing to let Janice have the upper hand. But her insinuation was filled with reality. Perry had replaced her. She couldn't go back, even if she wanted. Since she had nothing to do, she also yearned for law firm life. Since filing the applications, her only responsibility was to entertain Janice and answer patent law questions from Sung-soo.

"I hear they are so busy they are all working weekends," Janice said. "At least they could use me."

Addy was tired of the babysitting and figured that not having a paralegal would be better than this.

"Maybe you should go back," Addy finally conceded. "How many stock options would you give up?"

Janice slammed down her menu rattling the silverware. "Stock options? What options would those be?"

Addy cringed. She'd assumed Janice was given a lucrative package with stock options like herself. "I'm sorry. I just thought they gave you some."

"Zippo," Janice said forming a zero with her thumb and index finger. "And you know what else? Sung-soo is doing more than just eavesdropping on us."

"What makes you say that?"

"He's been logging in using my credentials and surfing the Patent Office databases."

"Are you sure?"

"I'm not stupid. I know how to check my history log. He

spends almost all night on their site."

"Maybe that explains why there's never any fresh coffee. What was he searching?"

"Looking at a whole bunch of patent applications. All fuel cell stuff."

"Probably just some prior art searching," Addy said, trying to sound unconcerned. It was one more thing to hash out with Quinn.

They ate their salads, mostly in silence. Finally Addy spoke. "I really need you to stay. It won't be long before we will be busy again. We can make a big difference in the world."

Janice buoyed up her curly hair. "I thought you said I should go."

"I didn't mean it. Please don't leave. Give it a few more weeks. It will get better."

"You said that last time I wanted to go back to Wyckoff."

"Tell you what. Give it a couple more weeks, and if it doesn't get better, we may both be looking for a new job."

Addy was so involved in her discussion that she didn't even notice the man seated two tables away wearing a black fedora hat pulled down low and a gray, wool jacket.

Agent Long waited for them to pull out of the parking lot, then paid his bill and climbed into his Buick. Before starting the ignition, he took another note. He'd been seated too far away to overhear their conversation, but he could tell from their animated tones that the discussion was at times heated.

But that didn't bother him. His assignment from the Justice Department wasn't to eavesdrop, just to see what times Addy was at WTG. His colleagues back at the office were monitoring her internet usage. They simply needed him to confirm that she was in fact at WTG.

# 20

ADDY FLUNG HER purse onto her chair, then strode down the hall and barged into Sung-soo's office. He frantically grabbed for his mouse and began clicking rapidly. The monitor was facing away from Addy, so she didn't get to see what he was trying to hide.

"You must knock," Sung-soo spat out.

"And you've got to let me know how to contact Quinn. I've got to talk to him now."

"It's the middle of the night in Korea."

"Quinn's a night owl." She picked up a phone on Sung-soo's desk. "Get me a phone number, now," Addy insisted.

"I'm not supposed to call him."

Addy strode over to his computer, hefted it up and threatened to send it crashing to the floor.

"If you know what's good for you, don't do that."

"If you know what's good for you, get me on the phone with Quinn."

Sung-soo reached into his desk and pulled out a mobile phone. "Calm down Addy. I'll let you call him, but we need to use this phone." He depressed a series of buttons and handed

Addy the phone.

Addy pointed to the door. "I want to be alone."

"Very well," Sung-soo said, scooting a laptop from his desk. Addy knew he'd be listening to her, but at least she didn't have to see his smirking grin.

After several rings, Quinn's groggy voice answered. "What do you want Sung-soo?"

"It's me, Addy. We need to talk."

"I heard about the two applications. I'm a little bit concerned."

"You're concerned. What about me? This is my job. I think I need to go to another state with another computer and do some more filings. They've obviously latched on to this computer address."

"Impossible," Quinn said. "Sung-soo makes sure it generates a new address each time you log on."

"And that's another thing. Sung-soo is using Janice's login to scour the Patent Office files. What is going on?"

The line went silent.

"Don't try to tell me you don't know," Addy continued. "We're not stupid."

"Yeah, I know about that. Sung-soo's a wannabe patent lawyer. He stays up all night monitoring our competitors' patents. That's all."

"That's a thirty-minute job, once a week. What's he doing the rest of the time, viewing porn?"

Quinn chuckled. "It's a little more complicated than that. You already know the Patent Office is watching my applications and trying to stop them from being approved."

"Yes."

"Your government is doing more than just trying to keep my ideas secret. They are stealing the technology. Remember those other cases that I told you about? We put bogus technology in them. A few days later, the Department of Energy filed their own cases with our secrets."

"But the US is a first-to-file country," Addy said. "If you win the race to the Patent Office, no one is allowed to come in and file after you, not even the government."

"I understand, but what they've done is take our ideas, further embellish them, and then file on the improvements.

They're clearly trying to hem me in. They've apparently got an army of scientists monitoring everything I file. I told you, there are powerful investors who don't want to see this technology come to market, at least not in the next decade. That's why I needed you to help me. Sung-soo is trying to find out who is accessing our filings so we can develop a strategy for getting some of my cases through without being stolen."

"What about the two from last week?"

"The ones with the secrecy order? They've been accessed by the same group. The DOE has seen what we filed."

"And?"

"We haven't seen anything filed by the DOE or any of their related entities, but we're expecting something any day. We've got to get one of our cases through. Any ideas?"

"Like I said, we may want to file using a different computer."

"That won't work. Sung-soo rerouted your filings through a half a dozen computers all over the country before they hit the Patent Office servers. The Patent Office is using some other strategy to cull them. I'm sorry I haven't called, but we've had some challenging production issues. I'm trying to get you a sample of the catalyst for the meeting with the examiner."

Quinn always seemed to have a logical explanation. And his confident demeanor always calmed her.

"I'm afraid that's my fault. I think I'm failing you. I thought my strategy would work. I'm sorry."

"No need for an apology. We knew it was going to be difficult. You filed a few dozen cases. Let's sit tight and see what happens."

"But there has to be something more we can do. More than just Sung-soo prowling around on his computer all night."

She needed some way to force the Patent Office to let her cases through, but without knowing why they were being systematically denied, she didn't know what to do.

An idea flashed into Addy's mind. Several years ago, the Patent Office had created a secret program to put the kibosh on "sensitive" patent applications they didn't want to see the light of day. These were patents covering ideas that, when poked fun of by the media, would embarrass the Patent Office.

It all started when Amazon received a patent on their one-click ordering scheme, and the press mistakenly reported that

Amazon's patent covered all online shopping. The Patent Office was accused of doing a poor job in filtering out ideas that weren't patent worthy, especially by issuing a patent that reportedly could shut down all internet commerce. The reality was that internet merchants were unfazed by this patent, and simply chose to let their customers check out using more than one click. However, the Patent Office didn't like the unwanted attention and created a secret program that allowed the Patent Office to monitor any technology that could be potentially embarrassing, and then give bogus rejections to make sure the patents were never granted.

Addy's partner, Perry, had heard rumors of the program and filed a Freedom of Information Act request about it. He was right. There had been such a secret program. He gave the story to the press, the Patent Office was embarrassed, and class-action lawsuits from harmed inventors followed.

"I'm going to file a Freedom of Information request today," Addy said. "They can't do this. We'll know soon enough if there is a systematic plan to protect US interests by copying foreign technology."

"How long will it take?"

"I know an attorney in D.C. who can move it to the front of the line. We'll know real soon."

# 21

THE NEXT MORNING Addy had barely taken a first sip of her coffee when Janice bolted through the door waving a paper.

"We got an office action!"

An office action was patent lawyer lingo for the document summarizing the examiner's review of a patent application. The fact that this paperwork had been issued by the Patent Office meant one of Addy's cases had gotten through the minefield meant to submerge her attempts.

Addy snatched it out of her hand. "What's it say?" She immediately began perusing the results of the examiner's findings.

For some of the applications, Addy had filed a special request for an interview with the examiner before he formally acted on the case. This was a response to her request, and contained a summary of the scientific literature the examiner had discovered during his search. Before proceeding with his examination, the patent examiner wished to discuss his findings with Addy. By filing this request, Addy could be made privy to whether the examiner thought the application contained any merit and then informally negotiate a way to get the patent without all the normal back-and-forth paperwork.

Addy ran her finger down the list of documents the examiner had uncovered during his search. "I need copies of these pronto," Addy said, handing Janice the last page of the report.

"Consider it done," Janice said hustling out the door toward her office.

Addy picked up the phone. "I'm gonna call the Patent Office," she said loud enough for Sung-soo to hear. "We may have some good news."

The examiner gave Addy the impression that he was skeptical of her claims about extracting hydrogen from water. The good news was that the examiner was located in the San Jose office, meaning they didn't need to travel all the way to Washington for a meeting.

Nearly every patent application is initially rejected, and the examiner's dismissal was nothing new to Addy. His position that this idea was akin to a perpetual motion machine was disheartening—but not unexpected. She'd already told Quinn that a demonstration with his catalyst would be critical to ensuring the examiner's stamp of approval.

"If you're going to make claims like this, I'm going to have to see it for myself," the examiner told her over the phone.

Addy was incredibly relieved that he spoke with an American accent. So many of the examiners struggled to speak English, making it difficult to explain any type of invention. As much as she cringed when Perry complained about the so-called diversity in the Patent Office, sometimes he had a legitimate point.

"The inventor is fully prepared to give you a demonstration," she told the examiner. "I admit that although I am his attorney I, too, was somewhat dismissive. But after studying the science and seeing it for myself, I can honestly tell you that this is sound technology, and one that could change all of our lives. When should we set up a visit?" she concluded.

"Since you filed this as an expedited case, I need to act on it in two weeks. That means I'll need to see your demonstration next week. Is that possible?"

"You're in San Jose?"

"Yes, and it looks like your offices are in Palo Alto."

"That's correct, so we can drive down for the interview. Would next Tuesday at ten work?"

The line went silent as the examiner checked his calendar. "Let's make it ten-thirty. I have a training meeting."

Before she hung up, Sung-soo was hovering over her desk, his morning drink on his breath. He plunged his hand into his pocket, tugged out a phone and tapped the screen to call Quinn.

"Thanks," Addy grunted as she snatched the phone.

"You're killing me," Quinn's scratchy voice answered.

"It's Addy, and I've got some news. You'll want to hear this." Sung-soo's breath was more than she could bear and she turned to walk to the corner of her office. "We got one through to an examiner. He's on a tight deadline and wants to meet next week. He's got his doubts, and we need to dispel them."

"Can you meet with him?"

"Yes, but I need the catalyst."

She listened as Quinn cleared his throat. This was it. She was going to find out if this whole venture was a ruse.

"Did I mention we're having some production issues? Jeyhu has his team working round the clock."

"You did, but none of that matters. If you want your patent, you'll be here Tuesday morning with the catalyst. We should leave the office by nine in case there is any traffic. I'll see you then."

Addy ended the call before Quinn could respond. She tossed Sung-soo the phone, who barely managed a two-handed grab, then plunged into her chair and kicked her feet onto her desk. "It's show time. Let's see how you boys perform."

Sung-soo stormed out just as Janice bustled in with an armful of documents.

"Sorry for the light reading, but this is what Examiner Daniel Johnston found in his search."

"What do we know about this Johnston fellow?"

"Next on my list," Janice said. "I'm going to run a report right now."

Because all of the patent filings were public documents, a host of analytics companies had scoured the Patent Office databases for statistics on every facet of an examiner's career, from how long he took to allow cases to how many went on appeal.

"Thanks, Janice. That's why you're here," Addy said, her head already buried in the first patent from the stack.

# 22

MOLLY PEELE WASN'T Long's boss, but she was responsible for his current assignment. With the cybercrime division of the Justice Department, she oversaw federal criminal activity where computer networks were used for crimes. At the request of the Energy Department, she'd been investigating whether Quinn Moon had stolen important trade secrets relating to renewable energy sources.

Long found Peele's door cracked open and peeked his head in. She was on the phone, speaking into a headset while she typed away. As soon as she noticed Long, she waved him inside and ended her call.

Long took a seat in front of her desk and sat down his cup of coffee.

"Sleeping these days?" she said.

"Last night was better. I think I can function today."

"I'll be quick," she said, looking down to finish her email. "I need to get your log."

Long pulled out his notepad and tossed it on the table. "Here it is."

"Cute," she said. "That's why I didn't bother asking you to email it. When are you going to get into the current century?"

"Old habits die hard," he said. "When you grow up on a cattle ranch, there aren't too many electronics."

Peele slid the pad toward her. "That's okay. I'll have my admin put it into a spreadsheet."

"What do you have so far?" Long asked.

"When Addy was with Wyckoff, her login ID to access the patent office website was used by several people at the same time. We've spoken with the Patent Office and they assured us that is normal. Most patent attorneys use paralegals to file their applications."

"But I assume the attorney is still responsible for what happens when someone uses her ID."

"Correct. When Addy joined WTG, the same thing happened, but it wasn't to file applications."

Long took a sip of his coffee. "Let me guess. We've got some Koreans snooping in the Patent Office records trying to steal even more technology."

"That's what we don't know. Could be that, or it could be Addy. That's where your log will help us. Most of the illegal activity is at odd hours. We want to match up when Addy is in the office with when her credentials are being used. If she's in the office when we've detected illegal activity, it's not going to bode well."

# 23

JANICE HAD TO remind Addy that she was scheduled to meet the judge to discuss Hindy's release from the impound lot. The hearing was scheduled for Monday morning, the day before her interview with Examiner Johnston.

Addy was stressed, fearing the loss of a day would mean less time to prepare for her meeting with the patent examiner. But she also knew Hindy's notoriety would be a key marketing element when they announced to the world that they'd not only invented a car that ran on water, but that the United States Patent Office had granted them a twenty-year monopoly. She'd envisioned leaning against Hindy's hood, a new silver blimp floating above, while Quinn held up the blue ribbon copy of the patent and explained how soon—very soon—every car would be running on water.

While her driver hustled down the 101 Freeway to the courthouse, Addy flipped through pages of the old patents the examiner had uncovered while researching Quinn's idea. She would leave the legal haggling over Hindy's release to Perry.

When they rolled into the parking lot, Perry was already there, standing tall and elegant in his suit, arms folded, leaning against the door of his silver BMW. It was as if he were a carefully crafted illustration of what she'd given up by leaving the partnership.

Addy slipped out of the sedan and quickly hugged her mentor, eliminating any possibility of an awkward moment. "You look dapper as always," she said. "Thanks for doing this."

"Anything for you," he said with a smile. "You should come back."

Addy pressed her finger against his lips. "We can talk about that after the hearing. This is really important. What should I know?"

"If you'd responded to the texts I've been sending all this past week, maybe you'd know."

She grabbed his arm and pulled him toward the courthouse. "That's my fault. My phone was out of commission for a bit. I should have called you, but I've been really busy."

"So I hear."

Addy frowned. "We had a little time on our hands, but now we're all business."

"Like you said, we can talk later."

They bustled up the granite steps and into the stately courtroom, where they passed through a metal detector. Perry took up his keys and briefcase, straightened his tie, and turned toward the second courtroom, where the hearing would be held.

"Here's what you need to know," Perry said while they waited for the session to begin. "This isn't just about getting a ticket from the Sunnyvale police. The investigation has now moved onto the FBI and DHS. Their lawyers are all going to be here, probably an army of them."

"That's fine," Addy said. "I'm sure they've inspected every inch of Hindy. Tell the judge I'll cooperate in any investigation. Just give me back my car."

"Understood, but you never know what could happen."

"But I have you representing me."

The judge entered, took her seat and got right down to the business at hand. From her elevated position, she asked for Perry to state his appearance. Perry gestured for Addy to stand. The judge took a swig from her giant mug, then shuffled some papers.

"I am Perry Thompkins from Wyckoff and Schechter, representing the defendant, Addeline Verges."

"Addeline is a partner at your firm?" the judge asked, peering over her bifocals.

Addy interrupted. "Please call me Addy. I'm a former partner."

Perry surreptitiously put his hand on her wrist. "Addy recently accepted an in-house position."

"Very well. I think the issues are relatively straightforward. I've got a busy morning, so let's get this taken care of. How does your client plead with respect to the charge?"

"Not guilty," Perry said. "Hindy, the defendant's car, actually runs on electricity generated by a fuel cell and a few solar panels. It's one of the safest vehicles on the road."

The judge slid her mug and again peered down. "Understood, but that's not the issue. "Did your client have a license to carry a flammable substance?"

Perry glanced at Addy who nodded.

"No, your honor, but it was such a small amount, and only used to float the blimp. It was just an advertisement. The fire would never have happened if someone hadn't taken a shot at it with a flare gun."

The judge held up her hand and shook her head. "That's a different issue, and is being handled by law enforcement, who are amply represented here. If you don't have a license, I'm afraid I'll need to impose the fine."

Addy whispered to Perry.

"My client understands. She is willing to pay the fine, but would like her car returned. There is no reason why it should still be impounded. The Sunnyvale police have had ample time to conduct any kind of investigation."

Four lawyers shot up from the adjacent table.

"Sit down," the judge snapped. "I've read your briefs."

"Your honor," said a stout man in a navy suit, "I merely wish to emphasize the delicate nature of this investigation. We've been diligently collecting evidence, but since several federal agencies are now involved, it will take more time to coordinate efforts."

"Did you ask for their help?" the judge asked.

The district attorney cleared his throat. "They have investigative resources and abilities that a small police department—"

"Just answer my question."

"They offered their services, and we mutually agreed it would be best to conduct a joint investigation. For public safety issues, that's all I can offer in open court."

The judge rolled her eyes.

"Your honor," Perry interrupted. "I think my client has a right to know what kind of crime is being investigated, and why a routine examination of her vehicle will not suffice. And can they tell us what they've done so far to bring the suspect to justice?"

"It's a fair question," the judge said to the opposing lawyer.

Another attorney, wearing a gray suit stood. "I'm Molly Peele, representing the Department of Justice. We can provide this information, but I'll need to give the details *in camera*. Can we have a sidebar?"

"That won't be necessary," the judge said. "You've got a week, and don't come back asking for more."

Both attorneys were seated.

"You can see the bailiff regarding the fine," the judge said. "I trust that the Sunnyvale police will have your car available for you no later than next Monday morning. The day after the Super Bowl, in case anyone here hasn't heard about that little event in Santa Clara this weekend."

A few of the attorneys gave a small courtesy laugh. Perry shuffled his papers and escorted Addy out of the courtroom to pause beneath a large redwood tree.

"Pretty much what I expected," he said when they were out of earshot of the retinue of opposing attorneys. "They've got the judge worried about some terrorist plot. She knew about it even before they stood up. Her hands are pretty much tied."

"And what is this giant plot?"

"Pingree knows the lieutenant governor. He called the governor's office and found out there are a few terrorist cells targeting alternative energy companies. Some kind of hopeless attempt by some radical Middle Eastern groups who are worried that America will wean itself from oil and their cash cow will dry up. They want to make sure it won't happen, so they are starting guerrilla warfare to stop it. I have to admit the whole thing sounds pretty far-fetched to me, but it's gotten some attention at the highest levels. The current administration in Washington will do anything to avoid another 9/11. I'm just sorry you got caught up in it."

"By doing what?"

"Hard to say. Could be the media attention that the Mustang generated recently. Could be the fuel cell company we've been doing work for. Who knows? I played naïve in front of the judge, but I need to warn you that this could be serious. I'm a bit worried about what might happen to you, especially now you're associated with this Quinn fellow."

Addy maintained eye contact and tried to seem unconcerned. Inside, she was burning. That he would mention Quinn angered her. At the same time, the threats against her life were no trivial matter. First the attacks in Vietnam, then while she was on her bicycle, now this.

"Addy, why don't you come back to Wyckoff?"

"Seriously?" Addy said. "I heard you've already hired my replacement. Jerry Cochran. Really? You couldn't do better than that?"

"Nobody can replace you, Addy. That's why I want you to come back. The place just isn't the same without you. Frankly, it's kind of lonely. Not fun like it used to be. You are such a breath of fresh air."

Addy felt her insides stinging. Perry was being truthful. She didn't want to admit it, but she missed his camaraderie. Just yesterday, when she realized the examiner's untenable position with regard to Quinn's invention, she actually got out of her chair to run down the hall and complain to Perry, then remembered he wasn't there.

"I don't want you to think I'm spying on you, but I looked into this WTG company. It's not adding up. They've got some shell company in the US that you're probably working for, but they have only two published applications. What have they got you doing?"

"I wish I could tell you. Just know that it could be revolutionary. Otherwise, I never would have left."

Perry combed back his salt and pepper hair and looked

up into the redwood branches. "Okay, I'm going to be frank, because that's how I am. Since you appear to be lacking any kind of common sense, I must insist that you sever all relations with that Korean kid. Get your head screwed on straight, and come back to Wyckoff before you get into this so deep you can never get out. This bit about some magic car that runs on water using some hocus-pocus catalyst is nothing but a giant hoax. Your career, and maybe even your life, are going to be finished if you don't see the light of day and quit chasing this little fairy tale dream of yours."

Addy wanted to slap him, just like she had done with Quinn. Even more, she wanted to dig Janice's eyes out. She'd been tattling on her, in direct violation of her duty of confidentiality. What else had she told Perry?

She moved closer and with gritted teeth said, "You've misjudged him, just like you always do. You're being intolerant, and you know it."

Perry looked down so that they were almost nose to nose. "That's where you're wrong. I'm watching out for you like the father you never had. How can you say that I'm selfish? I've spent two weeks trying to work out a deal to get your car released, and what have you done for me in return? You certainly haven't come back to the firm. You should be thanking me for trying to keep you away from that predator. What kind of spell did that kid cast over you? My bet is that you're sleeping with him."

Addy's blood went from simmer to boil. "Tell you what," she spat back. "I'll come back to Wyckoff as soon as you learn to accept someone for who they really are, someone who has a real dream."

"Who, Quinn?" Perry shot back. "Accept him for who he is? Now that is crazy. I already know who Quinn is. He is a giant scam."

"Well, I believe in him."

"So you won't trust me, but you'll trust him? He's nothing but a snake oil salesman."

"That's where you're wrong. I know his science is for real. Maybe you should quit feeling sorry for yourself and help us for a change."

Addy regretted saying it as soon as the insult left her lips.

She did love Perry, had loved Keri, and the jab was uncalled for. In his own narrow-minded way, he was trying to help her. Addy watched his face fall. Without comment, he turned and strode away.

* * *

Agent Long watched the heated exchange between Perry and Addy and sensed an opportunity.

"Could we have a few moments?" he asked her.

Addy gave him a blank stare and attempted to sidestep him.

"I'm Jesse Long. Remember, from the hospital?"

The appearance of a bald man asking her questions after she'd been thrown from her bicycle came back to her.

"FBI? You know my lawyer isn't here."

"I'll be quick."

"We didn't part on the best terms as I recall."

"I was just doing my job. I noticed that you told the judge that you were no longer with Wyckoff. Do you mind if I ask you what you're doing at WTG?"

"And this has what to do with finding the person who punched my guts out?"

"Are you filing patent applications?" Long persisted.

"You know my profession."

"You spend a lot of time logged onto the patent office's computer network."

Addy told herself to keep cool. He was clearly trying to get under her skin. But why would he care when she had accessed the patent office site? "Every patent attorney does. Usually all day."

"And night?"

Addy thought about Sung-soo and wondered what Long was getting at.

"Did Quinn ever claim to have a car that can run on water?"

Addy hesitated. "What are you asking? I'm the victim of a crime and you're interrogating me like I'm some kind of criminal."

Long continued with his line of questions. "Did Quinn tell you how he came up with that invention?"

"That is none of your business," Addy struggled to regain her lawyerly cool.

"Did he tell you where he worked after he graduated from Caltech?"

Addy stayed silent and folded her arms, considering how she was going to wedge her way past him.

"Did he ever mention the name of Jerry or Jerald Wilcox?"

Again, silence. She'd never heard the name.

"I know sometimes I'm brash, but there's a reason."

"Rude, not brash," Addy corrected him.

"Take some good professional advice. Divorce yourself from this Quinn fellow before you're in too deep. He's a shady character. You can't trust him."

"If he's so bad, why don't you arrest him?" she huffed.

"We may do just that, and you don't want to be a part of it."

Addy was seething. She knew she should probably shut her mouth and walk away, but she couldn't help herself. "You know the government lawyers just lied to the judge. That's not why they want to keep my car."

"Why else?" Long asked. "That's what we do, we investigate crimes."

"Then why don't you go investigate the man who broke my rib? Maybe Quinn really does have an invention and some freaking terrorist is trying to stop him."

"Maybe you could tell me what Quinn is doing that has so many people after you?"

"That's none of your business." Addy stepped forward and reached out to push her interrogator aside.

"Are you sleeping with him?" Long sniped.

"We're finished," Addy said pushing his broad shoulder.

Long stepped aside to avoid the physical confrontation. "I'm sure we'll see each other again—really soon."

Addy stormed off and by the time she reached the courthouse steps Perry was already in his BMW and speeding away. She wondered who had hurt whom more and felt sad when she realized she had probably done far more damage.

She slipped her purse on her shoulder and was sidestepping

down the steps in her high heels when her black sedan appeared around the corner and pulled up to meet her. The driver had barely closed the door when Sung-soo slid over and shoved a mobile phone under her nose. "Quinn stayed up late."

Quinn. She wondered whether she should confront him with the information Agent Long had just dropped on her. She snatched the phone. "Must be pretty important," she said.

"I wanted to hear if you got your car back," Quinn said. "Would be nice if we could drive it to the interview tomorrow."

Addy sat up. "Wait, you've got the catalyst? Where are you?"

"One question at a time. As promised, I do have the catalyst, at least enough for a demo. Yun has also built a miniature fuel cell. I've just got a few logistical issues to work out."

"Like?"

"Getting it into the States. Our investors insist that I personally escort the chemicals and run the demo for the examiner. That's posing a few problems."

"Where are you?"

"Don't worry about that. I'll be there by tomorrow."

Addy sighed. With Quinn, nothing was straightforward.

"You don't know how relieved I feel right now," Addy said nudging Sung-soo and his kimchee breath aside.

"I'm surprised you doubted me."

"You made it sound like making the catalyst was harder than enriching uranium."

"Close. We've only got a small amount, and I need to take anything we don't use back to Korea the moment the interview is concluded."

"Wait a minute," Addy said. "We've got a lot to go over before our meeting with the examiner."

"What are our chances?"

"At this point, it's hard to read. The examiner seems decent, about my age, with four years at the Patent Office. I think he'll give us a fair shake."

"What came up in his search?"

"Don't take this wrong, but you're not the first one to try to tackle this problem. There's an outfit in Munich that's been researching this for a couple of decades, and there's a Berkeley professor who's quite a prolific writer on the topic."

"I know about them both. They've hit around the edges, but they don't have what I've discovered."

"I agree, and I think we can convince the examiner. But he's still going to have issues if we can't prove it really works."

"It works. You'll see. Look, I've got to run, but first tell me about the hearing. Did you get your car back?"

"It didn't go so well," Addy said, the vision of Perry speeding away still fresh in her mind.

"So they're really going to keep your car? For what? I don't get it. I thought you lived in America, not China."

"The judge gave them a week to return Hindy. It's just that Perry—" She stopped herself. She was wasting valuable time, and she didn't need to unload on Quinn.

"Let me guess," Quinn said. "He's all bent out of shape that you left his firm and he wants you to come back. I can only guess the names he called me."

Addy paused. How would Quinn know about their discussion? She wondered what kind of surveillance network Quinn had tracking her.

"How'd you know?" she asked.

"Because he called me in the middle of the night."

Addy gasped. "What? Perry? How did he get your number?"

"Janice, I suppose—which is something else we need to discuss."

"Wait. Perry really called you?"

"Oh, yeah, he had all kinds of nice things to say, like how he thought I was scum of the earth, and how he was going to do everything he could to stop me from ruining your life. You know, things like that."

"I'm sorry," Addy said.

"That's okay. I understand. He's not the first one to tell me that my people are ruining America."

"He said that?"

"I think his exact words were that I took some true-blooded American's spot at a prestigious university, then used my education to prey on vulnerable girls."

Addy clenched her fists. So she was just a little girl to him? Why hadn't she punched him in the nose when he was still within reach?

"Sorry, I've got to run," Quinn said. "I'll see you tomorrow."

"Wait," Addy said, still wondering whether she should ask him about the name, Jerry Wilcox. There was no reply. She handed the phone back to Sung-soo. They could talk more tomorrow.

# 24

ADDY STARED AT her watch, then checked her email, watching for any sign of Quinn. It was already after eight, and they needed to leave for the Patent Office no later than nine o'clock. She'd intended to do a quick search for Jerry Wilcox, but was too busy preparing for the interview, mentally rehearsing every possible scenario. This was something she couldn't mess up.

Although she dreaded the thought, she needed to ask Sung-soo for an update. If Quinn didn't arrive soon, she'd need to call the examiner and postpone the interview, something she desperately wanted to avoid. Interviews were discretionary, and because of the examiner's deadline to act on the case, they might not get another chance.

She rang his line and learned that not only had Quinn's flight had been delayed, but he also had an issue with Customs. Their driver had picked him up at the San Francisco airport, and Sung-soo estimated they would arrive at the office shortly after nine. They were cutting it close.

Addy was ready the moment they arrived. Briefcase in hand, she darted into the parking lot and hopped into the back seat.

She scooted next to Quinn.

"I can't tell you how good it is to see you," she said. "Any issues?"

"Only if you call a body search an issue," he said, dusting off his lapel. "They also tore through my suitcases, but couldn't find anything related to a fuel cell or a catalyst."

"But you have them, right?"

Quinn smiled. "Of course. I used a mule, actually two mules," he continued as their driver sped them down the 101 toward San Jose.

Addy was familiar with the term mule from law school. A mule was someone who smuggled contraband into the States, usually drugs from Central America. In Quinn's case, it was a vial full of gray powder and a shoebox containing a fuel cell.

Addy peeked nervously into the rearview mirror, then swiveled her head to look out the back window. Placing his finger on her chin, Quinn brought her face back around.

"Easy, they're ours. I'm not taking any chances."

"How many?"

"Three vehicles. Nothing is going to happen to us. As soon as this interview is over, I'm getting back on a plane, and this little jar of chemicals is headed back to Korea."

Addy wondered whether she should ask Quinn about his brief employment stint after graduation and why Agent Long had thrown out the name of Jerry Wilcox. She decided that focusing on the arguments she was going to present to the patent examiner was more important.

The Silicon Valley Patent Office was located in the San Jose City Hall building, one of four Patent and Trademark satellite offices authorized by President Barack Obama in 2011. The other outposts were located in Detroit, Dallas, and Denver.

Since the main Patent Office in Alexandria, Virginia, was bursting at the seams, and patent examiners regularly clamored to work somewhere other than the crowded Eastern seaboard—with its expensive real estate, gridlocked roads and humid summers—politicians relented to test the concept of satellite patent offices.

While the hope had been to have patent applications examined by local examiners, patent applications were instead randomly assigned. So, an inventor in Dallas might need to travel to Detroit to visit with the assigned examiner. Addy knew they'd gotten lucky when Examiner Johnston told them he lived near San Jose. She'd take an hour car ride to San Jose over flying to the nation's capital any day.

At the steps of city hall, Addy straightened her jacket, tucked her hair behind her ear, and adjusted the stack of documents in her arms. Quinn repeatedly patted his pocket, assuring himself the catalyst was still in his possession.

"A few housekeeping things," Addy said, her heels clacking on the marble floor. "We'll need to go through security. It's kind of like going through an airport, with a luggage scanner and metal detector. They'll want to look at the fuel cell, but you can probably get away with keeping the vial in your pocket. Just make sure you get all the metal off you so the alarm won't beep."

"Got it," he said, once again patting his pocket.

"The examiner said he's arranged a conference room. When we arrive, you can set up the demo. But remember to keep your mouth shut unless I nod at you to speak. I've had enough inventors screw these things up by shooting off their mouths. Let me do the talking. Got it?"

"What if he asks me a question?"

"Let me answer unless I nod. That will be my signal that it's okay for you to open your mouth. And just because I give you the green light, that doesn't mean I can't turn it off. If you start saying something stupid, I'm going to kick you in the shin. That means you need to shut up. Got it?"

Quinn smiled and his white teeth sparkled in the sunlight. "It's why I hired you."

When they entered the front lobby there was already a queue at the security desk. Addy looked at her watch. They were five minutes early, but there was only one security guard carefully checking in each visitor, diligently following his intake protocol. Addy watched Quinn wipe his forehead, even though the outside temperature was in the sixties. In his suit, he reminded her of the evening in Vietnam when they first met, yet this time so much more vulnerable. He was on her turf now.

Addy pulled out her phone to call the examiner and explain their delay. It went straight into voicemail. The examiner was probably already waiting in a conference room, far away from his phone.

It took fifteen minutes before the security guard asked them for their identifications. Addy plopped down her driver's license. "Got your passport?" she said to Quinn, almost reaching into his pocket.

"You never told me," Quinn whispered.

The guard, a gentleman with gray hair and a bald top peered over his bifocals. "I'm going to need some official government ID. No exceptions."

Quinn frantically searched his pockets and tugged out his wallet. "Driver's license?" he said handing it to the guard.

The man turned it over a few times and studied the photo.

"It's Korean," Quinn said.

"Thought it was Japanese. I guess it will work. Put your goodies on the conveyor, take out any metal objects and walk through the detector."

Addy went first while the man started up the scanner and studied the screen while Addy's purse disappeared into the tunnel. Quinn dashed through as if he were a running back. The detector beeped the moment his body went through the frame. The guard looked up, waved him back and kept studying his monitor.

"What you got here?"

"Show and tell," Addy interrupted. "The examiner said he wanted to see it."

"I figured that, but what is it?"

"A generator," Addy quickly answered. "Kind of like a battery, but a little different."

The man scratched his head. "Okay, as long as it's not explosive."

"Not at all," Addy said.

"Take off your shoes," the man said to Quinn.

Quinn obeyed and walked through the detector. Again, it beeped.

"Going to need to pat you down."

Quinn swallowed and again wiped the beads of sweat that were forming on his forehead.

"It's my belt," Quinn said, tugging it off and handing it to the guard, who peered at it over his bifocals.

The line behind them was now five deep, and one of the patent attorneys called out and asked if he could cut to the front of the line, claiming his examiner only had fifteen minutes to spare. The guard stared the man down, then handed the belt back to Quinn and motioned for him to put it on.

"Remember to check out with me before you leave. I've got your licenses in my desk."

Quinn began to say something, and Addy kicked him while narrowing her eyes. "Examiner Johnston is waiting."

The conference room had a long, rectangular table, solid white walls, and no windows. Quinn set down his contraption and shook out his shoulders.

"I've been looking forward to this," Examiner Johnston said, after making introductions. He then slipped a red daypack off his shoulders, unzipped it, and tugged out a manila folder. The color of his pack nearly matched his hair, which hung in curls over his ears. He was short, and his chiseled face was heavily sprinkled with freckles. "I see a lot of patent applications, but not many like this."

Johnston was wearing a wrinkled blue oxford shirt with a yellow paisley tie. Addy noticed his sideburns were wet, like he'd just come from working out at the gym. Addy chuckled to herself. Techies—some things never change.

"I think you'll be pleasantly surprised," Addy said. "Quinn, the inventor, is going to set up the demo. If it's okay with you, I'd like to show you how the invention works before we dive into your rejections in the office action."

"Sounds good to me," Johnston said, hovering next to Quinn while he coupled an LED to a wire that extended out of the metal housing.

Quinn sheepishly shot a glance at Addy, who subtly nodded her approval. "What we've got here is a very simple setup. I've electrically connected an LED to the fuel cell, just to show that I'm generating electricity."

"From water," the examiner said.

"Correct." Quinn tapped the fuel cell. "This is a proton-conducting fuel cell. Are you familiar with those?"

Johnston nodded. "I've seen a few."

Patent examiners are assigned to certain technology groups, so it stood to reason that Examiner Johnston had reviewed any number of patent applications describing fuel cells.

"This one is a little different," Addy said, "but don't worry, after the demo we'll walk you through how it works. We can even take it apart and show you its insides if you want."

"Let's see how it goes. We only have an hour." Johnston opened his folder while Quinn continued with his setup. "I've read your application. I see you are using a catalyst to extract the hydrogen. How does that work?"

Addy grinned. Johnston was on the ball. Few examiners bothered to read the patent application, let alone dig deep enough to get to the heart of the invention.

Quinn again sought Addy's approval. Upon her signal, Quinn took the vial out of his pocket, retracted a small bin at the top of the fuel cell and tapped in about a teaspoonful of the catalyst like he was putting coffee into a coffee maker. "I've just dispensed a small amount of the catalyst. Next, I'll pour distilled water into a holding tank. This will be fed into a reaction chamber, where the water will react with the catalyst under a small electric charge."

"Which you are getting from where?"

"A very small battery. We don't need much current, just enough to start the reaction. The hydrogen atoms will separate from the oxygen, and will bubble to the top, where the hydrogen gas is collected and fed into the fuel cell. We've made the side wall of the reactor out of a transparent material so you can see it working."

"What kind of modifications have you made to the fuel cell?"

Quinn again sought Addy's approval. She narrowed her eyes. "Addy will explain those after we finish."

Addy wanted to keep Quinn on a short leash, just in case he strayed and said something that could hurt their case. Quinn made a few adjustments, checked the water reservoir and then said, "We're all set. Do you want to do the honors?"

"Sure," Johnston said. "What do I need to do?"

"Flip this switch, then slowly turn the dial to control the current to the reactor."

Examiner Johnston leaned forward and hit the switch with his finger, then slowly turned a black knob. In a matter of seconds, small bubbles floated to the surface. A second later, the LED illuminated.

Johnston scratched his head while lifting up the shining light. "Okay, I see it works, but how do you know that you're getting out more energy than you're putting in?"

"That's an easy calculation," Addy chimed in. "We're using a watch battery that draws about 20 to 30 milliamps. The LED lights up once the current reaches 100 milliamps. We're getting out about four times as much energy as we're putting in."

Johnston shook his head. "But that's impossible."

Quinn smiled. "Oh, but it's not. That's why we're here. You can see it for yourself."

"Don't worry," Addy interrupted, opening her binder. "I'll walk you through the physics."

Johnston leaned over and watched in awe while the bubbles continued to rise and the LED shone brightly.

"I don't know about this. What's the catalyst you've got here?" Johnston reached out and snatched the vial from Quinn's hand. Instinctively, Quinn reached out to grab it back. Johnston held it above his head, using the ceiling lights to visualize the powder as he rolled the vial between his fingers. "What is this stuff? It's not radioactive, is it?" he said quickly setting it on the table and stepping back as if it were a rattlesnake ready to strike.

"Totally safe," Quinn said.

A moment of silence followed while Addy collected her thoughts. The stillness during her brief hiatus was shattered when the conference room door flew open, slamming against the wall, and a team of federal agents with bright yellow FBI letters on their shirts barged through, automatic weapons drawn. They were all pointing directly at Quinn.

"Hands in the air!" the first agent shouted. Quinn hesitated, glancing at his fuel cell and the vial that the examiner had set on his folder. "Now!"

Quinn slowly raised his hands, palms forward. The second agent pressed forward, clamped onto Quinn's wrist and flung his right arm behind his back. Addy listened to the ratcheting of handcuffs while Quinn was subdued.

Addy noticed one of the agents was bald. Agent Jesse Long. She strode forward. "I'm Quinn's lawyer, and I demand an explanation. You can't arrest him without a warrant."

Long expanded his chest, his bulletproof jacket pushing her back. "Keep your mouth shut. He's not being arrested. Just detained long enough that we can search him."

"For what?" Addy insisted.

"It's all in the search warrant. Jake, pat him down."

The agent snapped the second cuff on Quinn's other hand.

"Okay, you're next," Long said to Addy. "We're going to need to cuff you. Policy, no exceptions."

"Me? For what?"

"You're being arrested for espionage and stealing US technology."

Addy couldn't believe it. Stealing US secrets. How? She looked down at the fuel cell and the brightly shining LED. Her arrest had to be related to the catalyst. Why else were they searching Quinn? But that didn't make any sense. She hadn't stolen anything. This was Quinn's invention. Could it be that he actually stole it from the US government?

"No, you've got the wrong person," she pleaded.

"Don't make this any harder than it needs to be."

Addy stepped back until the table blocked her retreat. Quinn had been right to worry about the Patent Office stealing his idea. Her own government. She couldn't believe they would stoop this low.

Addy watched while the agent completed searching Quinn. They wanted the catalyst, and she couldn't let it happen, not until she could sort this through. If it really was that valuable, if the federal government was willing to stop at nothing, she needed to protect it.

The vial was sitting on the table, in plain sight, directly behind her. These agents would soon swoop up the fuel cell and everything else in the room. She watched the agent physically go over every inch of Quinn's body, knowing she'd be next. If she snatched up the chemical, they'd quickly take it into custody.

She needed a diversion.

Abruptly, she whizzed around, stuck out her hand and flipped the switch on the fuel cell. The light flickered and went dark.

"Are you guys crazy?" she screamed. "Do you know what would

happen if you knocked this off the table while it was still on?"

One of the agents stepped back, throwing out his arm to hold back the rest of the agents. It was enough distraction for Addy to sweep up the vial without them noticing. In the same motion, she slipped it inside Examiner Johnston's open pack.

"I really can't believe you are so stupid," Addy yelled again.

The agent holding Quinn nodded, and the other agents converged on her. "Well, it looks like the danger is over." With one agent on each side, they manhandled her and forced her arms behind her back. A second later, cold steel was cutting into her wrists. She was a prisoner. A search followed, and a cleanup crew carefully secured the fuel cell. With an agent on either side of her, they took her outside the building.

The moment the sunlight struck her eyes, she could hear the clicking of camera lenses. The press had been tipped off to an important arrest. Instinctively, she lowered her head.

* * *

"Can you at least get me a newspaper?" Addy said to the guard when he passed by her cell during his morning rounds. Her head was pounding and her mouth was pasty.

After spending the night in jail, she was desperate for news of her arrest. She should have called Perry the moment she was booked, but she was too humiliated. She didn't want to admit he was right, and she held out hope that this was a giant mistake that would soon be sorted out. She assured herself that both she and Quinn had been set up, and that they'd be able to prove the governmental conspiracy to stop them.

She was scheduled for an arraignment before the judge after lunch, and she needed to call a lawyer. Addy wasn't sure she was ready to call Perry, especially not until she understood what the rest of the world had been told.

Someone brought her a copy of the *San Jose Mercury News* and tossed it onto her mattress. Addy tried to control her emotions when she saw her picture on the front page, biting her lip. Her photo—not Quinn's. The image of the dapper Korean inventor was conspicuously missing. She frantically scanned the article. It reported her arrest for stealing important technology from the United States. What exactly she had stolen the article didn't say, only that it was so important to national security that it was being kept under wraps. But the reporter said there had been rumors that it was tied to her locally famous impounded car.

There was a mention of Quinn's presence during the interview with the examiner at the Patent Office, and that he had been searched but not arrested. Addy shook her head, trying to clear the confusion—and anger.

Quinn's lawyers released a statement saying they were considering whether they would bring any civil charges against Addy for stealing WTG's trade secrets. *Damn him!* she thought. Brash as Perry had been, he'd pegged Quinn for who he was. She didn't yet know how, but it was clear she was nothing but a pawn, caught in some kind of crossfire. Quinn had used her and then thrown her to the wolves.

She crumpled the newspaper and hurled it against the wall, where it hit with nothing more than a rustle and drifted to the floor.

She'd trusted Quinn, breaking her vow to never trust anyone again. Why did she keep doing it? Every time she trusted someone, she got hurt. And now it involved much more than feelings. She was facing serious criminal charges, ones that could land her in a federal penitentiary for decades. Even if she could beat the trumped-up charges, she'd never be able to practice law again. No firm would want to touch her.

Exhausted, she curled up on her rickety bed and began to sob. She wished she had her father's shoulder to cry on, but that window had long since closed.

Instinctively, she slipped her fingers into her pocket, searching for her phone, for some comfort. No, wait. They'd taken it moments after her arrest, undoubtedly to mine it for every bit of data it contained. And she would likely never get it back.

She felt so alone, completely abandoned. It would have helped to know there was someone who cared about her. In just two days she was supposed to be with Lynda and her stepbrother and stepsister. But now it would be impossible.

She couldn't even call them to let them know. But they probably already knew. Thanks to modern media, half of America probably knew. She wondered how they reacted. Then she decided she really didn't want to know.

# 25

ADDY'S EYES WERE red and puffy when she was hauled out of the patrol car. This was her second trip to a courthouse in less than a week. But this time it was the United States District Court for the Northern District of California, located in the Robert F. Peckham Federal Building in San Jose. She was being arraigned on numerous federal charges. Bail was possible, but she had no way of knowing how much would be required, especially if federal prosecutors called her a flight risk. And, after deciding she couldn't face Perry, she decided to represent herself.

The police vehicle pulled up to the curb and a federal marshal opened the door. She blinked her eyes in the bright sunlight and wiped her eyes with her fluorescent orange sleeve. Not only did she stand out like a neon sign, but she also looked ridiculous in her prison garb.

She'd barely looked up when she spotted Perry's familiar figure waiting beneath a large elm tree. She rushed forward to embrace him, but the cuffs held her hands tight. Perry threw his arms around her, pushing the agent aside. Once again, Addy burst into tears.

"I figured you needed some help," Perry said, an arm over her shaking shoulders.

Addy could hear the bustle of photographers nearby, but she didn't care. She looked into Perry's eyes. "Sure—I mean yes. I want you to be my lawyer. I can't believe you're here, especially after the way we left things. You're all I have."

"I'm not much," Perry said. "I'm a patent lawyer, not a criminal attorney. I twisted the arm of one of my law school buddies, who's inside waiting for us. If we have any luck, we'll get you out on bail, and then we can try to sort all this out."

She wiped her eyes with the back of her sleeve while the federal agents hustled them into the federal building. Thirty minutes later, and fifty thousand dollars poorer from bail, they re-emerged. Perry's colleague had convinced the judge that Addy was not a flight risk and she posed no threat to society.

But she was still facing charges, including espionage, theft of trade secrets, and half a dozen others stemming from her alleged hacking into government databases, including those of the Patent Office. She was charged with trying to steal important technology relating to hydrogen fuel cells and hydrogen production.

* * *

"So, what are you going to do?" Perry asked, sliding behind his office desk while sipping his coffee. She could see the bags under his eyes, and wondered how much he'd slept since hearing about her arrest. She felt awkward being back at Wyckoff, and was grateful Perry had closed his office door.

Addy was sullen. "At WTG we had this IT guy named Sung-soo. Janice figured out that he was staying up all night and using my login to search the Patent Office databases. We had no idea this was just a pretense to illegally hack into the Patent Office computer network to search for patent applications that weren't yet publicly available. Quinn must have known they would pin it on me if they got caught. They sure played me. I'm so embarrassed."

"Any word from Quinn?"

"Nothing. He's probably back in Korea by now. I don't

understand why they didn't arrest him instead of me. He's the one who stole the catalyst and tried to claim it as his own invention."

"No probable cause. It was your account his IT guy used. The best the judge would give them was a search warrant to tear apart WTG."

"They must believe he has the catalyst."

"Highly likely. But if that's all they wanted, they didn't need to arrest you."

"But couldn't they see Sung-soo was using a WTG computer?"

Perry shook his head. "You weren't actually working for WTG. He set up the US company in your name—Addeline Verges P.C. His lawyers made sure he could have no possible connection to the break-in. He nailed you pretty good."

Addy squeezed her head, trying to make the dull ache go away. "I don't know what I'm going to do. I'm so terrified I can't think straight, Perry. How am I going to prove I'm innocent? I could be spending the next decade in jail. Stealing government secrets—people don't just walk away from that."

Perry didn't sugarcoat the situation. "It's certainly possible. The Patent Office has a list of applications for hydrogen production that were accessed from your computer using your credentials. All were assigned to the Department of Energy. It didn't help that some of the information in the applications you filed for WTG had many of the same ideas. This looks very, very bad. And the fuel cell they confiscated still had trace amounts of a chemical that was allegedly stolen from the DOE. If the government can prove they invented the catalyst first, you could be in a whole bunch of trouble."

Addy looked down and shook her head, her long dark hair slipping over her shoulders to cover her face. She was afraid to reveal to Perry what she had done with the vial holding the catalyst for fear of entangling him in her mess..

"Let me guess, every DOE application lists a guy named Wilcox as the inventor."

"They didn't provide me with that information. Why do you ask?"

"Probably doesn't matter now. Agent Long wanted to know if I'd ever heard the name. Anyway, did they search the office?"

"They did, but couldn't find anything. Quinn was clearly smart enough to have your computer's hard drive removed and replaced with a clean one. Your hard drive is probably already back in Korea.

"What's worse," Perry continued, "is that the hearing today was open to the public. This is sensationalist journalism at its best. You are going to be front-page news. I'll bet you're already the top story on most of the national networks. Addy and Hindy—you have to admit, the jingle has a nice ring to it."

Addy looked up and cleared her hair from her eyes, not bothering to hide the tears rolling down her cheeks. His regrettable sense of humor missed its mark, again. "Everything I've worked so hard for is gone. And for what? Because I was too vain to face reality? Why couldn't I see that this was too good to be true? Why couldn't I be happy as an ordinary patent attorney?"

"Don't be so hard on yourself. We all have dreams. If you never chased yours, you'd always have wished you had. You're young, you have time to learn from your mistakes and move on."

"No, even if I could beat these charges, I'll never be able to practice law. Who's going to want me for their attorney?" Perry's reaction was very subtle.

"I'd hire you."

His words sounded forced. As she'd suspected the firm would never vote to bring her back as a partner.

"Well, I guess you won our little wager. Quinn was everything you said. I was completely blinded, even though you warned me. I should have trusted you over him. I'd love to come back to Wyckoff, but you know as well as I do that it would never work. I'm probably going to be disbarred, which doesn't really matter, because you can't practice law from a prison cell."

"I've been giving that some thought. We're going to need a defense strategy, and if I'm going to be your lawyer, I need you to tell me what's been going on in your life. Everything. Let's take this one step at a time."

Addy sighed. She needed to trust him, even though they'd had their differences. Beyond that, every time she'd trusted someone, she'd been hurt. She'd believed Quinn would be the exception, and look how that ended. Why would Perry be any different?

She drummed her fingers on the table. She didn't have a choice.

"Okay, let's get going," she said, and began to summarize everything that had happened since the hydrogen balloon was torched. She told her mentor about the attacks and warnings in Vietnam, Quinn's too-good-to-be-true offer, and her introduction to the WTC hydrogen team. She retold the story of her tumble off the bicycle and the punch to the ribs, and Quinn rehabilitating her at his Half Moon Bay home.

She explained the office setup, and how she and Janice spent a week of total boredom while Sung-soo monitored their every move, at least while he wasn't snooping on the DOE's patent applications. When they were both about ready to leave WTC and come back to Wyckoff, Quinn appeared with the patent applications. She'd studied every word and convinced herself that the technology was scientifically sound.

And yes, Quinn had balked about bringing a sample of the catalyst, supposedly because of "production problems," but he eventually came through.

"What he showed to the examiner was real," she concluded. "There is a catalyst, and cars really can run on water."

Perry looked up from his notepad. "You were attacked while driving to work. So that's why Quinn got you a driver?" Perry said.

"At the time, I really believed he was looking after me. He was convinced some disgruntled gang from the Middle East was going to make sure the technology never saw the light of day. That much makes sense, especially when the man who attacked me recently looked Arabic and had a tattoo, and I could swear was the same guy who shot the balloon, and one of the two who accosted me in Vietnam. Plus, I doubt the people who threatened me were employed by the DOE, especially the ones in Vietnam."

"So do you think the attacks on you are somehow tied to same group that shot Hindy's balloon?"

"I'm pretty sure it was the same guy. Plus, you told me Homeland Security is investigating it as an act of terrorism."

"Sounds like you've got a lot of enemies."

"Including Quinn," Addy said, still fuming that she'd fallen for his slick, glib personality and the convoluted scam he'd created to trap her into—what?

"This is unbelievably complicated," Perry said. "Quinn hires you to protect his applications from being stolen by the Department of Energy, while at the same time he's using your login to steal technology from the DOE. Meanwhile, you're getting the crap kicked out of you, regardless of which continent you're on."

"It all seemed so legitimate. Quinn showed me two patent applications that he filed last year for WTG. Not only were they hit with a secrecy order by the Patent Office, but six months later the DOE filed its own patent application with the same invention. It was all bogus technology, but that's why Quinn was convinced they were planning to steal his inventions. That's the whole reason he hired me."

"I understand," Perry said, "but that's not going to help you in front of a jury."

Perry stood and sauntered over to the window. He folded his arms and peered at the foothills like he always did when he was seeking inspiration. While she waited, she fought tears over his last statement and wished he wasn't always so blunt.

"I have an idea," he said turning to look at her. "It's kind of crazy, but it may be your only option. Can you trust me?"

Addy tucked her hair behind her ear. Perry had bailed her out of jail. He'd also tried to protect her from Quinn. Still, that wasn't enough. "I'm not in much of a trusting mood right now."

"At this point, I'm not sure you have much of a choice." Perry strode across the room and perched on his desk facing Addy. "You told me I should start believing in someone, and I have. I believe in you, Addy. I know I say things that aren't politically correct, but I can't help it. I call it just as I see it."

Addy remembered Perry had called Quinn and said he wasn't wanted in America, and that he was preying on a vulnerable little girl. She wanted to confront him, especially about the little girl part, but decided to hear him out first.

"I know I can't relate to what you've been through, having parents who deserted you, and now this. I can only imagine how you must feel right now. Keri and I had a great marriage. Trust was never an issue. We shared everything. But I do know what it's like to be alone. I probably shouldn't tell you this, but over the past few weeks I've been so lonely I even considered ending it all, hoping somehow I could be with her in the next life."

"She would never have wanted that," Addy said. "You still have so much to contribute. Think about all the good you can do."

Perry smiled sheepishly. "Funny. In my most desperate moment, I came to the same realization. I don't know why, but I just did. And the next day I saw the news flash on CNN about a patent attorney who was arrested for stealing government patent applications. It was then I knew I had to help you. I figured that if you really believed in something that much, I should find out why."

Addy swallowed hard and wiped her eyes.

"That's really how you found out about me?"

"God's truth," Perry said raising his hand.

She took that as an apology. For Perry, it was the best he could do. "Okay, tell me what you're thinking," she said.

"First, tell me why you left the firm. I mean, I know it didn't work out, and it may seem like a poor decision in hindsight, but what really drove your decision?"

Addy leaned back. "I suppose there were lots of reasons," she said, "but I wouldn't have done anything if I didn't believe in the technology. While I was in Vietnam, I imagined what it would be like if those poor people could have their own cars and afford to drive them, or find a way to cook their meals without burning trash in the street. I realized that's why I'd spent years tinkering with Hindy. In my gut, I believe something like this is possible, and when I was shown Quinn's technology, I knew I couldn't walk away, no matter the price."

Perry slapped the table. "Then that's it. That is exactly what you should do. You should pay the price and make it happen."

Addy frowned. "I'm not sure what you mean. I'm looking at going to jail. I need a defense, not another silly dream."

"I'm being serious. You've seen the technology. You know the catalyst is real. You already see how this can change the world. You're the only one who can make this happen."

"It is for real," she said.

"Then fight for it. It is the right thing to do. The world needs this technology. If you can find a way to get the catalyst and prove it really works, I'm betting there will be such a public outcry that perhaps nobody will get the patents and everyone can use it. Isn't that what we really want?"

Perry might just be right. She knew the formula, and, perhaps more important, she knew where to find the vial of chemicals Quinn had used for their interview at the Patent Office. If she could show the world what was being kept from them, the court of public opinion might just win the day.

Addy nodded. "I agree with you. If Sung-soo was stealing inventions contained in our government's patents, WTG shouldn't be entitled to any patents, and if the US was also stealing WTG's technology, they are just as guilty. And, if the government is hiding this technology to protect big oil companies that's even more outrageous. Let's show the world the invention, and let them be the ones to demand that the technology be donated to everyone."

"That's right." Perry stood up. "You've got the fight in you. That's the Addy I've always believed in. Forget about the charges, forget about being disbarred, just give the world the technology, and we'll sort everything else out after that."

Perry *was* right. This was her dream. Spending the next three years defending herself with legal briefs and depositions was not going to get her anywhere.

"You're right, Perry, and thank you for helping me remember. Quinn has a technology to change the world, like the telegraph or the airplane, but everyone is fighting to control it. The result? I'm caught in the middle, and nobody gets the water-powered car. And the patent system is being manipulated by both sides to get what they want."

She leaned forward, the fog of depression dissipating. "I like your idea a lot! It's time to yank this out of the clutches of the Patent Office and the DOJ and Korea and WTG and the labyrinth of our courts and just hand it over to the world. Then, after the dust settles, maybe someone will figure out I'm innocent."

Perry nodded. "There's a point when you need to step outside the legal system and do what is best. There's precedent for this. Just look at our Founding Fathers. When the system fails and all the players are corrupt, you need to make a clean break."

"I'm in," she said. She uncrossed her legs, stood and gave

Perry a hug. "Thanks for believing in me."

"Just know that I'm here for you. Don't worry about the legal case against you. We'll be working on it from our end. All I want you do to is start putting together a plan. Can you get the catalyst?"

Addy pulled her hair back and tied it in a bun. Perry was risking his own career by helping her, and she needed to be as brave as him. The federal agents had come to the Patent Office with a search warrant looking for the catalyst. If Addy knew anything about its location and told Perry, it would place him in an ethical dilemma. He would be complicit in a crime. She was determined to shield him from harm.

"Leave that up to me. I've read the patent applications, so I know how they make it. The problem is that you need a billion-dollar factory to do it."

"So you don't have any?" he pressed. "I thought you had some to show the examiner."

"Had some," Addy said.

"They claim there's more."

"None that I have," she said truthfully.

"But you can get some?"

"I'll let you know. Let's leave it at that."

"Got it," Perry finally relented. "The first thing you're going to need is a car. You can use my hybrid. It's on level two. I have Keri's Mercedes, so I won't miss it."

"And I'm going to need a phone so we can communicate."

Perry tugged his wallet out of his pants and tossed a few bills onto the desk. "For now, get one of those prepaid phones."

Addy understood. The red tape in dealing with her current phone plan was going to be insurmountable.

She hugged him again, comforted by his body warmth as much as his encouragement and belief in her. She had to trust Perry. If he failed her, there was no one else.

# 26

THE FIRST THING Addy noticed when she pulled Perry's Prius into the WTG parking lot was that the building's front door was propped ajar. Tucking an empty cardboard box under her arm, she squeezed through, expecting to greet a beefy security guard. Instead, the lobby desk was unmanned. She sidestepped the body scanner and wandered down the hall, hoping there were at least a few of her personal belongings still in her office. Sung-soo's office was empty, but papers were scattered across his desk, with a few that had floated to the floor.

"Is anyone here?" she said.

"Just me," came Janice's voice.

Addy scampered to her office, finding Janice shuffling office supplies into a cardboard box. She tossed in a stapler, then a roll of tape.

"I'm only kind of sorry for you," Janice said looking up.

"You heard?"

"Who hasn't? Ever heard of CNN? By the way, everyone here's cleared out. I don't have a job, and you don't have any stock options." She tossed a paper at Addy, which fluttered to the ground. "Notice on the lease. I found it on the front desk. It's been terminated."

"Sung-soo?"

"Like I said, everyone's cleared out. They must have known this place was going to be ransacked by the Feds, because they cleaned out all the equipment and high-tailed it out of here. You know I love you Addy, but you did me wrong. I've got no job, no severance, no last paycheck. Nothing."

"Wyckoff?"

"Perry agreed to take me back, thank God. But I have to tell you that I'm really scared. How do I know I'm not next? What if they accuse me of stealing patent applications? Sung-soo was camped on my computer for weeks."

"You're going to be fine," Addy reassured her. "It's me they want."

Janice grunted. "WTG left me a text. They said if I ever speak to anyone, they'll make sure I can't ever talk again."

"WTG?"

"Uh-huh. They said they'd hurt me, and it wouldn't be like your bicycle accident."

Addy's heart nearly stopped.

"You lied to me," Janice continued. "That bump on your head—it wasn't an accident."

Addy fumbled for something to say. "You don't need to worry. I'll make sure you're okay."

Janice hefted the box and shoved her way past Addy. "Don't make a promise you can't keep."

Addy followed her. "You'll see. I'll make this all up to you."

"Tell it to the man upstairs," she said sidestepping to squeeze through the doorframe. "By the way, your request under the Freedom of Information Act came today. It's on your desk. You were right about one thing—the Patent Office was deliberately suppressing WTG's patent applications. It's all there in black and white—program 'Protect America'—and they're not talking about protecting US citizens from harmful weapons. They're talking about making sure the US knows first about every kind of alternative energy idea."

Addy nearly sprinted to her office. She scooped up the documents produced under the Freedom of Information Act and scoured their contents. It *was* true! The Patent Office had been directed to flag every new patent application that related to energy production. They were then forwarded to the DOE for scrutiny. If the DOE believed the technology could "impact domestic energy interests," it would be tagged with a secrecy order "until such time as the impact can be determined."

In other words, it was a way for the DOE to protect America's interests by refusing to grant patents to energy technologies detrimental to America's energy policy, which seemed to be protecting investments in oil production. All applications that in any way related to hydrogen production were to be specially culled from the stack.

Things were beginning to make sense. Quinn's applications were being watched—and suppressed. He was right to worry that the US would get its own patents and try to block any foreign interest from participating in the US market.

She folded up the documents and stuffed them into her pocket. Somehow, this information was going to help her case.

Addy's next stop was at a strip mall less than a mile away. She used Perry's cash to purchase a phone with a hundred minutes and thirty megabytes of data. That would be plenty, considering she'd only be sending text messages.

She thought about sending Lynda a text, but struggled over what to say. She should at least tell her she wasn't coming, though, something she'd failed to do with her father.

While she typed in a short message giving her regrets, Addy's fingers were trembling. Surprisingly, Lynda responded immediately.

*We understand,* the message said. *Let us know when things settle down. You're always welcome.*

That was all Addy needed, the assurance that someone else believed in her. *That is what family should be about*, she told herself.

For the first time in days, she smiled; it felt strange, but right. She could do this.

# 27

ADDY'S HOPE OF being exonerated and making the water-energy technology hinged on whether Examiner Johnston still had the vial in his pack. With any luck, it had fallen to the bottom along with pens, candy wrappers and whatever other mulch he had accumulated. Back in Perry's hybrid, she took back roads to San Jose, then ventured to the City Hall, watching to make sure she wasn't being followed.

The South Bay corridor looked like a Mardi Gras celebration, with NFL banners streaming from light posts, and flags draped from buildings celebrating the upcoming Super Bowl Sunday. This would be one Super Bowl she'd likely have to miss.

The moment she saw the white cement façade of the Silicon Valley Patent Office, her head felt light. It was less than a week since she was arrested, and these same streets had been filled with reporters poised to make her a household name. She circled the block twice, searching for something—anything—that would spark an idea for a strategy.

She couldn't just march in and demand to see Johnston. More problematic, even if they let her in, and Johnston still had the catalyst in his pack, why would he give it to her? If anything, he'd turn it over to the police, making sure to tell them that Addy was the one who'd secreted it away.

She decided to park across the street, then find a café for coffee and a muffin. Back in her car, she could wait until his day ended and see if he came out with his pack. It would be easy to spot, bright red, just like his mop of curly hair. The sun was shining, so Addy rolled down the windows and reclined the seat. With her feet perched on the dashboard, she waited. Twice she caught herself dozing off and shook her head to stay awake.

Just after five o'clock the short, energetic figure of Daniel Johnston emerged, his red curls bouncing with every step. Slung over his right shoulder was the crimson daypack. She nearly broke out laughing when she noticed his blindingly white legs, barely covered by striped running shorts that looked like they came from Richard Simmons' wardrobe.

Addy bolted upright, pressed the starter button, and waited for Johnston to turn the corner. Keeping her distance, she followed him for two blocks, where he climbed into a white Chevy Malibu. She stayed on his tail when he zipped onto the 280 Freeway, going north toward San Francisco. After ten miles, she wondered where he could possibly be going, especially wearing his outlandish running garb. Certainly not to a Pilates studio.

When he shot off the Foothill Boulevard exit, she figured it out. Rancho San Antonio park was an open space preserve in the foothills of Los Altos, and it had twenty-four miles of trails that both runners and nature enthusiasts flocked to for a retreat from the bustling city life. The Malibu was barely shoved into park when Johnston flung his door open and emerged. In a flash, he bolted down the gravel path, his pale legs glowing in the fading light.

Most serious runners pounded out at least five kilometers, usually ten or more. That meant she had a safety zone of around thirty minutes to get to the pack, inspect its contents, and hightail it back home. Addy parked several spots away and jumped out, squinting against the sun to make sure Johnston wasn't coming back, but he was out of sight after only a few hundred yards.

Addy prayed he'd left in such a hurry that he hadn't bothered to lock the doors. Otherwise, she'd need another plan. Breathing heavily, she ventured to the Malibu, pulling her shirtsleeve over her hands before she touched the vehicle. When she tugged on the handle, she heard a click and the door popped open.

*Sometimes you just get lucky*, she told herself. She quickly scanned the parking lot and, finding it empty, slipped inside and peeked into the back seat. The pack felt like it was filled with lead as she lugged it onto her lap. Addy yanked on the zipper and spread the pack open. It was jam-packed with textbooks. She shimmied the first one out. Torts.

Addy laughed. *He's going to law school.* One at a time, she hefted them out, setting the legal treatises on the driver's seat. Not having a phone, she didn't know how long she'd been inside, but already began to worry that time was running out. She glanced around the parking lot. A pickup had pulled into a spot on the other side of the lot, and a younger couple emerged and began stretching. In the rearview mirror, all was quiet.

Addy dove her hand to the bottom of the pack. With the exception of a stray peanut and a wrapper containing a wad of gum, it was empty. Again and again, she swept the bottom. Nothing. Frantically, she searched the pockets, but there was no sign of the vial with the catalyst. Addy rotated the pack upside down and shook it violently. Out came a paperclip and a pencil lead, but nothing else. *Where did it go? Had Johnston discovered it and turned it over to the federal agents?* If that had happened, her plan was ruined.

She peered out the driver's window and noticed a white SUV veer into the parking lot. She continued to monitor its progress while she mindlessly shoved the books back inside. Then it dawned on her. The bag's colors were the same, a dark red, crimson, like the Stanford colors, but it wasn't the same bag. When Johnston toted it into the conference room, he had it slung over his shoulder, but it was more like a duffle bag, kind of like the large bags tennis players used. This one was for school supplies, books and notepads.

Then where was his gym bag? Had he taken it home? Was it shoved into a corner in his office? She knew guys in college who wore the same shorts for weeks on end. Was he one of those?

The vehicle crept closer. She noticed it had yellow lights on the hood, some kind of official vehicle. It continued in her direction.

Addy picked up her pace and opened the glove box, where she found his wallet and phone. She flipped open the leather flap. His driver's license. At least she should could get his address. It was dusk, and the lettering was hard to read; she was thinking about using the flashlight feature on his phone when she heard gravel crunch as the SUV pulled beside her.

Her heart stopped. She needed to act unconcerned, like this was her car.

She craned her neck to see down the valley where Johnston had disappeared. The patent examiner could be back any minute. Calmly, she flung the phone and wallet into the glove compartment and looked up.

The SUV's white door had black and green lettering. SECURITY. Some kind of logo with a poppy was below it—the official flower of the State of California. A heavyset man inside rolled his finger as a signal he wanted to speak with her.

Not being able to roll down the window, she cracked the door.

"Everything okay?" said the security guard.

"Yeah," Addy said getting out of the car. "Can't let those cell phones run your life. I've got to get on my walk before the sun sets."

The officer nodded and shut down his engine. Addy closed the car door and pretended to stretch, pretended to be calm. Yet in the distance, she could see Johnston's bright shorts churning down the hill toward the parking lot.

She had to do something. She glanced back at the SUV, noticing that the man with the double chin was talking into some kind of radio. Addy once again studied the lettering on the SUV, realizing this wasn't an official parks and recreation vehicle after all. Her heart raced. Who was this? Johnston was getting closer. Addy realized she couldn't make a dash for her own car. This fake security guard would certainly follow her.

"Gotta go," she said, then zipped across the parking lot and onto the jogging trail, careful to stay clear of the returning patent examiner. As soon as she reached the trees, she made a beeline for the hills, disappearing into the forest.

After she'd gone about a hundred yards, she stopped and listened. Her heart was pounding in her ears, but she couldn't hear anything other than the sound of a bird chirping and leaves rustling in the breeze. The security guard hadn't followed her. She jumped up and darted through the bushes and downed trees until she reached a small clearing. Addy peered down onto the parking lot. Both the SUV and Johnston's Malibu were gone.

Still, she didn't venture out. The obese man in the SUV could be waiting for her, perhaps with reinforcements. How had he found her? Addy tried to calm her breathing and remained crouched behind a large eucalyptus tree until dark, shivering in the damp night air. Finally, she sneaked back to her car.

* * *

Addy had been prudently paranoid ever since Quinn smashed her SIM card. She'd learned that carrying a smart phone was equivalent to a deer wearing a tracking device during hunting season. She didn't have that problem with her prepaid phone. Now, however, she wondered whether a bug had been attached to Perry's car. That was the only way to explain what had just happened.

She was too scared to go home, since her address was a matter of public record. If someone thought she had the catalyst, they could easily find her there. But Perry often worked late, so she turned north and raced toward Palo Alto.

Reflecting on her next move, she came to the conclusion that it was time to quit holding back. She had to tell Perry about hiding the catalyst.

When she reached Wyckoff's office building, she was relieved to find his wife's BMW still in the underground parking lot. With her eyes glued to her rear view mirror, she made sure no other cars had ventured down the ramp into the parking garage. She hurried to the elevator, pushed the button for the second floor and was soon standing in Perry's doorway.

Her mentor had his sleeves rolled up, and his bifocals were resting on his nose while he studied a file. Startled at her appearance, he sat upright and peeled off his glasses. "Addy."

"Don't get up for me." Addy came in and sat across from

her aging friend. "I need your help," she said before she lost her courage.

"That's what I'm here for. I've been working on your defense."

"That catalyst," she blurted. "I might know where it is."

Perry cocked his head. "And why is that?"

"When Quinn and I were in the Patent Office interview, the agents burst in, and I didn't want them to take it."

"Because?"

"I didn't think they had a right to it, not since the federal government was trying to steal it."

"Or so you thought."

"I know," Addy said slapping down the papers she'd obtained from the Freedom of Information Act. "They call it project Protect America."

Perry reached out to inspect the documents. Addy explained how Janice had submitted a request on her behalf, and now they were certain the DOE was intentionally filtering out Quinn's applications.

"This is good—something to help us win public opinion. Now, tell me what you know about the catalyst."

She explained how she hid it in the examiner's gym bag, her run in-with the counterfeit security detail and her dash to the woods.

"You need to be more careful," he said. "Do you think the vial is still in his gym bag?"

"Could be, but I have no idea where that is."

"In his office?"

"It's a possibility. But I can't exactly hang out and wait for him anymore. Now that I got caught in Johnston's car, somebody is going to suspect Johnston has the catalyst. I don't know how I can get inside the Patent Office. But if I don't, somebody else will. I can't wait."

Perry scratched his head. "I do have an idea," he finally said. He spun in his chair and banged on his keyboard. A spreadsheet appeared on the screen. "Bingo, the firm has four other cases with Daniel Johnston. I can call him tomorrow to see if he'll let me visit him to discuss one of the applications."

Addy's eyes lightened. "Brilliant. You can see if he's got the gym bag. And if he does, you're going to need to find a way to look inside. Just look for a vial with a silvery grey powder, almost like graphite."

Perry frowned. "And how am I going to do that?"

"You're creative. Find a way."

Perry's scowl quickly changed to a smile. "I'll see what I can do."

"One more thing," Addy said. "I'm worried about what we're going to do when we get the catalyst."

Evidently lost in thought about how he was going to steal a container full of chemicals from the Patent Office, Perry wandered over to the one wall of his office, blankly staring at the display of sports memorabilia, including a signed jersey from Joe Montana.

He folded one arm and stroked his chin with his free hand. "Tell me what you're thinking. What's bothering you?"

"Our whole premise. The reason we need the catalyst is to show the world the world-changing solution that's being concealed from them—so that the world will go crazy when they realize that they could all be driving cars that run on water and demand I be set free. Remember?"

"Of course," he said, narrowing his gaze on the red and gold jersey.

"To do that, we're going to need to publicize it in a big way," she said. "The way I see it, I've got one shot to plead my case to the world. If that doesn't work, I'm going to look really guilty.

"Think about it. I stand accused of hacking into the Patent Office database and stealing government secrets for some phenomenal energy technology. When I get caught red-handed, I find a way to get my grubby hands on a sample, then try to prove my innocence by shouting out to the world I've got an invention that could be really cool, but I can't actually show them how cool it is." She paused for breath.

"What I mean is this—unless people can see this is a really, really big deal, they're not going to come to my defense. That's what I'm worried about."

"You need something like a Cuban missile crisis or a tsunami."

Addy frowned.

"Seriously," Perry said moving on to stare at a picture of the seventeenth green on Pebble Beach. "I've been worried about the same thing. We need something that not only dramatically demonstrates the technology to the world, but also reveals in a simplified way how you are the scapegoat—a pretty little patent attorney who got caught between powerful forces who are so caught up with their own greedy interests that nobody gets one of these cars."

Addy bristled. *He did it again.* "Pretty little patent attorney?"

"If that's what it takes to get the message out."

Addy shook her head, realizing this wasn't the time to put Perry in his place. "At least you see my point. Any ideas?"

"I thought about using the internet, but unless you already have traffic coming to a well-known website, just posting a plea isn't going to reach many people. Getting it to go viral is the key."

"Agreed. We'll have the same problem if we simply throw out a press release or pitch the story to the local media. The national news might be good, but I doubt they would want to touch it. Even if they did, I doubt a single run on the nightly news would have the impact we're going to need."

"Plus, you need to control the content. If you leave it to the media, they'll feel obligated to at least pretend to present both sides, and your message is going to get garbled, if not lost."

Addy leaned back and stared blankly at the wall where Perry was still admiring his collection. He'd reached the corner of his office, where a stand held an encased football signed by Steve Young.

"What we need is a Super Bowl commercial," she finally said in desperation. It seemed that every conversation in Silicon Valley eventually turned to the subject of the weekend's upcoming events.

"Are you serious?"

"No. I mean—well, I might be. Millions watch the Super Bowl every year, all over the world. You can't get better exposure than that."

"Got a few million dollars?" Perry said.

Addy frowned. "No, but you know what would be really cool? What if I got Hindy back, and I had a fuel cell like the one Quinn showed to the examiner. We could pop out Hindy's fuel cell and replace it with Quinn's. I could drive Hindy right onto the fifty-yard line. Now that would be dramatic."

Perry let his arms drop to his side. "But we don't have a slush fund with millions sitting in it, we don't have Hindy, we don't have a catalyst—and we don't have Quinn's fuel cell. For that matter, we don't even know if FOX has a slot available. Super Bowl Sunday is this weekend. That's only two days away. I'm sure these things are planned out months, if not years, in advance. Logistically, it's impossible."

"I'm not so sure," Addy persisted. "I read an article about how the network sometimes holds some Super Bowl ad slots in case of last-minute interest. And, Super Bowl commercials are so expensive that some years not all of them sell out, forcing the network to dump the empty slots just before the game. You have to admit, it would be pretty cool—a live commercial with me driving Hindy."

"It's not going to happen. Let's get practical."

"But if I could get the catalyst by tomorrow. Theoretically, we still have enough time."

Perry shook his head. Seeing this, Addy frowned. Perry breathed heavily and rubbed the back of his neck. "Tell you what, let's start with getting the catalyst. And if it will make you feel better, I'll put some feelers out about a commercial."

"Deal," Addy said. "Why don't you call Examiner Johnston right now?"

Perry stole a glance at his desk clock. "He's not going to be there. It's Friday night, and you already know he's been out running."

"Then leave a message."

Perry reluctantly took up his phone and dialed the number, switching to speakerphone mode. Addy watched the phone intently and waited for Johnston to answer. The call went straight to voice mail. Perry left a message about the case, asking if he could have a meeting to discuss the fuel cell technology in the application, and requested that the examiner call his cell phone.

Perry hung up and shrugged. "I tried."

Addy reached over and putted his arm. "Thanks. Let me know when he calls back. I'm going to shower and get some dinner. And I think I'm going to give your car back tomorrow."

"You were followed to San Antonio," Perry surmised.

Addy nodded. "I'm pretty sure your hybrid is bugged. I'm going to rent a car if that's okay with you."

"I'm worried about you. Sometimes I wonder if we're doing the right thing."

"Don't give up on me now," Addy said. "Once I'm in, I'm all in. I'm going to find that catalyst and give Quinn the butt-kicking he deserves."

Her car had barely left the Wyckoff parking garage when Perry's cell phone rang. Examiner Johnston was returning his call.

# 28

WITH HIS SECURE government job and plenty of seniority, Jesse Long rarely worked weekends. Now, as a new father, he loathed the thought of giving up a Saturday morning, especially after getting up twice to help his wife with the baby feedings. But Molly Peele insisted on an emergency meeting. The Justice Department had made a break in the case.

Long met her at a local diner in San Jose, avoiding any restaurant near Levi's® Stadium.

Peele was wearing baggy sweat pants and a matching hoodie. Long thought she looked like a different person compared to the one he was used to seeing in a business suit.

"Before we start, give me any updates," Peele said staring at the assortment of egg dishes on the menu.

"Addy's been spending a lot of time with her former partner," Long said casually.

"Going back to the firm?"

"I dunno, but yesterday I caught her tailing Examiner Johnston. She's not as innocent as she likes to pretend."

Peele lowered her menu and peered over her reading classes. "That's right, following him just like she was an FBI agent.

Appears that Johnston is an avid runner. She followed him to Rancho San Antonio and sneaked into his car when he went out for a late evening dash. But what's more interesting is that there were at least two other vehicles following her, and one of them had a fake insignia on the door."

"You could have pulled them over."

"I could have, but then I'd blow my cover."

Peele took a sip of her orange juice and nodded. "I wonder why they're all following this examiner. Really strange. Perhaps he knows about the catalyst."

"Makes sense. It was all spelled out in Quinn's patent application. It would fetch quite a price on the open market."

"Could have been WTG," Peele suggested.

"At this point, it could have been anyone."

"Not anyone," Peele said. "I've gone another lead for you. We found some information on our tattooed terrorist."

"Really?"

"His real name is Shaun Ritter, but he goes by Azhar Nejem."

"How'd you find him?"

"Wasn't too hard once we figured out his faux paus. You don't get a tattoo like that and keep it secret. Anyway, he grew up in Oakland. He's one of these self-proclaimed terrorists. He went to Syria for military training, and that's probably where he got himself branded."

"If he's received that kind of training, he's got to be extremely dangerous. Those folks like to behead people. Who's supporting him?"

"That's where it gets interesting. You'd assume some radical Muslim group who doesn't like any technology that could reduce the demand for oil, but that may not be the case."

"You've piqued my interest."

"We discovered that he's been hanging out with Jerry Wilcox. We have you to thank for that one." She reached down and unsnapped her purse, then placed a photograph on the table. "We enhanced the photos taken at the crime scene with Hindy. It's a little bit blurry, but you can make out his face next to the red Camry."

Long scooped up the glossy image and squinted. A broad grin crept across his face when he made the identification.

"So Wilcox is hanging out with the same guy who attempted to torch Addy's car and then cracked her rib."

"The odds are too great for it to be a coincidence. Even more so, because Quinn Moon was also there and pulled Addy away from the wreckage."

Long tapped the corner of the photo on the table. "The common thread appears to be the technology WTG is developing. Wilcox is convinced that Quinn stole it."

"Which is why we got involved—and why we arrested Addy for lifting the DOE's technology from the patent office. But the tie to Shaun Ritter is unclear."

"That's what you're going to find out. Sorry to ruin your weekend, but I managed to secure a warrant to search Ritter's apartment. He's still living in Oakland. It's got to be executed today."

Driving to the East Bay was the last thing he wanted to do on his day off. "Part of the job," Long said, handing her back the photo.

"Remember that we're under pressure to keep all this from exploding onto some front page until the technology can be sorted out and scientifically proven. Please don't shoot the place up. Addy's arrest and the missing catalyst haven't made my job any easier."

"Understood," Long said. "If you don't mind, I'm going to skip breakfast and get to work. With any luck, I'll be home in time to make dinner."

"Sorry about the baby's earache. Welcome to a parent's life. I've already done my stint, twice."

# 29

TO PERRY'S SURPRISE, Examiner Johnston was very eager to grant his request for an interview, even on a Saturday morning. In nearly thirty years of practicing patent law, he could remember only two other times when an examiner was willing to give up a weekend to discuss a case. Johnston said he could meet after his morning grocery run. Like nearly everyone else, his Sunday was going to be spent with a few other examiners watching the game.

Perry went to the office early, reviewing the case, and wracking his brain for an excuse to get Johnston out of his office so he could search his gym bag. The easiest way was to ask the examiner to print something from his computer, forcing Johnston to walk down the hall to the print center.

It didn't take long to drive from Palo Alto to San Jose, but he couldn't afford to be late. After passing through security, Perry was greeted by the red-haired examiner, who was sporting a two-day beard of bright orange whiskers.

"Too bad the 49ers aren't playing. Got my costume on my face," he said, rubbing his cheeks. "We're going to meet in my office if that's okay. I assume we don't need a conference room."

"Perfect," Perry said with a sigh of relief. "No demonstrations today."

Johnston directed Perry down a hallway. As they passed down the corridor, Perry noticed most of the offices were empty and the lights were out. It was nothing like his own firm on a Saturday morning.

"You heard about the last one?" Johnston asked.

Perry paused.

"My last interview. Addy used to work for you."

Perry grinned. "She did work for me, and I think every patent attorney in America knows by now. Fortunately, I think this interview will have a little less drama."

They reached his office, and Johnston motioned for Perry to be seated. While Perry unlatched his briefcase, he surveyed the area. The room was small, nearly the size of a cubicle. It had a window on the far wall, and a small desk with a computer screen on it that separated the guest chair from Johnston's workspace. To his right, a lone bookshelf took up half the side wall. It was filled with volumes of patent treatises and technology journals on fuel cells. The opposite wall was bare except for several hooks from which hung a colorful assortment of medals.

"Marathoner?" Perry asked, nodding at the awards.

"Yeah, even a few ultras. Do you run?"

"Used to, but the knees gave out. Just swim a few days a week to keep in shape."

"I can't swim, never could. That's why I run."

Perry looked outside at the low-hanging clouds. "You look Irish. Probably run in any weather."

"No, I'm not that tough. Usually hit the treadmill if it's nasty outside."

"Ultra Fitness?"

Johnston's eyebrows raised. "Yeah, how'd you know?"

"One of our clerks is a gym rat. He says Ultra has the nicest treadmills in the Valley."

"That's true. Will probably be going there today."

"He said he loves the executive locker room. He even has his own locker."

"Yeah, that part is nice."

Perry wondered whether Johnston kept his gym bag there.

So far, he hadn't been able to locate anything red other than Johnston's curly mop of hair.

"Well, enough about that. Should we talk about the case?" Perry asked.

"I already looked at it. My rejection isn't very good. I'm going to allow the case."

That almost never happened. Most examiners dug in their heels and rarely overturned themselves, and then only after a long, drawn-out battle. And it meant the interview was over. Perry needed time in this office alone. It didn't look like that was going to happen. He quickly rescanned the small room. No red bag.

"I'm sure my client will be thrilled," Perry stammered. "Are you sure there aren't any other issues we need to go over?"

"No," Johnston said. "I'm allowing the case."

"I guess that's it, then," Perry said. He stood to leave, hoping his height would give him another vantage point and maybe reveal the bag's location.

The examiner raised his hand and motioned him to sit. "Before you go, can I raise a personal matter?"

Perry cocked his head. "Sure."

"I need to ask you a few questions . . . about Addy."

*So that was why Johnston was so eager to meet,* Perry thought.

"Go ahead."

"I'm still wondering why was she arrested."

"It's been in all the papers."

"I understand what's been reported about her stealing national secrets, but I don't think that is the real reason."

Perry hesitated. "What makes you think that?"

"Can we talk off the record?"

"Certainly."

Johnston looked around the room like someone else was listening.

"I'm scared. Last night when I went running, something happened. When I got back to my car, somebody had gone through my things. Then somebody followed me home to my apartment."

"White SUV?"

"No, black. Why?"

"Just a hunch. Tell me more."

Johnston breathed deeply. As he began to speak, his voice quivered. "Three masked men came up behind me, forced open the door, and threw me down on the floor. They tore up everything. They said I had the catalyst, and that they wanted it. When I told them I didn't know what they were talking about, one guy punched me in the stomach. They said they wanted the catalyst Addy and her client brought to the interview."

Perry noticed a goose egg just above Johnston's right brow. "Do you have it?"

"No! The last time I saw it, Quinn was pouring it out of some container. I swear he set it down on the table. When the feds busted in, there was chaos. I have no idea where it went. I assumed the feds took it."

"But you don't have it."

"No, and when these guys couldn't find it, they banged my head into my kitchen floor. They said I have a week to find it."

"And if you don't?"

"They said they'll be back, and it won't be pretty. They mentioned torture, like cutting off my fingers. And they said if I called the cops, I'd be a dead man. What if the federal agents did take it? There's no way I can get it back."

Perry scratched his head. It was clear the federal agents who'd arrested Addy didn't have the catalyst. But it was unlikely they had roughed up Johnston, making Perry wonder who it was who threatened Johnston, and what they knew. Clearly he couldn't discuss any of this with the patent examiner, though.

"But you know how to make it," Perry said, taking a different tack. "Couldn't you just tell them?"

"I read the application," Johnston said, "and I generally understand what Quinn was doing, but that doesn't mean I could just go out and make a car run on water."

"It's something to give them," Perry said.

"They want the catalyst. I was hoping Addy knows where it went. Can you ask her?"

"I can, but I already know she doesn't have it."

Johnston squeezed his temples.

"Then I need some legal advice. I want to go to the police."

"I'm sure they told you it wouldn't be a good idea."

"Yeah, they said I'd lose another body part, one I can't live without. But I've got to do something. They're going to come back. Can't you ask Addy who these people are?"

Perry swallowed. He knew what terrorist organizations were capable of doing to people they didn't like. He was worried for Johnston, but even more for Addy. And now he'd injected himself in her defense, he realized he also wasn't immune.

"Let me do some digging and get back to you," Perry finally said.

"What do I do in the meantime? The clock is ticking."

"If I were you, I'd go blow off some steam on the treadmill, then get a good night's sleep. I'll get back to you tomorrow."

When Perry pulled out of the parking lot and into the street, he peered in his rearview mirror. He was sure he saw a black SUV peel around the corner after him.

# 30

ADDY HAD RENTED a black Dodge Challenger. Big engine and fast off the mark. Right now, it didn't matter that she was driving a gas guzzler. The car could move. She'd argued with the rental car clerk for more than thirty minutes after she insisted on paying cash. The clerk finally relented after Addy put up a two hundred dollar deposit.

The moment that was settled, she found a payphone in front of a convenience store to call Perry, who related how Johnston had scheduled the meeting as a plea for help, and that he was certain that Johnston's gym bag was not in his office. Perry said Addy's best chance to find it would be to follow Johnston to the gym. She could expect Johnston to arrive about half past noon, giving her a chance to test out the Challenger's engine as she rushed to a Target store to purchase some inexpensive workout clothing.

Ultra Fitness was ultra-crowded on a drizzly Saturday, with partygoers trying to squeeze in their last-minute workout before a day of cheap bar food and desserts that always seemed to accompany Super Bowl parties. Addy had to park five aisles away from the entrance.

The cool temperature dictated her choice of clothes—an old pair of black yoga pants and a matching top. In the cold mist, she rubbed warmth into her bare arms while she darted over the asphalt. She was greeted by a teenager wearing a black T-shirt with ULTRA printed across her chest.

"Any chance I can have a day pass?" Addy asked.

"I can set up an appointment with a membership manager."

Addy bit her lower lip. "I'm kind of in a hurry. You know, got to get my place cleaned up for the big game tomorrow."

"You and me both," the girl said.

"Can I get a pass for today, then come back and talk about a membership next week?"

"We're not supposed to do that."

Addy flipped two twenties on the counter. "Will that help?"

The teenager looked behind her, scooped up the bills, and nodded Addy inside. "I can't get you a locker, but you can use the cardio equipment."

"That's all I need," Addy said squeezing through the turnstile.

The main workout area looked as big as a soccer field, with row upon row of cardio equipment, each with its own television monitor. The other half was filled with every imaginable type of weight training machine.

Addy studied the layout. The treadmills were toward the front. Quickly, she darted over to a stair climber, realizing it would give her a bird's-eye view of the facility. She set the equipment to the slowest possible rate and began scanning the sweating bodies in front of her while she methodically stepped in rhythm. Off to her right was the free-weight section, occupied mostly with well-built men working on their biceps or shoulders. She noticed a group of three staring at her while they bantered back and forth. They'd obviously observed she was a newcomer. One, dressed in baggy sweats and a muscle shirt smiled and waved. Since she'd already made eye contact, she couldn't just ignore him. She waved back sheepishly, then looked down and pretended to change the speed settings.

Addy knew Johnston would have to be on a treadmill. She scanned the runners in front of her, searching for a familiar sight—curly red hair and bulky white legs in short, brightly-colored running shorts. She saw him, about four rows up, his glowing legs churning up the miles. Now all she needed was his gym bag. Sometimes runners put their gear off to the side of the treadmill, but Addy didn't see a bag near Johnston, just a white towel hanging from the front console. If he'd brought his bag, it was likely stored away in the men's locker room.

She hopped down and strode over to the back of the room, then hung a right down the hall toward the locker rooms. After passing the indoor lap pool, she came to a doorway with a sign showing a female stick figure. About twenty yards down she saw a similar sign with a male figure. She ventured inside the women's changing room, figuring the men's would have a similar layout. There was a long aisle with nooks of lockers off to the right side. The showers and vanity areas were off to the left.

Addy opened one of the lockers, studying the lock—a keypad and a handle that permitted the user to select her own combination. There was no way she could break in. Her only chance would be to follow Johnston into the men's locker room, wait for him to open his locker, then pounce on him, extract the vial, and hope to get out without being caught.

Another attendant wearing a black uniform rolled a large bin full of used towels down the aisle. She thought about hiding in one, but then quickly dismissed the idea. She'd need someone to wheel her inside the men's changing facility.

She hurried back outside to make sure Johnston was still on the treadmill. She found him standing off to the side, wiping his face with his towel. He pivoted and began walking toward her. Addy quickly bent over and pretended to tie her shoe, making sure to avoid any eye contact. But she could still see his bright florescent shoes as he headed toward the men's locker room.

The moment he left the main workout area she followed him, making sure to stay far enough back that he couldn't recognize her if he suddenly turned around. She ventured down the long hall until Johnston hung a right and disappeared. Now was her chance.

Addy paused at the door. She couldn't see any way other than to bolt inside and grab the vial, hoping nobody would try to stop her. Perhaps a room full of half-naked men would be too shocked to see a woman in a yoga outfit darting past them to do anything about it.

"Can I help you?" came a voice behind her.

Addy spun around. The three body builders who'd had their eyes on her were arrayed behind her. She grabbed her chest.

"You scared me."

"You passed the women's locker room," one of them said.

"But if you want to come in a sit in the steam room with us, you're more than welcome," said another.

Addy's eyes were fixed on the guy's enormous chest. It gave her an idea. "Well, that might be nice."

"Then come on in."

"No, that's okay, but you can do me a huge favor. Did you notice that creepy-looking guy, red curly hair and shorts that are way too short?"

All three burst out laughing. "Yeah, we know the guy. Always wears those Richard Simmons shorts."

"Yeah, that's him," Addy said. "I'm embarrassed to say this, but we dated for a bit. It was a huge mistake. We're lab partners in my geology class, or at least we were until we broke up. Look, he took it really hard, and stole one of my lab samples, hoping that I'd have to come back to get it from him. He's a real jerk. Anyway, he's hiding it in his gym bag, a red one, like his hair." She started talking faster. "It's in a vial, a small bottle. I think he stashed it right in the bottom. Any chance one of you could get it for me? My project is due Monday morning. I'll buy you all a drink."

The body builder in the muscle tee pushed his other two compatriots aside. "Come to our Super Bowl party?"

Addy shrugged. "Maybe. Depends on what you're drinking."

"Whatever you're bringing."

"Bottle of tequila I brought back from Mexico last month?"

"Perfect," he said. "It would be my pleasure. Be right back."

"This could be fun," said another.

Addy stood motionless next to the door, trying to calm her breathing enough to hear what was happening inside. All she could hear was the blood pumping in her ears. She turned and looked down the hall, but it was empty. If an attendant came, she was prepared to head him off.

Finally she heard a squeal, then, "please don't hurt me."

A moment later, the three well-built men emerged. The one

in the muscle tee was holding the vial in the palm of his hand as carefully as if it were a butterfly.

"Here it is."

"Did he put up a fight?"

"No, he was more than willing to give it up."

Addy snatched it from his hand, realizing she had to get out of there. She turned, then noticed the disappointed look in the man's face. She spun back around and threw her arms around his broad shoulders, jumping off the ground to reach his face. Hanging from his large frame she pecked him on the cheek. "I owe you all a drink."

She slid back down to the floor. All three had a giant grin.

"Gotta go and finish my project."

"You know where to find us," he said.

Vial in hand, Addy tore down the hallway, only slowing at the counter so she wouldn't look suspicious.

She broke out into the cool air and nearly sprinted toward her rental car. Guessing she'd reached the fourth aisle, she turned and began searching for the dark-colored Dodge. Two cars in front of her, a black figure shot out, halting her progress. He was wearing a black ski cap, and from his thick beard he looked Middle Eastern.

A wave of nausea disoriented her. She'd been mugged in Vietnam, beaten while riding her bike, and shot at while driving Hindy. And now it was happening again. She was the bait to get the catalyst. Now she had it, this thug figured it would be easy pickings.

"Give me what you've got in your hand and nobody will get hurt," the man said. She'd heard his voice enough times to know their paths had crossed before. A tight-fitting, long sleeve black shirt covered his arms, preventing any identification of his tattoo, but she didn't need to see it. She knew.

"No," she said and pursed her lips. "This is mine."

Addy got ready to run, but the man pulled a gun. The barrel was long, like it had a silencer attached. Addy knew he was more than willing to kill for what she was holding in her hand.

She held up both arms like she was being arrested. "No, don't shoot. It's not worth my life."

"Then hand it over."

Addy paused, hoping an idea would come. "Okay, you win."

The man reached out his free hand. "Easy, take one step forward and place it here. One false move and you are dead. I already broke your ribs, next time it will be your skull."

So this *was* her attacker. Her blood start to boil. There was no way she was going to let him do this to her again. She clasped her hands, pretending to beg while she switched the vial to her off hand.

Addy slowly moved closer, then began lowering her loosely clasped fist toward his hand. When her hand was only a few inches from his, she tightened her fist.

From her MMA training, she knew how to lay him out. Instinct took over. In an instant, her fist flashed through the air and landed on the man's chin, stunning him.

He reeled back a step. Addy knew she had to move fast. The moment he recovered, he would certainly aim and pull the trigger. She remembered how she'd been taught to land a hard blow, by lowering her shoulder and pivoting her hip. Using all of her weight, she loaded her punch and let it fly, aiming at the middle of his face.

When her clenched fist crashed into the man's nose, she heard it crunch, and knew she'd broken his nose. But it wasn't enough. He shook his head and began raising his pistol.

Addy short-hopped closer, reeled back her shoulder and punched again with all her might. This punch caught him in the right eye at the same moment she felt a pop in her hand, just above her pinky finger, followed by searing pain.

This time, the man crumpled to his knees and grabbed the side of his face with his free hand. She did the best roundhouse kick she could muster, and caught the side of the man's face with her foot, knocking him flat. She kicked him again in the chin, knocking his teeth together. Then again and again, until he dropped the revolver.

After kicking it under the Suburban next to her, she turned to run, but then stopped. The memory of being punched in the stomach wouldn't leave. She spun around and kicked him hard in the abdomen, feeling her foot sink into his fleshy midsection. "Now you know how it feels," she snarled.

Running on adrenaline, she bolted for her car. A moment

later, she was streaking out of the parking lot. In her rearview mirror she could see her three new friends watching her car. But they weren't alone. Standing behind them was Johnston, on his cell phone. *He'd called the police,* she thought. *And he probably got the number on my license plate.*

Addy took the Sunnyvale exit, debating whether she dared go to her condo. She turned onto El Camino and tried to gather her thoughts while she waited at an endless series of stoplights. She noticed that the side of her right hand was swelling. When she tried to clench her fist, a mind-numbing pain shot up through her arm. There were no visible signs of a break and she could still move her pinky finger. Still, it was a serious injury.

She needed medical attention, or at least some kind of painkiller, but if she went to the hospital, she risked being reported to the police. For now, she could wrap it and take some ibuprofen. There were probably a couple of caplets left in her purse that she could take right now. But her throbbing hand was the least of her worries. She was a fugitive.

Using the wrist of her injured hand, she slipped her newly purchased pre-paid phone from the glove box and dialed Perry's number.

Perry was at work, and she quickly filled him in on what had just transpired.

"Get off the roads," said Perry. "You need to get to a place where police cars won't be roaming."

Addy hung a quick right and shot into an empty parking spot at a busy grocery store. She'd need a place to spend the night, but this would be good for now.

"I've got the catalyst, we've got to execute," she said. "What have you got so far?"

"Lots of balls in the air, but making progress. With our limited budget, the local media is going to be our best bet. I've got our PR firm working on some options. They're pretty sure they can get an exclusive with the local CBS affiliate. This was before you took out a terrorist. It can only get better from here. If the story gets traction, it will run nationally. At the same time, our PR firm is going to roll out a social media blitz. You probably haven't noticed, but we've completely revamped your website."

She hadn't been on the internet for days. "I keep dreaming

about the Super Bowl. I guess I need to get realistic."

"That's the other news," Perry said with a hint of enthusiasm. "I called about an opening for a Super Bowl commercial. The network says they do have an open slot, several in fact. You were right. It seems like there a lot of people who want to run ads, but not at the price demanded by the network, especially for time slots that could be a bust."

"Like at the end of the game if it's a blowout."

"Exactly. This year's matchup between two mid-tier market teams isn't commanding top dollar. The network will hold out as long as they can, but tomorrow morning they will start slashing prices. I discovered that they still have a pretty decent spot— right after the halftime performance, but they want cash up front. The other problem is that we don't have time to make a commercial. We'd be doing a live commercial on the field. For that, they want top dollar."

"How much?"

"How about $4.5 million for thirty seconds."

Addy's stomach lurched. She'd held out hope that if she could only get the catalyst everything else would work out. Now she knew it was wishful thinking. "Ouch. I'll quit dreaming."

"Don't do that," Perry shot back. "I put down a deposit."

"What? Are you crazy? How much?"

"A hundred grand. It's refundable if we cancel by noon tomorrow—assuming they can resell the spot."

"But Perry, you can't do that."

"It's all for a good cause. And it's the least I can do."

She wasn't going to let Perry waste a hundred thousand dollars. There was no possible way to raise more than four million dollars in a day. Or did Perry know something she didn't? "No," she insisted, "we can find another way to get the word out."

"You probably haven't been listening to the news, but you're somewhat of a national enigma. People are wondering if there really is some sort of government conspiracy to suppress important technologies, and you're their champion. When I pitched the idea of a live commercial about a water car to the Super Bowl producers, it had a ring of truth to it. They even called me back a couple of hours later, with news they'd floated the idea to Zissy."

"Wait! They really told Zissy?"

"When I put down the cash, they had to. You'd be coming onto the field right after she finished her halftime show, so they had to get her approval."

"And what did she say?"

"She was all for it. She wants to personally make the introduction."

Perry's voice had a level of excitement she hadn't heard in years. She, too, knew of the belief of many Americans that valuable technologies never came to light because of some kind of conspiracy, be it a bully corporation, an illegal trust, or even the government.

Now she had the opportunity to be their champion, and prove it really was true.

"Thanks Perry," she said. I wish you were here so I could hug you!" With Zissy on board, she knew she'd get traction. But it was too early to celebrate. "This is all great, but they still want the money."

"They do, but I'm working on it."

"I really don't know what to say. I mean how are we going to come up with that kind of money? If I'm lucky, I might have fifty thousand of equity in my condo."

"I'm not going to lie. It's going to be a challenge. I know a few wealthy venture fund capitalists who understand the importance of technology. They've made their money and want to give back. I've got some feelers out. What else can I help you with?"

She wanted to ask him for a doctor. Her hand was throbbing, but there were clearly no time-outs for injuries in this race. "We're going to need to build a fuel cell to demo the invention. I know you've got a couple of clients who manufacture models that I could modify, but I'd need access to their shop and probably a couple of their engineers to help me make the modifications."

"Are you sure you know enough to build one that will work with the catalyst?"

"You don't need to worry about that," Addy said.

"You stole a copy of the patent application?"

"Let's just say I printed off an extra copy, just in case something happened. With the help of a few sharp engineers, I know I could put one together."

"Already have a call into them." Perry sounded a bit smug, and she couldn't blame him.

"Okay, then the biggest problem is that showing a fuel cell on national television is going to be pretty boring. It's not like you can see it churning out gobs of electricity. What I really need is my Mustang. It seems like everyone knows about Hindy. She's got selling power."

"Agreed," Perry said. "Then why don't we just go pick her up?"

"How?"

"Finally got the FBI to release it."

"When?" Addy shrieked. "Why didn't you *tell* me?"

"I just found out last night. They kept stalling, so we threatened an interlocutory appeal to get it in front of an appellate judge. That was all it took."

Addy looked at her dashboard clock. It was already three-thirty. Government offices never worked past five, and especially not on a weekend.

"We need Hindy today. If we show up tomorrow morning, there's going to be a boatload of federal agents waiting to pounce on us. Besides that, I could work on the fuel cell all night. With any luck, it could be ready by tomorrow." She stopped herself, realizing she was still short of more than four million in cash.

"You're correct on that point. I'd be surprised if the local cops haven't already called the feds. We've got to hurry."

"Are they open on a Saturday?"

"Yes, until five and not a minute later."

"Tell me where to meet you and I'll be there," Addy said.

When Perry told her it would take him about a half an hour to get to San Jose, Addy had already started her engine.

# 31

LONG KEPT HIS search team to a skeletal crew. He needed to execute the warrant with minimal fanfare. He often wondered the real reason for keeping the investigation of Quinn and WTG a secret. It stood to reason that big oil didn't want Quinn's catalyst coming to market, but delving into that issue was a sure way to end his career. Right now he wanted to know what a suspected terrorist was doing on the loose.

Long wound his Buick past a half of dozen nearly identical buildings in a sprawling apartment complex until he reached building 11. He parked the car and surveyed the scene, immediately noticing a motorcycle parked in one of the stalls. He wondered whether it was the same one used to run Addy off the road.

The judge had signed a no-knock warrant, meaning that the FBI could pound down the door. Long chose to have an agent trained as a locksmith pick the lock. The unit was 1101D, a two-bedroom apartment on the ground floor of a three-story building.

Long stood back as the lead agent checked the door handle and applied pressure. The door immediately popped open and the agents drew their weapons. The door wasn't locked.

All three agents barged into the living room. Long followed.

The air was stale, and the room smelled like a garbage dump. It didn't look much different. Pizza boxes were stacked three feet high, and crushed beer cans were strewn everywhere. What caught Long's attention were the four inflatable air mattresses squeezed between a television set and a couch, half covered with bed linens.

Keeping to protocol, the agents swept the kitchen and the two bedrooms. Blankets were piled high on each of the beds, and more air mattresses were strewn on the floor.

"Okay, tear the place apart," Long said. "See what we can find."

In less than thirty minutes, the agents had dismantled every piece of furniture, emptied all the drawers and boxed up all the garbage. Besides extra underwear and dirty socks, they'd found nothing to link Shaun Ritter to any crime.

Long decided to slice apart the air mattresses, hoping to find any evidence. He stripped off one of the blankets and tossed it in the corner. As he did, a brass shell pinged against the wall. Long picked it up in his gloved hand and carefully placed it into an evidence bag. Far from a flare, it looked more like it was from a Glock or a SIG.

Long panned the strewn assortment of air mattresses. He wondered if Ritter was housing an army.

Long's phone rang and he looked at the number that popped on the screen.

"What's up Molly?" Long said.

"Where you at?" she asked.

"About to wrap up the search at Ritter's. Place looks like a barracks. Even found an empty handgun shell. Addy should be worried."

"How soon can you get to San Jose?"

"At least an hour. Seeing it's a Saturday, traffic should be light, but you never know. What do you have in mind?"

"Got a homicide. Examiner Johnston. Nasty crime scene. You're going to want to see this."

Long jumped to action. "Any suspects?"

"He had a run in with Addy Verges two hours before the time of death. It appears that Johnston placed a 911 call from Ultra

Fitness reporting that Addy engaged a few large body builders to rough him up and tear apart his gym bag. Evidently that was where Addy hid the catalyst during the raid we did during the interview. Anyway, Addy tried to get away but she was attacked in the parking lot."

"Ritter?"

"Not sure, the subject was masked and hobbled away after Addy managed to escape."

"What about Quinn?"

"We know he's somewhere here in the States."

"Okay, you can fill me in later. I'll let these guys wrap up the search. Keep everything in place until I get there."

# 32

THE RAIN HAD stopped, but it was still chilly. Addy was still in her yoga outfit, wishing she had packed a jacket. The impound lot was on the outskirts of the city in an industrial part of town. After passing several blocks of weathered warehouses, Addy reached her destination at exactly four-fifteen.

The small cinderblock building was perched in front of a large, gravel-covered parking lot filled with every make and model of car and truck, and a chain-link fence topped with spiraling barbed wire surrounded the impounded vehicles.

Addy pulled into one of the empty spaces and checked the dashboard clock. Nearly five minutes passed, and there was still no sign of Perry. She reflected on why Agent Long had asked her about Jerry Wilcox. She'd done some quick internet research, but discovered nothing.

She decided to wait a few more minutes before calling Perry. Three more minutes passed.

At this rate, the shop would close before they got Hindy. She snatched up her phone and was instantly reminded of her injured hand. She winced and tried to hold her hand still, hoping the shooting pain would subside. Just as she began dialing,

Perry whipped in beside her, flung open the door and squeezed out of his car. Addy followed suit.

"Sorry I'm late," he said, buttoning his sports coat. "Been busy trying to tie up a lot of loose ends."

"Were you followed?" Addy said, glancing back down the street.

"I don't think so."

"Come on. Let's get this over with and get out of here."

At the front of the cinderblock building, Perry tugged on a heavy metal door and waved Addy inside, where they were greeted by a heavyset woman wearing a police uniform. Addy and Perry introduced themselves and handed her a set of papers he'd snatched out of the printer on his way out. "We're here to collect the hydrogen car."

"I know which one it is," she said slipping on a pair of bifocals that were hanging from her neck. She flipped through the documents without looking up, "Got any ID?"

Addy plunged her non-injured, "off" hand into her purse and fished out her wallet, then fumbled out her driver's license that Perry had obtained from the FBI after her arrest at the patent office. The officer spun it around, then swiped the magnetic stripe through some kind of reader. She studied a computer screen, running her finger along as she read.

"That's funny," she said continuing to run her finger back and forth.

"Problem?" Perry finally asked.

"I'm surprised they're releasing your car. There's a lot going on here. I'm going to need to call the station."

"That's unacceptable," Addy said slamming her good fist on the counter. "We have papers from the court. That overrides anything you have there on your screen."

The woman snatched up the papers and read them again, shaking her head. "Well I guess so, but I'm still going to call in."

Perry reached out his hand. "Call all you want, but give me the keys first."

"And open the gate, please," Addy chimed in.

The woman shook her head. "It's in stall 86. You can pull the car up, but I can't open any gate until I get the okay from HQ."

Perry shoved his way through a side door that led to the

lot where the impounded vehicles were parked. Addy scooted in front of him, studying the stall markers. In a few moments, she spotted Hindy, tucked between a monster truck and a VW bug. Addy snatched the keys from Perry and hopped into the front seat. "There should still be hydrogen in the tank," she said flipping a few switches. "Enough to get it back to Palo Alto." Her right hand flinched each time she lifted it up, and the ever-present pain ratcheted up exponentially. If Perry noticed, he didn't stop her.

Then she noticed that none of the indicators lighted. "That's funny," she said. "There's no power. I put in a new battery less than six months ago."

She reached down with her left hand and pulled a lever. The hood popped up and Perry propped it open.

"You're not going to like this," he said shaking his head.

Addy shot out of her seat and shimmed around to the front end. The moment she looked beneath the hood, her jaw dropped.

There was *nothing* under the hood. Hindy, the already-castrated Shelby, was completely gutted.

"They can't do this," she shouted at Perry.

"No wonder they were willing to let us have her."

Addy stared into her mentor's eyes. He was staring blankly at the empty shell, arms folded. What about Perry's $100,000 deposit? What about the commercial? What about her freedom?

"How much work do you think it's going to take to rebuild her?" Perry said without feeling.

Addy shook her head. "A ton of work. I'd have to start from scratch. Even if your client could help me build a fuel cell, Hindy's still missing all her internal organs. There's no electric motors, no steering column, no nothing. It would take me weeks, if not months, assuming I could even get the parts I need. No way could it be finished by tomorrow afternoon. There's not going to be a Super Bowl commercial in our future, that's for sure."

Addy folded her arms, rubbing her good hand over her bare skin to keep warm. She looked skyward, trying to think of a way out of their predicament. How could she demonstrate the catalyst without Hindy? There had to be a way they could still do the commercial, even if she didn't have a car. But how?

She looked over at Perry and noticed his jaw muscles flex.

She could tell his mind was racing, also trying to find a solution.

Then it hit her and she froze for a moment before reaching over and grabbing Perry's arm.

"Perry, let's get out of here. This is a trap."

She watched his eyes widen. He understood. Before he could say anything, she began using both hands to tug him toward the office. She winced and stifled a whimper when her pinky finger flexed backward. "We've got to give up on Hindy. We've got to get out of here. The police officer saw something on the screen that prompted her to call HQ. If we can't get through that office, we're certainly not going to be able to hop this fence."

Together, they zipped toward the cinderblock building, weaving through the mass of vehicles. When they reached the side door, Addy calmed herself, deliberately opened the side door, and quietly made her way down the hall. As they neared the front desk, she could hear the officer's conversation. Something about a death.

She cocked her head so she could hear the discussion. It was about Examiner Johnston. Based on the officer's responses, Addy surmised they'd found his body, with his red curls shaved off and his eyes missing. And apparently he'd been murdered only an hour after he called the police to report Addy's theft of the vial.

She reached out her hand to halt Perry's progress, then motioned with two of her fingers for them to dart past the lobby and out the front door. They took off in unison, Addy's eyes fixed on the front door.

"Hey wait!" the officer said reaching for her holster. "You're wanted for questioning. You can't leave."

But Addy's shoulder was already slammed against the door, shoving it open. They each sprinted to their cars. "I'll find you," Addy yelled to Perry, nearly out of breath. "Let's get the fuel cell built first. I'll figure out the rest," she said as she threw herself into her car. Addy slammed her door and started her ignition. With tires squealing, they both peeled out of the parking lot and into the darkness.

* * *

Keeping to side streets, Addy plotted her next move. Without Hindy, she needed another plan—another car, and a new fuel cell—otherwise the catalyst was of little use. And time was running out. The gridiron classic was less then twenty-four hours away.

Her eyes were burning. Oncoming headlights were no more than blurred dots on the horizon. She'd been wearing the same pair of contacts for two days, and they had to come out, but her glasses were still in her condo—a place she didn't dare go.

But her fuzzy eyesight was the least of her worries. Her hand was throbbing, and a visit to any hospital was out of the question. If she went to her condo, she could probably jury-rig a splint and possibly replenish her supply of painkillers at the same time she retrieved her glasses.

She meandered along vacant streets, through Los Gatos, then Saratoga, and dropped down into Sunnyvale. She was just inside the city boundaries when she noticed a lighted yellow icon in the shape of a gas pump on her dashboard. Addy looked down at the dial. The red pointer was well below the empty line. She'd been feeling so crazed and cornered she had completely forgotten to check her gas level.

Her wallet was in her purse, on the passenger seat next to her. Keeping her eyes on the road, she reached over and rummaged through the contents, wincing every time she moved her fingers. When the pain was too severe, she relented and pulled over to inspect her cash. A ten, two ones, and some change.

Using her credit cards was out of the question. If she swiped her credit card or tried to withdraw cash from her bank account, there was no doubt they'd be all over her in a New York minute.

She needed to get off the grid. She was also going to need money for a hotel room. She could get cash from Perry, but she worried that if she got him any more involved, he could end up like Johnston. For now, she could pump in a few gallons with the money she found in her purse.

Addy pulled into a Shell station and pumped in a few gallons. She paid the attendant, then hung her head while she ambled back to her car, sorting through solutions. Where could she hide the catalyst? Not in the car; that would also be an obvious place to search. She decided it would have to be someplace easy to retrieve when she needed it, but in a location where nobody would think to look.

Addy noticed a row of hedges at the back of the gas station, separating it from an apartment complex. Cobblestones were stacked around the roots as ground cover. It was as good a place as any. Addy took out a Ziploc bag from her purse, emptied out the last of her pain-killers, swallowed them, and slipped the vial inside, and zipped it shut.

She looked around. It was a quiet evening. An elderly man was filling up his Cadillac, but otherwise nobody was around. She scurried over to the hedge, bent over, and hefted up a few of the cobblestones before gently nestling the vial in the dirt. Then she carefully replaced the rocks, taking special note of their arrangement. She studied her work. It was impossible to tell anything was hidden there.

By now, nearly blinded by her increasingly blurred vision, it was time for her to get back into her condo. Besides needing her glasses, she was thoroughly exhausted and needed some cash for a hotel room.

Her emergency stash of bills hidden in the freezer wasn't a lot, a few hundred dollars, but it could get her a place to stay for the night.

Addy turned the key in her ignition, and stabbing pain in her hand dizzied her for a full minute. She blinked her eyes in a feeble attempt to clear her vision. As much as she hated the thought of what might happen, she must get into her condo, at least for a few minutes, to grab what she needed. To be incognito, she could park a few blocks away and sneak into her complex the back way.

As she crept closer to her residence, she peered into her mirror, trying to detect any would-be followers. She debated about how close she dared to park. She settled on five blocks, probably far enough away that anyone staking out her place wouldn't notice her arrival.

The Crescent Condominium complex was laid out in the shape of a horseshoe, with the front office and pool at the main entrance. Addy's condo was on the right leg, facing the parking lot. She decided not to try the main entrance, but to flank the complex on the left side, sneaking behind a four-foot brick wall.

When she was parallel to her unit, she put her hands on top of the wall, but her pain kept her from scaling the rampart. She jogged back and took a running start, leaping and pressing her foot a few feet up on the wall. The rubber on her sole gave her just enough traction that she was able to fling her left arm over the top of the wall, the cement cap digging into her armpit. She surreptitiously zipped between parked cars, crept between adjacent buildings, and made it to the inner courtyard. She looked around.

When the weather was good, teenagers tended to hang out and talk there. Luckily it was a cold night, and the courtyard was empty. Acting as casual as she could, trying not to draw attention, she ambled across the grass, inserted her key into her back door, and slipped inside.

In the mud room, the only light came from the courtyard lamps. Addy didn't dare turn on any more lights. Feeling her way through the pantry, she entered her kitchen, mentally making a list of what she needed.

Eyeglasses were a must, so she scampered up the stairs and into her bedroom, where she took out her contact lenses, put in some eye drops, and slipped on her glasses. Then she opened several drawers and found an old ACE bandage. Downstairs she should be able to find something to use as a splint, maybe some spatula handles.

Back in the kitchen, she opened the freezer door and fished through a stack of veggie burger patties until she found the Ziploc bag containing cash. She tried to stash it in her pocket, but realized she was still wearing yoga pants. A pair of sweats would be nice, but that meant another trip upstairs, and she was worried that she was running out of time.

She needed something warmer to sleep in, though, so she shut the freezer door and went to the hall closet near the staircase where she kept her jackets.

She heard the floor creak somewhere near the front door. She looked out through the breakfast nook into the darkness, but couldn't see anything. If the front door had opened, she would have noticed either the sound or the light coming through.

She slowly stepped back, reached out with her good hand, and opened the knife drawer. She slipped out her only butcher knife, holding it in a death grip, her heart pounding in her ears.

Heart thumping, almost panting with fear, she heard another noise coming from the front room. This time it was a rustling sound, almost like someone had rubbed up against her window blinds.

Knife in one hand, money in the other, she steadied her workout shoes on the tile and rocketed toward the pantry. The moment she did, there was a clatter behind her, like her blinds were being ripped from the wall.

She bumped into a shelf full of soup cans, which clattered across the floor. When she reached the back door, she tried to turn the knob without dropping the cash, but her fingers only slipped, and a sharp pain shot up her arm. She dropped the bag of money and, grimacing, turned the handle and pulled the door inward. As she did, a massive figure tackled her to the floor, pinning her arm beneath her. With all the weight on top of her, she couldn't free her arm or use the knife. She could feel the cool concrete on her cheek.

She tried to buck her hips to throw off her assailant. But he was too heavy.

She opened her mouth and took a breath to scream, hoping someone would hear and come running. The moment she shrieked, a forearm smashed into her open mouth. She tried to bite down, but the man was wearing a thick leather jacket.

The fragrance. It was cologne she'd smelled before, but where?

Her hands were now free, and she swooped them across the floor, searching until she clutched the handle of the butcher's knife. Then she heaved upward with all her might, ready to stab the man in his side. He sensed the movement and deflected the blow, crushing her arm to the floor with his knee. He reached out and dislodged the knife from her hand.

The next thing she felt was the cool steel blade pressed against her throat.

"Don't do anything stupid," the man said, easing his forearm from her mouth.

Now she remembered where she'd smelled the cologne. "Quinn."

"Just hand over the catalyst, and I'll be gone. I'm not here to hurt you."

"Funny, then why have you got a knife to my throat? Quinn, why are you doing this to me?"

"It's for your own good. If you give me the catalyst, they'll leave you alone."

*What did he know that she didn't? And why was he threatening her?*

"That's not true. I know too much. I know the formula. All because of you."

"You don't know who you're dealing with. You should be thanking me. Now tell me where you have the catalyst."

"You son of a bitch."

"We don't have much time for name calling, Addy. Just give me the catalyst, go back to your old job, and nobody will get hurt. Don't make this any harder than it needs to be."

"I don't have my old job, or did you forget that little detail?"

"Wyckoff will take you back."

"I'm not going back, and I'm not giving you the catalyst."

She felt the blade sink into her skin. He wouldn't.

"You can't beat the forces against you. Just give me the catalyst and this will all go away."

"Do you really think that's possible? Johnston is dead, and for all I know, you killed him. Am I going to be next?"

Addy began crying. "I trusted you," she said between hiccupping sobs. "I can't do this anymore. You win. The catalyst is in my car. Just get off me and you can have it."

"You're telling me the truth?"

"What, do you want me to take a lie detector test? Where else would I have it?"

"It's not in here?" he said.

"It was so nice of you to invite yourself in. Now get your bony ass off me and maybe we can walk to my car like civilized people."

She could feel the pressure on her throat relax and Quinn sat up straight, still pinning her to the ground with his legs. "Well, nobody has ever accused me of that before," he said, lifting his left leg to unsaddle himself.

The moment he was in an unstable position, Addy bolted upright, slamming her forehead into his face and shoving him back. She heard the crack when the cartilage in his nose crushed. Dazed, he dropped the knife and grabbed his face.

Addy threw him onto his back with such force that his head crashed on the floor. She grabbed his thick black hair and pounded the back of his head repeatedly onto the hard tile, cringing every time his head hit the floor. When he stopped struggling, she fumbled for the knife, and brought it to his throat, making sure to nick him.

"If you ever treat me that way again, I'll kill you. Understand?"

The fight drained out of her when Quinn started making strangled, gurgling noises. Oh, no! Was he dying? But then he coughed, and a thick plug of blood and mucus shot out from his mouth, some spraying onto her yoga shirt.

"Are you crazy?" he croaked, his pupils visibly dilated, even in the dim light. Then he coughed again.

"Now you know how it feels."

"I'm sorry," he muttered.

Suddenly shaky, she tried to suppress her tears. "You were the one person I thought I could trust. I even thought I liked you."

"I'm sorry," he said again. "I'm desperate. If I don't get the catalyst and ensure my investors will be paid, they are going to make mincemeat of me."

"Just like with Johnston? Are they going to gouge your eyes out, too?"

"The examiner?" he said through bloodstained teeth. "I'm so sorry, I didn't know. But it couldn't have been my people. Somebody else got to him, and they'll get to us if we don't leave right now."

"Not until you tell me the truth about what you did to me."

"*Reader's Digest* version, then," he said. "We've got to disappear."

"I'm all ears."

He squeezed his eyes shut, then opened them slowly.

"All right, I admit we used you to help spy on the US government. We suspected the US was taking our ideas and suppressing our applications, and we had been baiting them to find out for sure. I was ready to introduce our technology, but the Board wouldn't let me do it until we had patents in place to protect us. We all wanted to know if the US was taking our ideas and putting them into applications with earlier filing dates. We used you to confirm this. It was wrong of us, but at least now we know. I'm truly sorry."

Addy gritted her teeth. As much as she was furious with Quinn, the thought of a branch of the US government tampering with patent applications in order to steal foreign technology totally set her off. It was unconscionable.

"Wait, did you say that the patent applications I filed ended up in another inventor's application, with a filing date that predated ours?"

Quinn nodded.

"I can't believe it," she muttered. The Patent Office had stolen their ideas, put them in another application, and given that application a forged earlier date stamp. Tampering with filing dates was nothing new with the Patent Office, but the last instance Addy knew of was over a century ago in a debate over whether Alexander Graham Bell's patent application for the telephone was moved to the front of the line.

"I'm sorry," Quinn repeated. "I wish is wasn't true."

Addy tried to process her predicament. WTG was stealing from the Department of Energy, and vice-versa. But if the DOE got the earlier filing date, they would be able to control the patents. And with her arrest, they could cover it all up rather neatly.

"At this point, an apology is not going to help," she said.

"I understand, but at least I wanted to come clean."

"You haven't yet. How did you come up with the idea for a water-powered car? You never told me."

"We've got better things to talk about right now."

"Oh, really? What can you tell me about Jerry Wilcox?"

Addy watched as Quinn's jaw dropped.

"Not now. We really, really need to get out of here."

"We're not going anywhere until I get an explanation. I want to know how you invented the catalyst."

Quinn swallowed hard. "Okay, I did work for a company called HydroGen just after I wrapped up my dissertation. It was founded by Jerry Wilcox, but he didn't invent the catalyst. Wilcox is crazy. He thinks I stole his idea, which I didn't. Yes, I did get the idea of a water car from him, but his catalyst wouldn't work, and he wouldn't listen to me when I tried to explain why. I got fed up with him and left. I'm the one who found a better catalyst, but it was after I was already in Korea. I think his real problem is that the Energy Department owns the rights to all of his inventions, and he's mad that I have my own company. That's why he sicced the Justice Department on me. This bit about stealing trade secrets is nonsense. The reason they haven't arrested me is because they can't find any evidence that I stole anything."

Quinn always had an answer for everything, but Addy wasn't convinced, remembering the charges against her for stealing US technology. "There's also this bit about hacking into the PTO database using my ID to lift a few ideas from the Department of Energy while you were at it."

"Is that what you think? No, *they* were stealing *my* ideas."

"So you never stole any intellectual property from Jerry Wilcox?"

"Absolutely not."

"Then please explain this bit about Sung-soo illegally accessing his patent applications, which, need I remind you, is what got me into this mess."

Quinn rolled his eyes. "We don't have time for this."

Addy raised her fist. "You do that again, and I'll pop you in the mouth. Out with it."

"Okay. WTG knew Wilcox was crazy and would stoop to anything in order to stop me, including stealing my ideas. So they had Sung-soo watching every application with Wilcox's name on it. None of his patents ever issued, probably because he didn't invent anything. He couldn't get his idea to work. I did, and he's jealous."

Addy shook her head. "But that's not who took down my blimp. I know the guy. He's Middle Eastern."

"I've had more threats on my life than you care to know about. There are all kinds of people who don't want this to come to market."

"But what you were doing was wrong. Admit it."

Quinn coughed again. "It was."

"And Sung-soo was probably stealing technology, not just

monitoring Wilcox's applications."

"I'm afraid so, but it was without my knowledge," Quinn insisted. "In fact, I knew nothing about it until later. It was Sung-soo, under orders from Jeyhu. I'm so sorry. I never intended for any of this to happen. If I'd known WTG's true intentions, I would never have involved you. Now I can never face my father. My whole family is going to be dishonored if this ever gets out. I need to find the catalyst."

"Your family! You really want to talk about your father at a time like this?" Addy practically shrieked. "What about *my* father? At least yours is alive."

Addy watched him struggle to swallow. Looking into his bleeding face, she felt a small niggling of compassion. There was a reason she'd had feelings for him.

"Did you really like me?" he muttered.

It sounded so pathetic, yet somehow sincere.

"I shouldn't have said that," Addy said. "We've got more important things to discuss."

"I feel terrible about Johnston. My dream to change the world has turned out to be a horrific nightmare that keeps getting worse."

"That pretty much describes how I feel, too."

"You've got to believe me. When I met you in Vietnam, I really believed you could help me, not just as a patent attorney, but in seeing my vision and helping to bring it to the world. I loved your enthusiasm, your drive. I really was going to use Hindy to make the announcement."

Addy nibbled on her lower lip. She wanted to trust him, but every time she had, it had brought an unbelievable avalanche of disaster, guilt, and heartache.

"This is my baby," he continued. "Everything I've ever dreamed of accomplishing. I've put every emotion, every cent, every bit of energy into changing the world. And now I'm going to lose everything."

"Unless you get the catalyst," Addy reminded him.

"I'm not going to lie. I've got to get it back for there to be any chance to put this right."

"I thought you could make some more; that's what you told me."

"Yes and no. I know how to make more, but the refining process is very expensive and WTG is out of money. I need the catalyst so WTG can show proof of concept to the investors, just like we did with Johnston. That's why they didn't want me to take it. WTG needs a massive influx of cash to finish the production facility. Without the catalyst, it's really hard to drum up that kind of investment. And if I fail, my investors are going to come after me. It will be ugly."

"Well, you can forget about the catalyst, because I'm not giving it back. And I think you'd rather deal with me right now than with them."

"Then I'm a dead man," he groaned. "You've made your point," he said looking down at the knife. "Would you let me up? My head is killing me."

"You know what I think?" Addy said ignoring his request. "I think getting the catalyst is the least of your problems. You've got to secure the patents, or your investors are going to get skittish. Why would they be willing to cough up that much money when it's just going to be copied?"

Addy searched Quinn's eyes. They were flashing back and forth like he was trying to process her logic.

"You should have thought about all this before Sung-soo did his little invasion of the Patent Office database. I don't think the PTO is going to be too keen to give you anything since you've stolen the government's technology, and it looks like you've knocked off one of their examiners. Have you mentioned that to your investors?"

Quinn remained silent.

"Well that's all water under the bridge now," Addy continued, trying to sound blasé. "I'm going to end up going to jail, and you will never get any patents. Seems to me like you've got a bigger problem. At least I'll be safe in prison."

Addy paused and listened, wondering if anyone was closing in on them. Except for Quinn's heavy breathing, it was quiet.

"What can I say besides I'm sorry? I thought I had everything figured out, but I didn't realize I was being used. I let my ego get to me, and now it's going to cost me everything."

"One thing is for sure, they won't be selling water cars in the US If the DOE has patents on any part of your technology, they are going to put the hammer down. This little boy from Korea is not going to beat Uncle Sam."

Addy expected another groan, but he was silent. Instead, Quinn's face brightened with a wry smile.

"But you could."

"Don't try to sweet-talk me," she said. "And I already told you, when this is all over, even if I can get out of doing any prison time, I'm not going to have a license to practice law."

"I know you have a plan," Quinn persisted. "You wouldn't go to prison without a fight. Whatever you've conjured up, I want to help. It will be my way of making things right."

"What makes you so sure I have a plan?"

"I know you too well. You do have a plan. Admit it."

"I do, but I'm not going to tell you what it is."

She stopped. She was almost certain she heard the hum of a car's engine. It could be one of her neighbors, but it could be someone else.

"Did you hear that?" Quinn said. "We need to get going. Now will you accept my offer?" He reached up slowly and took the blade of the knife between two fingers and pushed it away. "I want to see everyone driving a water car. I don't care about the money. The only thing I want is credit for my invention. I've studied history. I don't want to be another Eli Whitney, who spent his life trying to enforce his patents. Life is too short. I'll leave WTG, and we can work together."

Addy set the knife down on the floor, but stayed atop his chest. She didn't trust him, but he had something she still needed. She could use him just as he'd used her.

"There's more," Quinn continued. "I think there's something between us—"

Addy could feel the heat in her cheeks. Even if she did have feelings for Quinn, she wasn't about to admit it. And she was still too furious to even like him. But when she gazed into his bloodstained face, something struck her heart.

"Maybe I do too," she muttered, "but there's still this trust issue."

"You can trust me. Is there anything I can do to prove it?"

Addy sensed her chance. "How much are you worth—in cash?"

"If that's what we're going to talk about, can't you at least let me sit up?"

Addy got up and off him and waited while he hoisted himself up. Quinn rubbed the back of his head.

"Are you okay?"

"I've got a goose egg the size of a softball."

"I'm sorry about that, but I think you understand. Now, about my question."

"How much do you need?"

"A little over four million."

Quinn's head whipped around, his eyes wide. "What, are you kidding?"

"You said the money didn't matter."

"It doesn't. But what makes you suppose I have that much money?"

"Your stock in WTG. How much is it worth?"

"I couldn't sell it all at once. They wouldn't let me."

"Don't you have a marketing budget or some kind of other slush fund?"

"Getting that much money isn't easy. It will set off all kinds of alarms."

"Tell you what, you come up with the money, and I'll trust you. Perry needs it by tomorrow morning."

Quinn grunted. "You know we're not exactly on speaking terms."

"I know how Perry is, but he still needs the money—by ten tomorrow. You know how to contact him."

Quinn smoothed his hair and tapped his fingers gingerly around his contusion. "You really need that much?"

"You were right. I do have a plan. I'm going to tell our story to the world, tell them that if it weren't for a few corrupt governments and some unsavory companies, we'd all be driving cars fueled by water. Then I'm going to recruit humanity to fight for me. It's the only way I can prove my innocence."

"I agree with you, but I don't see how you're going to do it."

"Just trust me with your money and you'll find out."

"And if I don't?"

"You're the one who said something about becoming mincemeat."

The sound of a car door closing interrupted their conversation. Addy flinched, quivered, then whispered while she felt around for her money, "Let's go."

They slipped out the back door, scrambled over the brick fence, and made their way to Addy's rental car. Addy fumbled with her keys to unlock the door.

"Where's your car?" she said pressing the key fob.

"I took a cab," Quinn said, staring at her swollen hand. "I don't dare get in the same car twice."

"Get in. We can talk while I drive."

"I think you should let me drive. What happened?"

"Never mind," Addy said opening her door. "We should be going."

Quinn winced the moment his head encountered the headrest. Addy started the car and pulled into the street. "Where can I take you? Half Moon Bay?"

"No, they'd find me there. I gave up that place. How about the Stanford Park Hotel?"

"Got it," she said as she turned north toward Palo Alto.

"Where are you staying?" he asked.

"I can find a place," Addy said, since she still had serious trust issues.

"Have it your way. So tell me about your plan."

"I need another Hindy," she said without further explanation. "Perry and I went to get her out of impound, but she was gutted."

He laughed, then grabbed his head and moaned.

"What's so funny?" Addy said. "I'm being serious."

"I know you are. You forget that using Hindy to announce the discovery was my idea. You stole my idea."

"I had that idea long before you ever did," she said, then pursed her lips. "Anyway, Hindy is out of the question. She's still in the impound lot, doesn't even have a transmission or drive train, and I can't get her out, even if you gave me a fuel cell."

"So, let me see if I understand. You don't have a fuel cell that will work with the catalyst, and you don't have a car for the fuel cell."

"Something like that," she admitted.

"And you need me, not only to get your hands on a few million dollars, but also to provide a car with one of my fuel cells in it."

"We can call it an even trade. You get me the money and the car, and I'll forgive you for ruining my life."

Quinn took a deep breath. "Let me get this straight. You want me to give up my company, get you a few million in cash, add to that a new car, and risk my life, all without telling me what you are planning."

"That's right. You'll need to trust me."

"No. You won't be safe. You need to let me help you."

"I can take care of myself," Addy insisted.

Quinn raised his eyebrows, then adjusted the rearview mirror and studied the headlights behind them.

"Why won't you tell me? I want to be a part of what you're doing. After all, it is my invention."

Addy sighed. He was right. He needed to be as passionate about her plan as she was. Just asking for money and a car wasn't going to do that.

"I suppose that's fair," she began. "Perry and I have planned a massive public relations campaign. We are going to make this story go viral. We've set up everything we need for it to take off, social media, major news networks, freelance reporters, everything. But we need a spark, something to get the world's attention. If we could do that, everyone would want to chatter about it. Everyone would demand a car that runs on water."

"And what kind of spark are you thinking about, the one that is going to cost me the pittance of four million dollars?"

Addy paused to let the tension build. Quinn shifted in his seat, turning to face her.

"A Super Bowl ad," she finally said.

This time Quinn didn't laugh. "So you're going to make a commercial, driving a new Hindy that runs on water."

"Actually, it will be a personal appearance on the playing field, but you get the point. It would be seen by more than a billion people. And when they realize there might be a world without gas stations, and all the pollution, poisons, and politics associated with the petroleum industry, they are going to want to know more.

"We've got websites, pages on social networks, everything set up to feed them the truth. Your patent application is going to be published for all the world to see. And I'll have a blog with my story, how I was set up, how our government tried to stop this. I'll plead my case to the world."

Quinn's face remained stoic while he absorbed her idea.

"Well?" Addy said when he didn't respond.

He opened his mouth to speak, then closed it.

"What?"

"It's a good plan," he finally said, "but—"

"But what?"

"The Super Bowl is tomorrow."

"And that's why I need the money pronto, and a new Hindy. It's going to be a live commercial."

Quinn clapped his hands. "I like it," he said. "In fact, it's brilliant! It's worth betraying WTG, and it might just work."

Addy felt herself grinning, the first time since she'd walked up the steps of the Patent Office with Quinn before their fateful interview with Examiner Johnston.

"I'll see if I can get the money, but it's not going to be easy. I'm not sure what restrictions our banks have on our accounts, especially for a transfer in less than twenty-four hours. And it is the weekend. All I can say is that I'll give it my best shot."

"And the fuel cell?"

"That one is a little easier. We always knew we'd need a show car when the catalyst was finished. We built one each for Asia, Europe, and the US To avoid problems with US customs, we had it built here. It's got the same fuel cell that we showed to Examiner Johnston, only on a much larger scale. I would have brought it to the interview, but you said a small model would be good enough, so I didn't bother with the car."

"Where is it?"

"Good question. We keep moving it around so it won't be discovered. But it's somewhere close. It hasn't left the Bay Area."

Addy smiled. Looked like her plan just might work.

"The problem is that you have the only available catalyst," Quinn said.

"Understood, but I won't give it to you. That's my only leverage."

"If I'm going to get the money, it would really help if could show them I have the catalyst."

Addy knew she wasn't going to give in, no matter what Quinn

offered. "I'm confident you can find a way without it."

Quinn raised his eyes, fiddled with the rearview mirror and said, "I need you to hang a quick left, then floor it. Now!"

Addy obeyed, squealing the tires and sending agonizing bolts of pain from her injured hand while she cranked on the wheel. Quinn gave her a few more directions, telling her to keep her foot glued to the pedal. Every time she turned, he looked into the mirror and shook his head. "We've got to shake them."

"How? I can't drive any faster without killing us. We're going to run into the Stanford campus."

"That's the idea," Quinn said. "I'm taking you close to the dorms, where there will be plenty of students. Then we're going to ditch the car and make a run for it. Find any way you can to blend in. We'll find each other later."

Addy wheeled the car to the right, feeling the tires separate from the pavement and settle back down as they shot onto Campus Drive, Addy doing her best not to hit one of the students pedaling away on his cruiser.

Quinn pointed to her left, and she screeched into a small parking lot next to a two-story sandstone building. "This is as good a place as any," he said. "Leave your phone in the car."

"It's okay. I bought one of those cheap reloadable ones."

"No," Quinn shot back. "As long as you are connected to the phone network, the feds will find you. They know where you've been, and they can map that up with calls made from the same area. By now they know your phone number."

"Then how can I call you?"

Quinn dove his hand into his jeans pocket and fished out a smart phone. "Here, use this one. It can't connect to the phone network. The only way it works is using local Wi-Fi hotspots. Coffee shops are usually good places. You can't be tracked this way. And, it's got some apps that might come in handy."

Addy pulled in behind a row of scooters and shoved the car into park. She swiveled around to see who had been following her. Quinn yanked on his door handle. "Don't look, just disappear."

"Wait, how will I find you? And the money? And the car?"

Quinn reached out for her hand and slipped a wadded-up gum wrapper into her uninjured hand, closing it into a fist. "Don't lose this. It has my phone number along with a simple code to decrypt my geolocation, just in case our messages get intercepted."

"You're going to send me GPS coordinates?"

"Yeah, like in Vietnam. I've got to find the car, then text you the location, but I can't risk letting anyone else find it. I'll set up the warehouse as a cache, then encrypt the location coordinates. We've got a lot of people chasing us right now."

"But you said our phones were safe."

"They should be, but with technology these days, you never know. If the text is discovered, I suspect some of them are smart enough to crack the code and figure out it's a geographical coordinate, but the encryption will slow them down enough to let you make your Super Bowl appearance."

Addy raised her eyebrows.

"You have a better plan?"

She leaned over and kissed his cheek. "It's brilliant."

# 33

ADDY DIDN'T BOTHER closing the car door before she fled, sprinting over a cobblestone path between two dorm units, clutching Quinn's phone in her good hand.

She darted across a large field and disappeared behind a row of hedges, gasping for breath while she peeked over to see if she could glimpse her pursuers.

The spacious lawn, dimly lit by a few streetlights, was empty. She'd managed a clean escape. She wondered whether Quinn had been as fortunate.

The sun had long disappeared, and the damp, cool evening made her shiver. She remembered Quinn wanted to stay at the Stanford Park Hotel, which was just on the other side of campus. Her problem was that she only had the money from her condo that she'd stuffed down the front of her top. She fished it out and unfolded the wad. A hundred and six twenties. Not nearly enough. Rooms in Palo Alto never went for less than two-fifty.

With her adrenaline rush seeping away absent immediate danger, Addy's body began to crave sleep. She couldn't remember how long she'd been running on empty. She told herself to keep pushing on. There was still too much to do. With the Super Bowl only a few hours away, sleep was hardly an option.

If Quinn could get the money and the car, she still had a chance at making her debut. She had to let Perry know Quinn was back in the picture, and that Perry should start making plans to finalize the live commercial and to kick off their PR campaign.

Her biggest problem was how to communicate. The phone Quinn had given her could send a text, but only if she found a Wi-Fi hotspot. She considered walking to Wyckoff's offices, hoping to find Perry working late. But she worried that she'd been detected and might possibly endanger Perry's life.

Her best bet, she decided, was to find an all-night coffee shop, settle her nerves, and send Perry a message. There would be plenty near the hospital; strategically positioned to serve those with loved ones waiting to hear the latest updates. With her injured hand, she would fit right in.

Keeping in the shadows, she made her way across the enormous campus until she found Tully's Coffee Shop, across the street from the emergency entrance. She found a padded booth, ordered a cup of coffee and asked for the Wi-Fi password.

She tapped out a text to Perry, then waited. Her coffee arrived, and she slowly sipped from the cup, feeling the beverage warm her core. Perhaps he didn't recognize her new phone number. She considered putting her name in another text, but figured that was too risky.

So she waited several minutes and typed out another message to Perry, asking him to at least confirm he received her message. Again, no response. She wondered whether he, too, had been overcome with exhaustion. She could feel her own eyelids drooping. She wanted to send Lynda a text message, asking her to make sure she watched the halftime show at the Super Bowl, but her gut told her it was a bad idea. She could only hope Lynda would be watching.

When Perry still didn't respond, Addy decided a catnap would do her good, just a few minutes while she waited for Perry's reply. She switched off her phone, leaned over on the table, rested her head on her arms, and dropped into a deep sleep. It was about four-thirty when she felt a hand shaking her. A long-haired woman wearing a pinstriped uniform hovered over her.

"Sorry," the waitress said. "I let you sleep long enough. Time to move on. They've got places over at the hospital if you want to crash there."

"Sure," Addy said, rubbing her eyes. "Just let me shoot off a text."

Addy turned on her phone. Still no reply from Perry. She quickly tapped out another message to him, saying that they urgently needed to meet. Then she switched off the phone, scooted across the crosswalk, and ventured into the emergency room entrance. It was filled with half a dozen people either milling around or fast asleep on one of the several couches. Addy found one with split vinyl and plopped herself down. She let herself doze a few more minutes, then turned her phone back on. No messages.

She again wondered whether Perry might not answer because it was from a different phone. Since time was running out, she didn't have a choice. She had to know about the arrangements for the Super Bowl. She tapped out another message saying she had a new phone, then waited. Still nothing.

Addy found a bathroom and splashed water on her face. She inspected her hand, which was now bulging and severely discolored, a sickly black and blue. She wiggled her fingers. It was painful, but at least she still had the full use of her hand. She wondered whether she should admit herself to the ER, but knew they would have to enter her name into their computer system. And she didn't have time to wait for a doctor.

Instead, she put on her game face and walked to the law offices of Wyckoff & Schechter. Until she found Perry, she couldn't do anything. She was almost certain the place was staked out, but she didn't have a choice.

She walked down University, peering into the shop windows until she came to another coffee shop. She ordered another cup of coffee and a cream cheese-covered bagel. She wasn't hungry, but knew she had to eat to keep up her energy.

An older couple who were in line behind her were speaking in hushed tones. When she overheard the words "patent examiner," she paid attention. The woman was horrified by what they had done to his body, cutting off body parts and reassembling them in grotesque positions.

Addy couldn't listen any longer. She turned and left the shop.

When she was within a block of Wyckoff, she turned off and went around the block. While visitors entered through the front door on Waverly, she remembered she could get into the parking lot from Lytton, then take the back staircase to the second floor, where Perry had his office.

She hurried into the parking lot and crouched behind a Chevy Tahoe. When she flipped on her phone, she noticed it was almost eight o'clock. Most of the parking stalls were empty, and it would be nearly eleven before they were filled. Perry had not returned her message, and there was no sign of his car. He was usually in well before the sun rose.

Addy peeked over the hood. If she'd been followed, she couldn't tell. Maybe they'd wait until after she left.

She zipped across the garage, jogged up three flights of stairs, and opened the door into the front lobby. On a Sunday morning, the receptionist's desk was obviously empty, so she made her way down the hall to Perry's corner office.

"Is that you Addy?" came a voice from behind just as she was ready to slip inside.

Janice—who never clocked in until nearly ten in the morning and never worked a weekend. *What's she doing here on the day of the Super Bowl?*

Addy slowly turned. "Oh, hello, Janice. I had an appointment with Perry. Nobody was at the front desk, so I let myself in."

Janice looked her up and down. "Dressed like that?"

"He said he had something for me. It shouldn't take long. I just came from the gym."

"Well he's not in yet. He left early yesterday. Said he had some business to attend to," she said with a smirk. Janice tapped her lips. "I think he's got tickets to the game."

"He might have left me a folder. Do you mind if I look?"

"I guess that would be okay, but you know Perry. He never leaves anything on his desk."

Addy didn't wait for an escort, but hurried into Perry's office and flipped on the lights. His desk was barren. If he'd intended to leave her a note, it wasn't there.

"Told you," Janice said, swaying her hips as she entered.

"I really need to get him a message."

"Did you try to call his cell?"

Addy nodded. It was strange Perry hadn't replied. He was always glued to his phone, constantly checking his messages. When they fled from the impound lot, she told him she'd find him so they could work out a new plan. He had to be expecting a text or some kind of communication.

She also worried about the money he'd put down for the commercial. If Quinn didn't come through, the funds would be forfeited. That could happen at any moment. Maybe Quinn couldn't get the money, and that's why Perry wasn't answering. Perhaps he was upset that Addy didn't have a workable vehicle and that he'd lost his money. That would explain why he wouldn't answer her.

"Well I can't just let you hang around here all day. You know, firm policy. Perhaps you want to leave him a message."

"Did he say anything to you about a commercial he was working on?"

"A commercial? Like on television? Why would he do something like that?"

"Long story. Anyway, he was supposed to leave me some information."

Janice's eyes went round. "Now that you mention it, I was in his office when he was talking to someone about wiring money. That must have been for your commercial. Tell you what, I'll ask him next time I see him, then have him email you. Will that work?"

"Text is better," Addy said. She pulled out the desk drawer and scribbled a number on a yellow note pad. "Here, use this number."

Janice took the paper, noticing the bulge on Addy's hand. "Are you okay Addy?"

"Fine, just a lot going on right now."

Janice looked deep into Addy's eyes. "Look, I know we didn't part on the best of terms. I was upset about what happened at WTG and said some things I shouldn't have. Can we put that behind us? I know you're in a lot of trouble, and I want to help."

Addy smoothed back her hair. If she hadn't recruited Janice, they'd probably have still been friends. "Sure. I'll give you a call. And please let me know as soon as you hear from Perry."

Addy's spirits soared. It sounded like Quinn really was going to send the money. Their plan was going to work. But where was Perry and why wasn't he answering her texts? Addy knew she couldn't simply wait for him to come to the office. Something wasn't adding up. While she could ask Janice to use her phone, she didn't want Janice eavesdropping on their conversation. She decided that she needed to find a hot spot and send Perry another message. She could also try Quinn, to see if he'd wired the money and located his hidden car.

The Four Seasons hotel was about a ten-minute walk, and she could freshen up there and check her messages. If Perry hadn't responded, she'd catch a taxi to his home.

She'd barely gone a block when she spun around to make sure she wasn't being followed, and saw a figure dart behind a large oak tree two blocks down. She continued walking backwards, keeping her eyes on the dark brown trunk.

Then she noticed a car door open, a black sedan less than fifty yards away. A dark-skinned man wearing a 49ers cap and sunglasses stepped out and began striding down the sidewalk toward her. He was carrying a newspaper under his arm and was constantly adjusting it with his free hand, which probably meant it concealed a gun. When she peered further down the street to the oak tree, she saw another man slip on the concrete, hurrying to catch up to the man with the baseball cap.

They were gaining on her. She didn't hesitate, sprinting in the direction of the hotel. She veered to the right, turning toward University Avenue. There was always a stream of cars venturing along that boulevard. Maybe even a cab.

At a full sprint, Addy looked back over her shoulder. There were now two men and a woman, all in hot pursuit. Just then, directly in front of her, the door of a truck opened and a heavyset man in a black ski mask bolted out and pointed a gun right at her head.

"Stop!" he said in a deep voice.

If they wanted the catalyst, she figured they wouldn't kill her. Perhaps capture and torture her, but not shoot her on the street. University, with its line of cars, was within sight, but she had to get around this hulking man. Instead of trying to cross the street to avoid him, she continued straight at him, increasing her speed.

The man was so astonished he didn't have time to react. She barreled into him like she was a running back taking on a linebacker. She knocked him on his back, falling to her knees as she catapulted him backward. When she jumped back up to run away, she noticed that he'd left the engine running.

She darted inside and slammed the door shut. The glass in the passenger door shattered, and she felt a bullet whiz past her head. She ducked behind the dashboard, turned sideways, and ignoring the pain, ripped the gearshift down with her injured hand while steering with her left hand, and floored the pedal. She couldn't see where she was going, but knew the truck was pointed toward University.

Two more shots ripped through the cab, and then the steering wheel pulled to the right. One of her tires had sideswiped the curb. She turned the wheel, only to hear the screech of metal scraping metal as she clipped another car.

She kept her foot glued to the accelerator, gaining speed. When she reached the intersection, she looked up. A school bus was directly in front of her, and she spun the wheel to avoid a collision, sending the truck over the curb and across the front lawn of a colonial mansion. After crossing the lawn, she weaved in front of the bus and ducked into the line of cars streaming along University. At her first chance, she hung a hard left, then roared through quaint bungalows into the heart of Palo Alto.

She had no way of knowing if she'd shaken her pursuers. There was only one way to be absolutely sure, but it would cost her valuable time. She headed west, into the hills. She wound her way along Page Mill Road until she found a gravel turnout sheltered by two giant redwoods. She pulled in and cut the engine.

They would never find her here, but she also couldn't get a signal for her phone. With kickoff just hours away, she couldn't stay here.

She considered her options, debating whether to ditch her freshly stolen vehicle, but decided against it. Whoever she'd stolen it from couldn't exactly report it to the police. And she needed transportation. Still, the entire Bay Area was going to be crawling with spies hunting for it.

Her next problem was communication. She'd planned to get an internet connection at the Four Seasons. Here she had none and needed to know if Quinn was going to make good on his promise to deliver the car and the money. By now, Perry would have figured some way to communicate with her, even if he was busy working on the logistics behind her commercial.

Her eyes began to droop, the urge to sleep almost overwhelming, and she realized she was functioning on only two hours' sleep in forty-eight hours. Even the constant nagging pain in her injured right hand wasn't enough to keep her head from bobbing, then falling on her chest.

She dimly remembered she needed to access Quinn's geo site, but she couldn't do that without a signal to her phone. Her eyelids felt like concrete.

She jerked herself awake and switched on her phone. It was nearly nine o'clock, and she was out of time. She needed a signal.

Addy retraced her steps, heading back down Page Mill Road and into Palo Alto. After she'd gone several miles, she veered onto El Camino Real, found a McDonald's restaurant and parked the truck. She hustled inside and switched on her phone while standing in line. While she waited for the Wi-Fi connection to register, she ordered a burger and fries along with a large cup of coffee.

The moment her phone detected a signal, an alert popped up. She recognized the phone number. Janice had sent her a message. It was the only one. Nothing from Perry, even though she was sure he had her number. She clicked on the notification and read the text. There were a series of numbers along with wiring instructions.

"Six fifty-three," said the cashier.

Ravenous, she toted her meal to a back corner table and gobbled it down while sipping coffee in between bites.

Why was Janice sending her the wiring instructions—and with no explanation? Janice had said Addy would know what to do with them. Did Perry instruct Janice to send them to her so she could forward them to Quinn? But what wouldn't Perry just give them to Quinn himself? Where was Perry? Was this a trick, some kind of scam?

*How much?* Addy texted back, trying to figure out if Janice was trying to get the money wired into her own account.

Addy read the reply: *4.5*

There were only two people who knew the amount—Perry and Quinn. Her stomach sank. Was Quinn going to give her the money in exchange for the catalyst, only to have it wired back into his own account? Was Janice still working for WTG? She began to wish she'd never trusted Quinn. But there was a chance Perry had asked Janice to send the instructions. Perhaps he was so busy setting up her campaign that he didn't have time to type it in?

Addy shot back another text. *When will I make my appearance?*

She waited for the reply.

*Perry is working on it.*

Addy was confused. Janice had always been reliable, and Addy had no reason not to trust her. But why would Perry tell her the details of the wire transfer and nothing else? Perry could simply be overwhelmed, but that didn't ring true. Addy switched off her phone, worried that she'd had it on too long already.

# 34

ADDY KEPT AN eye on her rearview mirror as she barreled down El Camino, but all she saw was the usual steady stream of vehicles.

Time was running out. The Super Bowl was less than six hours away, and if the money wasn't wired now, there would be no Hindy on the 50-yard line.

She regretted not forwarding Janice's text to Quinn while she had an internet connection at McDonald's. But something in her gut told her not to trust Janice. It still didn't make sense that Perry wanted her to give wiring instructions to Quinn. She wanted to do some research on the account, to see if it was a legitimate bank, one that a major network would have used. But there was no way she could connect to the internet.

Addy rolled her phone in her injured hand, ignoring the pain, too worried that she still hadn't heard from Quinn with the geocache message. She slammed her good hand against the dashboard. "No!" she shouted. "Why is this happening to me? Can't I trust anyone?"

At the next intersection, she cranked on the wheel and made a U-turn, heading back to Palo Alto. Perry lived just a few miles from the office. She didn't care if an army of assassins had his place staked out. She had to find him. Even if he was overwhelmed with her publicity campaign, he would never have gone this long without an update.

Feeling an increasing sense of urgency, she pressed down harder on the accelerator, weaving through the traffic, cutting off a Lexus sedan. A horn sounded, but Addy pressed on.

When she reached Frost Avenue, she let her foot off the gas, momentarily debating whether she should try to remain incognito. But it was probably a waste of time. If Perry's place was being watched, they'd spot her even if she tried to sneak in.

So she whipped into the driveway and marched to the front porch. She didn't bother knocking and was surprised to find it wasn't locked. She half expected the furniture to be overturned and the carpet torn up. She found the sofa upright and a half filled glass next to an opened Coke can on the coffee table; a John Grisham thriller was face down next to it.

"Perry, are you home?" she called out.

Perry's Persian cat wandered in from the kitchen and rubbed against her leg. She reached down and scratched between her ears.

She thought she heard a noise from the back of the house where Perry had his bedroom.

"Perry?" she repeated as she walked down the hallway.

The familiar chatter of ESPN's Sports Center emanated from the master suite.

"Are you in there?" she said, pausing to listen. A vignette on one of the Super Bowl pieces shouted back at her.

Slowly, she pushed the door ajar, then craned her neck to peek inside.

"God, no!" she screamed and flung herself back, crashing into the sheetrock behind her. Addy buried her face in her hands. She slid down the wall, curled into a ball and began shaking.

"I'm so sorry," she began sobbing. "I never meant any of this to happen."

Perry's rigid body dangled from a cord, chin down, black tongue protruding from between his lifeless lips. Her insides churned with the vision of Perry's eyes bulging out of their sockets.

She clutched her stomach, but it was no use. The hamburger and fries she just inhaled came rocketing up. On hands and knees, she kept vomiting until she had the dry heaves.

Addy took a deep breath and reached her hand out, then jerked it back. *Suicide? Murder?* She wanted clues before calling the police. Careful not to leave more fingerprints, she nudged the door open and studied her surroundings.

The bed was still unmade, with several throw pillows scattered in front of the footboard. Perry's open laptop sat on his maple writing desk. Addy leaned over and listened. She could hear a faint humming. His computer was in sleep mode. With the corner of her phone, she tapped the space bar, and the screen came to life. The only application running was Microsoft Word, and she studied the document. It was an outline of her advertising campaign, mostly bullet points of what they'd discussed. *Whoever killed Perry saw this,* she thought.

She quickly scanned the details, hoping to discover any updates on the Super Bowl commercial. She saw the name of a woman he'd spoken to—a Claire Charnes—and that they'd agreed on terms. But there was nothing about where to send the money, or even the name of the agency.

Addy debated about whether to check Perry's email, but since the program wasn't already running, she decided against it.

A few papers were strewn on the desk. She scanned their contents, using the knuckle of her index finger to move the sheets around—notes to the web master running her website, and the names of several local reporters and their contact information. Another note had the phone number for a local pizza joint and the price for a small Hawaiian pizza. She wondered if he'd even made the call.

Addy stepped back to think. *Where would Perry have saved Claire's phone number?*

She thought about how he loved to scribble messages to himself, usually on yellow sticky notes. But his one quirk was that he never stuck them in a prominent place like they were intended. Instead, he folded them in half and stuffed them into his pockets. He'd keep them there as a reminder until he returned the call or filed a document. The problem was that half the time they ended up at the cleaners.

Her knees wobbled. Her head started to spin and she felt faint. Slowly, she turned around until she was facing Perry's waist. She kept her eyes on his belt. Another deep breath and she dipped her fingers into his front pocket but couldn't stretch her fingers low enough to reach the bottom of his pocket. She stood on her toes, but it wasn't enough.

Not daring to let go and have the rigid body spin, she hooked the leg of Perry's stool with her foot and scooted it over.

She stepped up on the stool and came face-to-face with Perry's pitiful, purple tongue. It smelled of death. That, mixed with the lingering vomit in her mouth reignited the heaving. She tightened her stomach muscles and dove her hand into his pocket. His leg was hard against the side of her hand, like a cold tree trunk. She gritted her teeth and dug down further until she reemerged with a fistful of creased-in-half yellow papers. Then she stepped down carefully and let the notes scatter across his desk.

Using her knuckle again, she stirred them until she found one with a series of numbers. She pried it apart and studied the row of digits. They were in the same format that Janice had sent her, but they were not the same numbers. There was a second row, a number with nine digits. A phone number, with a New York area code.

*Claire Charnes?*

Finally! She had what she needed.

Addy leapt from the front porch, leaving the door open, hoping someone would notice and report Perry's death. She'd wanted to cut him down and cover him with a sheet, but there was no time. And she wanted the police to see him just as he'd been after the murder.

She revved the engine and squealed out of the driveway, flying along the side streets, leaving streaks of rubber through every intersection. In her rearview mirror she noticed a white Lexus SUV hugging her tail. If they knew about the commercial, they were obviously waiting for her to lead them to the catalyst. That explained why she'd been allowed to find Perry's body.

Addy needed a phone that could connect to the cellular network so she could dial the number on Perry's hen-scratched note. Quinn's useless piece of hardware wouldn't fit the bill.

Addy headed north toward Menlo Park until she found an open-air mall with a coffee shop, café, and cupcake store. Normally, she'd be salivating for a cream cheese-covered cupcake, but after seeing Perry, she wasn't sure she could ever eat again. Her mouth was pasty, mixed with the acid from her stomach. If nothing else, she needed a bottle of water.

The narrow parking lot was full of vehicles, and Addy had to park five stores down in front of a tax preparation shop.

The bell on the door rang when she entered, and a teenage girl wearing a pink apron smiled and said, "Welcome to Belle's Cupcakes. Got a pre-order?"

The small store was packed, with six people working behind the counter. Addy noticed a handwritten sign: *Super Bowl Orders Here.*

She'd almost forgotten. Today virtually every household threw some kind of Super Bowl party, whether or not they understood the first thing about football. Addy turned to leave and find a less crowded alternative.

"Wait, don't you want to hear about the flavor of the week?"

Addy hesitated. The melee of shoppers could work to her benefit. She needed a cell phone, and there must be about a dozen within a few feet.

"Sure, I'll take one, whatever it is. And a bottle of water."

"No problem. It's lemon meringue." She reached down and snatched up a pair of tongs. "Water's over there in the corner."

Addy knew she didn't have time to strike up a conversation with half a dozen busy shoppers to see if she could use their phone.

"Do you have a phone I can borrow?" she asked the girl. "Left mine at the gym. I need to call their lost and found."

The girl frowned but slid her hand into her jeans pocket and handed over the hardware.

Addy plucked it out of her hand and dialed the number.

"Is this Claire?" Addy said the moment someone answered. Addy reached into her shirt and flipped two twenties on the counter, then kept talking. "Can we still do the commercial?" she asked.

Addy listened while Claire explained that Perry had worked out a deal for a live commercial during halftime, right after Zissy

Spaeth performed, just as Perry had told Addy. It was a major concession from the network, Claire continued, one without precedent. It was only because of the intense public interest in such a politically hot topic that they'd allowed it. That, and the fact that Zissy believed in Addy's cause and insisted on making the introduction.

"Then we're still on?" Addy asked, worried that Claire had either given away the spot or would demand an immediate payment.

Claire explained about a problem with the final payment, one that they were working to resolve. If not, they'd be forced to cancel the contract and slip in an automobile advertisement instead.

"No, don't do that," Addy said, knowing she needed to beg for more time. "I've got the money and the wiring instructions. I'll have the money in your account within the hour."

Addy felt sick inside. The number Janice had given her was not the same as the one she'd found in Perry's pocket. If Janice's number originated with Quinn, then Quinn had no intention of ever paying for the commercial.

"Why don't you hang tight for a few minutes?" Claire said. "I'm hoping to have the issue resolved shortly."

"But how?" Addy said.

"You're lucky to have such a good friend. To hold the spot, Perry put up two million of his own money, and he assigned us title to his house in Palo Alto and condo in Tahoe. We typically only do cash deals, and that's what's holding it up. Our lawyers still need to sign off on the documents, then our chief executive needs to give the final approval."

"What?" Addy said, astonished. "Let me see if I understand this. Perry gave you his retirement money and both of his houses?"

"It appears so," Claire said. "Like I said, he's quite the friend."

Addy knew all about legal protocols and requirements for attorney approvals. "Do you have any initial indications that they'll approve?"

"Wait just a minute. Someone is on the other line."

Addy's phone went silent.

Claire returned a few moments later. "I think we're all set.

Our lawyers have verified that the value of the two properties is well over the amount needed to pay for the commercial, and our CEO said we can run the commercial."

Addy swallowed hard. Before his death, Perry had given up his life savings, retirement, and virtually all of his other assets. He'd believed in her that much.

And that could only mean that Janice had given her a fake bank account.

Did that mean Quinn didn't have her car? Had he lied to her? Was Quinn just trying to find a way to get the catalyst back?

Claire said that they were moving forward and reminded her that the script had already been written. She would be allowed one lap around the field, and that she could use the giant screens to explain her invention. But, they needed the car by kickoff. Security would need to perform an inspection, just to confirm there were no safety issues, meaning it didn't have any explosives.

"What if I'm late?" Addy said, wondering how she was going to find Quinn and get his car to the stadium all before kickoff. "I mean, I don't plan to be, but what if something happens? The commercial is paid for, right?"

The line was silent and she thought she heard Claire sigh. "Yes, it's paid for, but please don't make my day any more difficult than it needs to be," Claire said. Addy ended the call and handed back the teenager her lifeline. "Keep the change," she said. "You got Wi-Fi?"

"For that kind of tip, you bet. *Topping*. That's the password. Kind of cute, isn't it?"

Addy pulled out her phone and squatted to retrieve the crumpled note from Quinn that was wedged between her sock and her shoe. She un-crumpled the wrapper and began furiously tapping the screen. When she finished, she shoved it back into her shoe.

"Wait, I thought you lost your phone," the teenager said as Addy straightened up.

Addy simply nodded at the two bills on the counter.

Addy typed a note to Quinn: *I need it NOW!*

A few minutes later, Addy's phone buzzed. She jerked out her phone and read the screen. It was a series of numbers separated by periods. A geocode from Quinn.

Now she had what she needed, the location of the car. But could she trust it? Did Quinn really have the car, or was it a trap to lure her to a remote location where he could retake the catalyst?

# 35

LONG WAS RESTING in bed, flipping through channels, looking for interesting Super Bowl stories. With the volume down so as to not disturb the sleeping infant, he could barely follow the commentator's game day analysis. He rarely slept in this late, preferring to arise early and exercise.

Today was different. His sleep had been restless, not so much because of the feedings, but because of the ghastly images of Johnston's cut-up corpse. Long couldn't ignore the obvious conclusion that Johnston had been murdered because of his knowledge of the chemical makeup of the catalyst. Now it appeared that Addy Verges was in possession of the physical sample. He didn't want to think what her corpse would look like if she were caught.

Long's phone rang and he answered quickly. It was headquarters calling in a traffic incident in Palo Alto involving a woman fitting Addy's description. Shots had been fired and a team of ragtag hit men, most of them appearing to be of Middle Eastern ethnicity, were giving chase. The one piece of evidence for Long to inspect was a shell casing from one of the weapons.

Long was on his way.

* * *

Traffic on University Avenue in Palo Alto was still being funneled onto parallel side streets. Long was standing on the yellow divider studying one of the empty shells. It was from a .357 SIG, the same kind of casing he'd found in Ritter's apartment. Still, it was too early to jump to conclusions. It was a popular weapon.

Long placed the shell back down onto the pavement and proceeded to the sidewalk where agents were interviewing several witnesses. He listened in while a gray-haired woman with a terrier tethered to her hand complained about some black truck jumping the curb and tearing up her neighbor's landscaping just to pass a bus.

Long was about to interrupt and ask for a description of the truck and its driver when his phone rang. Headquarters, again.

"What you got?" Long answered, still watching the elderly lady's free arm flailing as she spoke.

"Another potential crime scene," the dispatcher responded. "Possible homicide. Name is Perry Tomkins. Lives at 847 Parkinson Avenue."

"Wait," Long said. "Addy's former partner at Wyckoff?"

"That's him. His body is hanging from his bedroom ceiling. And, one of his neighbors is claiming to have seen a woman fitting Addy's description leaving the home and driving away in a black truck with large mud tires."

*First Johnston, now Perry. Who will be next?* Quinn shoved his phone into his pocket, dashed to his Buick and sped away.

# 36

A BEARDED MAN wearing a Ravens jersey caught Addy's attention as he wedged his way through the front door and worked his way to the end of the ordering line. For a moment, their eyes locked. Addy turned to leave the cupcake store. Suspecting the man was more than an admirer, she spun her head and glanced backward, noticing the man's gaze suddenly shift away from her and to the menu displayed on the wall. Keeping one eye fixed on the man, she made her way closer to the exit. Once again the man set his eyes on her, a dark cold stare.

Addy bolted from the cupcake store into her stolen truck, digging her fingers into her shoe to extract the wadded gum wrapper while she craned her neck to see over the dashboard. Steering with the wrist of her injured hand, she once again uncrumpled the paper. The encryption scheme was simple. Quinn had randomly assigned a number from one to ten for each single digit. Her task was simple enough, match each number of the geocode with the identical number on the gum wrapper, then find its counterpart. But she couldn't manage that while driving.

She needed another hotspot to run her geocode app on her phone and identify where Quinn had stashed Hindy's replacement. Her best bet was the Shell station where she'd hidden the catalyst. She could do a two-for-one: connect to the internet, get the location of the cache, then unearth the catalyst. The danger, of course, was that the moment she had the catalyst, all hell would break lose. Addy was convinced a tracking mechanism had been attached to her truck. She'd thought about trying to find the bug, but then realized she didn't know the least thing about electronic surveillance and it would be a waste of time to try to find it. Which meant that the truck had to go before she retrieved the catalyst.

Addy was still a good eight miles from Sunnyvale, and ditching her only mode of transportation this far away from the catalyst was problematic. Addy looked at the clock on the dashboard. It was nearly noon; only one hour left.

Her options were limited. A bicycle would be too obvious, even if she could find one and figure out how to steer with an injured hand. Walking was out of the question. That left the train, one that ran on a single north-south line from San Jose to San Francisco. She didn't have a train schedule, but she recalled that it was scaled back on weekends. Even then, what would she do when she got to the Sunnyvale station?

She looked at her speedometer. She was going fifty on a residential street. Her foot was as frantic as her mind. How was she going to dump the truck, get the catalyst and rush to the geolocation all within an hour? She had to have the new Hindy to Levi's® Field before kickoff.

Taking a gamble, she raced toward the bed of cobblestones hiding the vial, remembering there was a Starbucks across the street. At least she could get close, run the app to tell her where Hindy was being stored, and from there make a plan to get the catalyst.

She tapped on the radio dial, and scanned the available stations, hoping to get a traffic report. All the buzz was about the game. She listened to one DJ summarize the commercials that had already been leaked onto websites.

Then he changed topic to read a breaking news story, one that many of the local stations had been following. Yesterday, there had been a grisly murder of a patent examiner, one who had been examining a patent application about a car that could run on water. He mentioned that the patent attorney who had filed this patent application was a so-called "person of interest," because of an incident involving the examiner and this same patent attorney at a health club right before the examiner's death.

Now, the announcer said, the case had turned to the bizarre, when Palo Alto police had discovered the body of Addy's former partner hanging from his bedroom ceiling. One neighbor reported that they'd seen a woman fitting Addy's description and driving a black truck with large mud tires exiting the home earlier that morning. Police were reportedly putting together a reward for information on her whereabouts.

"I don't know about you," the DJ concluded, "but this is totally crazy. Who would have thought that a patent attorney would break into the Patent Office databases to steal US technology, then kill an examiner for not allowing a patent application that purportedly covers a car that can run on water, then murder her former partner? And, I might remind you that this is the same attorney who, just a few weeks ago, started a fire on El Camino when the blimp hovering over her hydrogen-power car exploded in rush-hour traffic."

Addy was furious. Her hydrogen storage tank didn't explode! The jerk neglected to tell his listeners that it went up in flames because it been shot.

Why wouldn't anyone believe that she wasn't a murderer, that she had been set up, a patsy for the schemes of competing government and corporate interests, and that she really did have a car that could run on water?

Addy's knuckles were white as she gripped the steering wheel, gritting her teeth through the ever-lingering pain in her hand. If she was viewed as a fugitive, as some kind of crazed serial murderer, she wondered how much sympathy she was going to generate during her Super Bowl commercial.

But seeing was believing. She absolutely had to get to the stadium. It was her only chance. Otherwise, she was doomed to a life behind bars. If she was lucky.

She swung the monster truck into the first available parking stall and rushed into the Starbucks. She found an empty table and switched on her phone. She didn't bother looking to see how many other vehicles had made their way to the coffee shop.

As she waited, she smoothed out the gum wrapper and began decoding the seven-digit number for the longitude. The first number was a six. That corresponded to a three. Then an eight that matched up with a two. She continued the process until she had decrypted Quinn's code.

When the phone had finished booting up, she searched the icons, desperately searching for the geo app where she could type in the translated coordinates. She scanned through the four rows of square icons, noticing apps on calculators, the weather and stock quotes, but couldn't find anything on GPS coordinates. Had Quinn forgotten to include it?

Then she realized there were more screens. She swooshed her finger across the screen to another page. *There it is,* she told herself, *in the middle row.* She tapped the screen, uploaded the program and feverishly typed in her code.

Her heart sank when a map of the address popped up. The new Hindy was stored in a warehouse in South San Francisco. Did Quinn realize that the 49ers didn't play in San Francisco anymore? Candlestick was long gone. Their new stadium was in the South Bay, nearly a forty-five-minute drive in good traffic.

Staring blankly at her phone, she remembered seeing a familiar icon on the second page. She exited the geo app and went back to the main screen. She hadn't been imagining it. In the row above the geo app was one from a taxi service.

Quickly, she tapped the screen to see if it worked. It loaded instantly. And, Quinn had set up a prepaid account. Quinn was definitely making it easy for her to get to South San Francisco. She wondered whether she should take the chance. There was no time for debate. If she didn't have a car, she didn't have a commercial.

Addy threw together a new plan. She asked to have a driver meet her in the back parking lot of the apartments behind the row of hedges. In a matter of seconds, her phone buzzed as she received a text. She pumped her fist when she saw the banner at the top of the screen. *Be there in three minutes.*

She leapt into the truck, revved the engine and illegally darted across four lanes of traffic, barely avoiding a collision with a yellow Corvette. She maneuvered parallel to the first pump and hopped out. Addy shoved the gas hose into the tank and hurried to the back of the convenience store to the bathrooms, head down, eyes raised, trying to remember the exact bush where she'd buried the vial in the Ziploc bag.

She remembered it was four bushes to the right. Her dart across the street hopefully slowed down her pursuers enough so that they wouldn't see what she was doing, but she didn't dare underestimate them. Even so, if she didn't get the catalyst now, everything she and Perry and Quinn had been through would have been for nothing.

Crouching, she scurried over to the spot where she found a familiar, slightly pink cobblestone. She had chosen that one so it would be easy to find. She quickly hefted off the three cobblestones, expecting to find a plastic bag. Her heart sank when the only thing beneath the stones was bare ground and a few ants.

Addy looked to her right at the next bush. No, she was sure this was where she'd put it. But now they all started looking the same. She shuffled to the adjacent bush and tore away the stones. Again, bare ground. This time she went to her left, checking beneath the stones of the next two bushes, all with the same result.

Addy squeezed her temples. This couldn't be happening. After everything she'd been through.

She sank to her knees and pounded the dirt with her good fist. Someone had watched her deposit the catalyst and had taken it. *But who?* There were plenty of others who still believed she had it.

She looked over her shoulder. Parked at the pump in front of her truck was a sedan with tinted windows. A man was standing, arms folded, watching her while he pumped his gas. She remembered the sunglasses. It was the same man who had passed her in the muffin shop. He quickly looked down and fiddled with the gas hose.

She heard a vehicle on the other side of the hedge. From her vantage point, she could see into the parking lot of the apartment complex. It was a green and white Prius. Her taxi had arrived.

"Are you looking for something?" came a voice in a thick Spanish accent.

She lifted her head and spun around. A short man with a

dark, leathery face and wearing jeans and a long-sleeved button-down shirt was peering down at her. It had a logo embroidered just above his bulging pocket—the name of the convenience store.

"No, I mean yes. I've misplaced something. I figured someone may have found it and put it in the rocks."

The man patted his shirt just over his heart. She could see the bulge in his pocket. "I saw you put it there. It must be valuable."

Addy shot out her hand. "Please, I'll give you anything."

"At first I thought it was drugs, but I tasted it. It tastes like dirt."

Addy moved her hand closer. "Please sir. It's a chemical. I need it for my chemistry class. My boyfriend tried to steal it when we had a fight."

It was the same story she'd told before, but from the blank stare she could see it wasn't registering.

"Okay, how much do you want for it?"

Now the man smiled.

"How much do you have?"

Addy figured she had about a hundred in change left in her purse. She offered him all her money.

"A rich girl like you driving a truck like that, you've got to give me more. I wish I could drive a truck like that."

"It's yours," Addy quickly offered, having no intention of getting back into that truck. "The keys are in it, and my wallet too."

The corner of the man's eyes crinkled, as if he were being played for a fool.

"No, I'm serious. Take it. Just give me what's in your pocket."

The man looked back at the truck with its chrome package and oversized tires. "It's a nice truck."

"And it's yours. Just give me back my chemicals."

Slowly, the man unbuttoned his pocket, removed the plastic bag containing the vial and placed it into Addy's outstretched hand. She shoved it down her shirt, the plastic pressing against her skin. The clerk's body was positioned so that the man pumping gas could not see the exchange.

"Go get your truck," she insisted, and she went down on all fours and crawled through the hedge. When she emerged on the other side, she brushed off her yoga outfit and opened the back door of the Prius.

"To the San Francisco Hilton?" the man asked.

"Yeah, for now," Addy said. "And make it quick. I'll give you a hundred-dollar tip in cash if we get there in thirty minutes."

"Sounds good to me," he said gunning the car before she'd even closed the door. Addy strained to look through the row of bushes as the car gained momentum.

Peeking through a gap, she noticed that the black truck with big mud tires had already pulled away from the pump. Her stomach sank. If the man was followed, who knew what might happen to him? She didn't know if she could handle another death on her conscience. She hoped it turned out to be the FBI and not some terrorists.

"You should have waited another hour until the game starts," the driver complained as he turned onto the 101 Freeway. "This traffic is impossible. For a Sunday afternoon, there's a lot of congestion."

Addy leaned forward and stole a glance at the digital clock. Kickoff would be in two hours. Even if the driver managed to reach the warehouse in South San Francisco in thirty minutes, that left her less than an hour to retrace her path and continue south to Levi's® Stadium in Santa Clara.

She did a quick mental calculation. She had a thirty-minute buffer, but the number of vehicles on both the north and southbound lanes could easily eat that up.

"What's going on at the Hilton?" the driver continued. "Super Bowl party?"

"Something like that," Addy said, fidgeting with her phone.

"Are you going to watch?"

"No, I've gotta work. Besides that, I'm not into American football. Where I come from, the football is round and you can't touch it with your hands."

"Soccer," Addy said, staring unfocussed at the brake lights in front of them.

The driver reached over and switched on his radio to an AM news station. The host was discussing the strange case of Examiner Johnston's murder.

"Can we listen to another station? I want to hear what's

going on at Levi's® Stadium."

The driver held up his hand. "Just give me a second. I want to hear about this. You been following this case? Some patent attorney kills an examiner and gets accused of stealing government secrets. Just today her former partner is murdered in his house and a neighbor saw her running away."

"He'd already been dead a day," Addy said, then instantly regretted it. "How about listening to the Super Bowl, something a little less depressing?"

"You're the client," he finally said, switching the channel. "But she sure seems guilty to me."

Once they passed Hillsboro, the traffic broke free, and the Prius reached nearly eighty miles an hour. At the last second, Addy gave a new set of instructions.

"I need you to exit right here on Grand Avenue, then take a left on Linden Street."

His head swiveled around like an owl's and he scowled. "I'm the client, remember?"

He swerved the Prius and shot down the exit ramp, following her instructions. In a few blocks they approached a warehouse in the shape of a giant barn with red walls and a corrugated metal roof. It had five bays for semis to dock and unload their wares. Two dozen unhitched trailers were stacked and waiting for a hookup. A wide chain-link gate blocked the entrance.

"This is it," Addy said.

The driver handed her his mobile phone, and Addy approved the payment with the promised tip, then jumped out and waved the driver on.

The taxi sped away, and Addy rolled away the gate and slipped through, nervous and uncertain. Would some masked men take her down and conduct a thorough body search?

She darted across the pavement and crept along beside an unhitched trailer. She wondered which one, if any, held Hindy II. When she reached the set of bay doors, she noticed one was a few feet open. This could be a trap, she thought. She might never come out alive. Could she trust Quinn?

Time was running out, and she was out of options. Addy flung herself down on her belly and wiggled her way through, hoping to find Hindy all ready for her Super Bowl appearance. A sharp pain shot up from her bandaged hand, but she had no time for medical attention. Ignoring the pain, she pushed herself upright.

Inside, the air was cool and damp. With no windows, the warehouse was dark except for the light streaming in from underneath the bay door. Addy waited for her eyes to adjust. The warehouse was nearly full of cardboard boxes, none of them large enough to store a full-sized vehicle. As she took in the scene, her neck and shoulders prickled as she half expected to be clubbed from behind.

"Quinn," she softly called out.

An eerie silence followed. Addy could feel the blood thudding in her ears. Then she heard a faint bang, like a door slamming. Addy turned in that direction while feeling her way along the wall until she encountered a light switch. Turning it on would give away her position, but she needed light to find her way around the stacks of boxes. But time was running out, so she shrugged and flipped it on. A row of incandescent ceiling lights banished the gloom.

Now she could see the entire warehouse, which was big enough for a 49ers practice. There were brown cardboard boxes everywhere. But nothing that would hold something the size of a car.

Off to her left she could see another door, which she assumed led to the front office. The slamming door had come from that direction. Addy dashed over and gently turned the handle, wondering if this would be the end of her quest.

She cracked the door a few inches, and suddenly she heard another loud bang, then another, then someone rustling papers. She pushed the door open far enough to poke her head through and peek inside.

By light from a small desk lamp, she could see Quinn frantically flailing his arms, tossing documents out of drawers, then slamming them shut. Sweat was dripping from his nose and his pupils were dilated.

She nudged the door further and it struck something on the floor. Instantly, Quinn pivoted, yanked out a gun from his pants and pointed it at the door.

"Quinn," she whispered with her finger over her lips.

He slowly lowered his weapon, his eyes focused on her small

frame.

"Is that you, Addy?" he said stepping forward.

She held up her hand. "Wait, don't come any closer. Are we alone?"

"Unfortunately," he said. "I could use a little help."

"Do you have any idea what you've done?"

Quinn wiped his forehead with his shirtsleeve, but remained silent.

"Let me tell you what you don't want to hear. Perry's dead. He's been murdered. And you know what he did right before he died? He paid for the commercial with his own money."

Quinn's jaw dropped. "I'm so sorry," he stammered.

"Oh, no you're not. You know what else I found out? Janice tried to give me fake wiring instructions. You were going to wire the money back into your own account and make it look like you'd paid for the commercial, just so you could get your catalyst back. But it didn't work. Perry beat you to it. And I'm not going to let you tie me up and take the catalyst."

Quinn ran his fingers through his saturated hair. "Addy, none of that's true. I called Perry last night, right after you and I separated. I told him about our plan, and that I was supposed to get him the rest of the money and track down the car. But the problem was that there was no way I could get the money.

"When I called Korea, it set off all kinds of red flags. They froze all the accounts. When I explained that to Perry, he said not to worry, that he'd already arranged for payment, and all he needed me to do was to get the car to Levi's® Stadium.

"He said that no matter what had gone on between us, he was sorry for how he treated me and that he believed that I was the only one who could help you. He said that if anything happened to him, I needed to make sure I got the car to the stadium in time. He said it was your only hope, but that he knew I could do it."

Addy folded her arms. If what Quinn was telling her was true, Perry had not only given all his savings, but he'd also admitted that he needed Quinn, and had even asked his forgiveness. Her chest felt tight. She'd misjudged her former partner, but too late to thank him.

"What about Janice?" Addy said.

"She must still be working for WTG. That explains why they froze my accounts. They knew I was trying to get money for the commercial even before I called. They must have given Janice the wiring instructions, hoping to prevent your Super Bowl appearance."

Addy swallowed and blinked hard, trying to contain her emotions. "Are you telling me the truth?" she finally asked.

"I'm truly sorry about Perry," he said. "I misjudged him. He was an amazing human being."

Addy couldn't hold back her emotions any longer. She rushed to Quinn and threw her arms around him. His tight-fitting black shirt was damp and hot. She felt his strong arms pull her tight, then drop.

"I'm afraid I've let you both down," he whispered. "The only task Perry gave me was to get Hindy to the Super Bowl. It seems like I can't even do that. I've got Hindy in one of those semi-trailers out there, but I can't find the truck keys. Without the keys to the tractor, I can't hook up the trailer, and the game is ready to start."

She stepped back and looked into his brown eyes, then smoothed back his rumpled hair. All she felt was relief that he hadn't betrayed her.

"Don't worry, we'll find them."

He shook his head. "I've torn this place apart. They're supposed to be here."

"Are you sure?"

"Yes," he said, sinking onto the floor, utterly exhausted. "Without a car, Perry's death is going to be in vain. What are we going to do?"

She pulled the vial from out of her shirt and held it up. "No, Perry didn't die for nothing. I've got the catalyst, and we are going to find those keys. We didn't come this far to fail. Perry wouldn't have wanted that. He believed in both of us. Now it's time to prove him right."

Quinn raised his eyes and she could see a glimmer of hope. "I'm not sure where else to look."

"I have an idea," Addy said and raced back into the warehouse. She remembered hitting her head on the corner of a thin cabinet next to one of the bay doors while she was feeling for the light switch. At full speed, she ran back and found a small oak cabinet the jutted out a few inches from the wall. She swung it open as Quinn raced to her side. The interior held five rows of brass hooks from which dangled an assortment of keys. She plucked off a half dozen and slapped them into Quinn's hand.

"Start with these. I'll bring the rest. One of them has to work."

He quickly leaned over and kissed her, then raced for the big rig.

The tractor Quinn was going to use to haul the semi-trailer housing Hindy was bright blue, with *Jerry's Trucking* emblazoned on both doors. It had polished chrome exhaust pipes running along each door. Quinn was standing on the runner shoving each key into the lock. Addy noticed his hands were shaking.

"How much time do we have?" he said.

Addy switched on her phone. "Forty minutes."

Quinn threw a key to the ground and tried another. "It takes that long just to drive there, and we've still got to figure how to hook this thing up."

"Keep trying. One of them is going to work."

The next key slid into the lock and he turned it clockwise. The door popped open. "Someone is watching over you," he said jumping inside and starting the diesel engine. A dark plume of smoke billowed out the exhaust pipes.

"Have you ever driven one of these?" she asked.

"Never," Quinn said. "Have you?"

"Only once. The father of one of the families I stayed with in high school was a trucker. He said I was a terrible driver when I drove over one of his sprinklers, so I bet him I could drive his big rig through the McDonald's drive through and order a hamburger."

"Did you?"

"Not even close. I ground the gears so many times getting out of our neighborhood that he said the bet was off."

"At least you know how they work."

Addy screened the mass of semi-trailers strewn out over the parking lot. "Which one has Hindy?"

"That one," Quinn said, pointing to an unmarked gray trailer at the front of the second row. "You stand in front of it and help me get this tractor truck lined up."

While Addy ran to the front of the second bay, she heard Quinn grind the gears. The truck lurched forward and died. She laughed when she saw Quinn bang the steering wheel. He tried again, and this time was able to direct the cab to the front of the line of trailers.

"Keep coming," Addy said, beckoning with both hands while Quinn shoved the cab into reverse and gently released the clutch. When the hitch was aligned, Addy held both hands high in the air. "Okay, stop," she yelled.

Quinn kept the engine running while he ran behind the tractor and began cranking a handle to lower the trailer onto the hitch. "There's got to be some kind of electrical connection. See if you can figure it out."

Addy found an assortment of wires dangling from the trailer and found mating connectors on the semi-truck. She plugged them together.

"Good enough," Quinn said. "Hop in. We're going for a ride."

"Don't you want to test it first?"

"No time."

"I'd feel better if I knew we were legal. Stay here," she commanded.

Addy darted to the cab and pumped the brakes, then turned on one of the blinkers. "See anything?"

Quinn studied the back of the trailer as a yellow light flashed on and off.

He gave her a thumbs-up signal.

This time it was Addy who ground the gears as she searched for first, then gently let out the clutch. Addy watched her side mirror as the truck and trailer began moving in unison.

Quinn held up both thumbs. "That works for me," he yelled. "Let's get out of here."

The truck was still edging forward when Addy heard the roaring of an engine, followed by squealing tires. A black Suburban roared into the lot and skidded sideways, blocking the entrance.

"We've got company," Addy muttered.

Quinn raced to the front of the big rig and hopped onto the runner. They both watched while three figures, all wearing bulletproof jackets, leapt out, weapons drawn.

"Your friends from WTG?" Addy asked.

"I don't think so, but I can't say for sure. I wouldn't have thought my colleagues were capable of murder."

Addy squinted her eyes. At least two of them had heavy beards, one with a bulging top lip. The third had hair flowing to the shoulders—a woman.

"My friends are back. We're dealing with terrorists."

A fourth person followed. "Wait, that can't be!" Quinn stammered, "but it is. That's Wilcox. He doesn't want the secret to get out. These guys killed the examiner—and Perry. They're not here to negotiate."

"What now?" Addy said.

"I'm going to slow them down. You get out of here."

Addy reached out and grabbed his arm. "No! I can't leave you. They'll kill you, cut you up just like they did to Johnston."

"Yes, you can. Just get to the stadium. I'll find a way out of this. I'm an Olympic fencer, remember?"

Addy's eyes began to burn. "This isn't a time to joke around. I'm not leaving you. I can barely drive this thing. And they blocked the entrance."

Quinn ignored her and reached behind her seat, emerging with a crow bar. Then he slipped off the runner and onto the pavement.

"Get back in here!" Addy shrieked. "I need a copilot."

"You can figure it out. You've made it this far," he said, maintaining eye contact with the three assailants.

"Don't go," Addy begged.

Quinn kept marching forward, slapping the crowbar against his open hand. Addy released the clutch to keep pace. The big rig jolted forward.

"It's the least I can do," Quinn continued. "I owe you this one. Two people have died because of me."

"It wasn't your fault," Addy said through her tears. "Get inside."

"Just do what I say. Okay?"

"But they will kill you."

Quinn kept up his steady pace, continuing to pound the metal rod in his open hand, ready for a fight. As he got closer, the first two men left the cover of the Suburban and rushed forward, leaving Wilcox and the woman behind.

"Don't be a fool," one of them yelled, their weapons still drawn. "Get down on the ground and put your hands behind your head."

Quinn continued toward them, undaunted. A shot kicked up a puff of dirt at Quinn's feet. This time he stopped. He turned to look at Addy and waved her on. Another shot rang out. The crowbar fell clanking to the ground and Quinn grabbed his shoulder.

"Get down," the assailant again commanded.

Quinn obeyed and began to kneel, still clutching his wounded shoulder.

The first man sprinted forward and swung behind Quinn, then kicked him in the back, knocking him face down on the asphalt.

Addy reacted, grinding the gears as she hunted for second, then found it. She floored the pedal and the semi accelerated.

The second man yanked out a baton from his jacket and swung it down on Quinn's back. Addy had to look away, and the engine was revving too high for Addy to hear the impact.

The big rig gained speed, but still not fast enough to stop the thug from striking another blow. Addy propelled the truck at the man, causing him to leap sideways. At the last possible second, Addy swerved to avoid hitting Quinn.

The man who had kicked Quinn to the ground jumped to the runner and hung onto the side mirror, his other hand holding a revolver. Once he regained his balance, he pointed it directly at Addy's temple. His oversized lip and black eye gave him away. The man with the tattoo, the same terrorist who had shot Hindy's balloon, punched her in the ribs and tried to stop her at the gym.

"Stop the truck!" he bellowed in a deep baritone voice.

Addy kept her eyes straight ahead while they bore down on the Suburban. She found third gear and increased her rate of acceleration. Now she was only a few yards from impact. She made eye contact with the woman who'd held her tight while the man who was now hanging on to her mirror had crunched her ribs. Her gaze moved to Wilcox, who she now knew to be the mastermind behind these acts of terror. She hoped they wouldn't move. She wanted them both dead.

Out of her peripheral vision, she sensed the man with the tattoo who'd caused her so much pain was perfecting his aim. At the last possible second, she ducked, just when the man pulled the trigger. The bullet whizzed through the cab, and a second later the semi broadsided the Suburban.

The impact slammed her head against the steering wheel, leaving a gash over her left eyebrow. But it knocked the gunman off the runner, sending him headlong over the windshield of the Suburban.

The momentum of the semi pushed the crushed vehicle aside, and Addy shot into the street. Bullets whizzed through the cab, and Addy kept her head down. She could hear bullets tearing into the side of the trailer and its precious cargo, and she wouldn't be able find out whether they'd disabled the new Hindy until she reached the stadium.

She kept the pedal down, veering left, then down the middle of the road toward the onramp for Grand Avenue.

She never had the chance to check her sideview mirror to see what had happened to Quinn. After what Wilcox and his clan had done to Johnston and Perry, she had a sick sense that she already knew what was in store. She wanted to stop, turn the rig around and finish off Wilcox. But she knew it would be useless. They had an arsenal, and she had nothing. Quinn had given her his final wishes.

Whatever happened to him, it was up to her to make sure his sacrifice was worth it.

# 37

JESSE LONG WAS sitting in his Buick, contemplating his next move. He'd wrapped up his investigation and was wondering if he should go to the station and talk with the other agents. Or, maybe he should call Molly Peele and give her an update. What he really wanted was to find Addeline Verges.

His stomach growled. He hadn't even had his morning cup of coffee, let alone any kind of real meal. He had a better idea. Go home to his wife and baby and watch the Super Bowl. He turned the key in the ignition. With any luck, Laura would have a nice dinner waiting, and it would be a close game, something to take his mind away from the exceptionally grisly deaths he'd witnessed over the past two days.

Traffic was heavy as he headed north toward the city. Long debated whether he should call ahead to warn his wife, or just surprise her. He decided the latter, just in case something else came up.

The Buick was pulling into his subdivision when his phone buzzed. His gut instinct was right. He pulled over, pried it out of his pocket and took the call. They'd found Addy.

"Where's she at?"

"We're texting you the location now. We don't know if she's still there. A taxi driver dropped her off at a shipping warehouse off Grand Avenue. He called us about fifteen minutes later."

"Anyone there yet?"

"You're the first one we called."

"I'm two exits away. I'll be there in five minutes."

"That's what we were hoping."

# 38

WITH TEARS STREAMING down her face, Addy barreled down the 101 Freeway. The heavy traffic she'd experienced on the way to get Hindy had subsided, because fans were now glued to their television sets.

She switched on the radio and turned the dial until she found the station broadcasting the football classic. They had a live feed from the field, and the captains of both teams were watching the head official flip the official coin to see which team would receive the kickoff.

Addy did a quick mental calculation. At her current speed, she estimated she had another thirty minutes, well past her allotted time. She only hoped Claire would hold her post-halftime spot. She assured herself that if Zissy had insisted on introducing her, they wouldn't yank her from the lineup just for being late. Addy pressed down harder on the accelerator. Going a few miles an hour faster could shave off a few precious minutes.

Addy listened while the kickoff punched the ball into the end zone, and the game officially began. A car commercial blared over her speakers, followed by one from a fast food chain. Addy prayed for something—anything—to stall the game. Her prayer was answered when a wide receiver went down on the following series, and she listened while the announcers speculated about the extent of the injury.

By the end of the first quarter, Addy had reached the 237 Freeway leading to the East Bay. She gently veered the semi left, then took the exit onto Blazingwood Drive. She slowed for the first light that had just turned yellow.

As she did, she noticed steam boiling out from the hood, near where she'd collided with the Suburban. She held her breath when the light turned green and she put her foot on the accelerator. Just a few more blocks, she pleaded. A few lights later, she took left on Tasman and Levi's® Stadium loomed in front of her. A wave of emotion came over her as she realized her ordeal was almost over.

The cargo entrance was on the far side of the stadium, requiring Addy to pull her load past the length of sports temple. She could hear the roar of the crowd as play resumed. The game was now well into the second quarter. Halftime was only minutes away.

She attempted to take her first right past the stadium and into the main parking lot, but it was barricaded. A Santa Clara policeman in full uniform was standing in front, arms folded. He shook his head when Addy slammed on her brakes to avoid a collision. He waved for her to continue on.

Addy stuck her head out the window. "I've got an important delivery for the halftime show."

The officer stepped forward, then halted as he studied the mangled front end of the semi. He continued sauntering past the front tire of the tractor until he noticed a small round hole. He poked his finger into it. Steam was still billowing from her engine and the officer reached out and fruitlessly waved his hand through the cloud.

Addy didn't wait for him to ask any questions.

"I should be on the VIP list, or whatever they call it. There's going to be a live commercial, right after Zissy performs. In fact, she's announcing me. I've got to get the props into the stadium so that they can be set up in time."

The officer lowered his sunglasses. His face was oversized, with a thick moustache. A clipboard was tucked underneath his arm.

"Got a name?"

Addy hesitated, wondering if she should tell him her real name. If the officer realized she was wanted for questioning, that would be the end of her quest. But Claire wouldn't have given any other name.

"Addy, and the future age car we are going to demo is called Hindy."

The officer's forehead puckered. He studied the first page, then flipped through the remaining sheets. The crowd inside the stadium roared again.

"Please," Addy pleaded. "It's almost halftime."

"Sorry, I can't find you on the list. Everyone's checked in by now. You'll have to move on."

Addy considered punching through the barricade, just like she'd done with the Suburban, but realized that would only attract unwanted attention and an army of law enforcement.

In her side-view mirror she watched a white, boxy-looking van pull up behind her. The door opened and a woman wearing a white jumpsuit emerged. Her matching white cap contrasted against the black hair billowing out beneath the cap. Addy watched her, wondering why this truck had boxed her in.

"Okay, if you're not going to move, I'm going to need to see your driver's license and registration," said the officer holding out his hand. "And I'm going to want an explanation of how this happened," he said as he pointed to the wisps of steam rising from the mangled hood and the bullet hole just a few feet below.

"Please," Addy pleaded. "I'm telling you the truth. I've got to get inside that stadium."

The woman in the white jumpsuit reached the officer. "What's the problem here?" she said. "She's blocking traffic. Lots of people have jobs to do around here. You know how many linens I've got to clean tonight?"

The officer raised his hand to halt her progress. "I'm taking care of this. You'll have to wait."

Out of her peripheral vision, Addy watched in the mirror as another white-clad figure slipped out of the van and disappeared behind the trailer. Then she understood. This woman was there to distract her.

"Your license ma'am," the officer insisted.

Addy was out of options. If she didn't do something now, she'd be arrested and never make it into the stadium. And in just a few moments, this second linen cleaner would be inside her trailer, dismantling her new Hindy. Even if she got through security, she wouldn't have a functioning car.

She did the only thing she could think of. With both fists, she leaned hard on the horn.

The semi belched like a trombone on steroids. The officer yelled in her direction, but she could only see his lips moving. She looked toward the stadium, avoiding eye contact. The officer began pounding on the door, but she wouldn't release the pressure on the horn. The banging continued, then she heard a loud *crack* when he hammered his baton against the window. He struck again, and she felt a shard of glass cut her face. Still, she kept the horn blaring.

Then she saw a woman half-dashing, half-waddling through the parking lot as if she were a penguin, followed by a host of security guards and men dressed in suits. When she got closer, she began flailing her arms, almost a warning to stop the shrill screaming of the horn.

*Claire?* Addy wondered. From her dainty voice on the telephone, Addy had expected a slim, shapely-looking woman, someone you might find on a morning news show. Instead, Claire was short and heavyset, with close-cropped hair that was thinning on the top. And she swayed from side to side while she lumbered toward the semi.

Addy watched the linen cleaners climb back into their van, reversing course. Addy released the horn and watched Claire stomp around the front of the truck and tug on the officer's shirt. He stepped down to confront her, and Addy opened the door to eavesdrop.

"What are you doing?" she insisted. "This is the halftime show. Are you crazy?"

The officer's mouth hung open, clearly nervous that maybe he'd crossed the line.

The woman shook her head. "I can't believe this." She shoved him aside and flung the door wide open.

"Addy?" she said.

"You must be Claire. Sorry I'm late. Are we still on?"

"That depends on whether we can get you set up. Can someone please move these barricades, and get the bay doors open? We've got to pull this semi inside."

Addy didn't argue. She waited for a few of the security guards to part the barricades and wave her through. With Claire as a pacesetter, Addy followed suit, winding her way through the parking lot and up to the loading bay where the large door was just being raised. She pulled through and entered the safety of the tunnel.

* * *

It took a few moments for her eyes to adjust from glaring sunlight to the artificial lights in the tunnel. With her eyes widened, Addy watched Claire use hand gestures to beckon her onward until she reached a giant staging area.

Side halls veered off to the coaches' offices and the players' rooms. Directly ahead was a column of light opening onto the grassy field.

Organized chaos—and maybe not even organized—was the only way to describe what was going on. Straggling players from the AFC team were hammering their cleats on the cement surface in their hurry to reach their locker room.

But they were overwhelmed by the hundred or so dancers nervously prancing in place as their moment of fame had arrived. They'd be doing a floor routine while Zissy belted out the words to songs like *You're My Man,* while lasers and fireworks burst throughout the stadium.

Zissy was a safe choice for the network, young with a tinge of innocence, yet with an air of seduction, no chance of a wardrobe malfunction, and immensely popular, especially with the millenials.

And Zissy was into all things green, was a practicing vegan, lived in a solar-powered home, and drove an electric car.

Like an army of ants, makeup artists, costume designers, and choreographers were frantically putting the final touches on the dancers, dotting on a smidge more rouge here, adjusting headdresses there, and checking necklines.

Addy spied Zissy near the end of the tunnel. A producer was adjusting her microphone while she smoothed on a final coating of lipstick. She watched Claire push her way through the dancers and whisper a final set of instructions into the ear of the platinum-selling artist. For a moment, Zissy's eyes met Addy's. The singer gave her grin and a thumbs-up.

A wave of relief made Addy dizzy and weak for a moment. She was going to get her introduction, and the live commercial was going to happen. The world was going to learn the secret, and then nothing could stop it from becoming a reality.

What amounted to a makeshift pit crew swung open the trailer doors, connected a ramp and rolled Hindy down. Addy rushed over. The first thing she noticed was the bullet hole through the driver's side window. She ran her hand along the doors, then the hood, searching for any other damage.

"Somebody shoot at you?" said one of the pit crew.

Addy wiped her brow. In all the commotion, she'd almost forgotten what she'd just endured, and what Quinn was probably suffering even now. "Long story, and we don't have time. Just know that what you see here is more valuable than solid gold. You'll hear it all when I get out on the field."

She felt a tapping on her shoulder. Claire was beside her with the producer and a cameraman. "Boy am I glad to see you here! Zissy's been driving me nuts asking about you, not to mention everyone at the network. We have ten minutes until you're out there. I need to walk you through the logistics. Meet our producer, Nate. He'll be running the show. Any questions, he's your man."

Addy took a quick glance, seeing a tall, slim figure with no hair. She immediately turned back, still fixated on Hindy, carefully watching as her pit crew polished her car, wiped the windows and inflated the tires. "Good to meet you, Nate. Can we talk while I'm getting Hindy ready?"

"Sure," the producer said. "And yes, you get started, we'll tag along. By the way, I love the name of your car—got a cute ring to it."

"It's named after the Hindenburg airship," Addy said, "not because of how it went up in flames, but because it was a totally new way to quickly cross the Atlantic."

With Claire and the producer in tow, Addy made her way to where the pit crew was furiously finishing up the shine on her car. The producer had his own headset, perched on top of his bald head. Like the rest of his crew, he was wearing black jeans with a matching T-shirt.

"It's going to be tight. You've only got a ninety-second slot, which isn't enough time to take a lap around the track and then give a speech. So here's what's going to happen. The moment Zissy finishes her song, there will be three loud pops from the last of the fireworks. The house lights will come on, and Zissy will give you a plug. By that time, you've got to be on the track, making your lap. The announcers will come on, say how great the performance was and how they are all looking forward to the second half. You should then be past the far end zone. That's when the live feed officially begins."

"So you'll capture the last part of my lap?"

"That's right. When you get to the fifty, hang a hard left and come right out onto the field. There will be an army of stagehands poised to clear the field, but they'll be on the other sideline, behind you. If I've timed it correctly, all that will take thirty seconds. That will give you a full minute to tell your story. As soon as you get out of Hindy, there will be another cameraman and a microphone stand. Got it?"

With her eyes still trained on Nate's shiny head, Addy nodded while simultaneously leaning down to fish for the hood latch. Her swollen hand knocked against the grill and she jerked it back with a gasp and stifled a moan. She tried again with her other hand, and it slipped through.

Claire looked at Nate and raised her eyebrows. "You get bitten by a snake?" Nate said. "Your hand looks like a balloon."

"It's nothing," Addy said as she tugged on the latch and the hood popped open a few inches, hoping he wouldn't notice the gash above her eye.

"You have a change of clothes?" Claire asked.

Addy looked down at her yoga outfit. The vial holding the catalyst was half poking out above her breast and she could see a ketchup stain on her right thigh. Thank goodness the blood was invisible. She hated to think what her makeup looked like, or how oily and stringy her hair must be by now. At least she still had her ponytail.

"It's been a long day," Addy said. "Got anything I can wear?"

Nate snapped a few commands into his headset. "I'll see what we can dig up. And, do you have your speech ready? Remember, you have one minute."

Addy froze. How could she have spaced out about something this important? She had no idea what she was going to say. Telling what had happened just in the last two weeks could take hours. She needed a documentary, not a few sound bites.

Addy lifted the hood to reveal the fuel cell. It didn't look anything like the one she'd had in the original Hindy, or even the one Quinn had used for the demonstration with Examiner Johnston.

The vivid stadium lights were suddenly dimmed, lowering the luminescence in the tunnel. It was then Addy realized that the team of dancers who'd been chattering like magpies had disappeared onto the field. The fans hushed their chatter.

Addy heard the public announcer boom out the name of Zissy Spaeth. The crowd suddenly erupted when they heard the first familiar chord of Zissy's most recent number one hit.

Claire stripped off a page from her clipboard. "I was afraid of that. I've made an outline, based on some of the things Perry told me. I'll put it on your seat."

*Perry.* Her eyes burned with tears that would have to wait until later.

Claire reached over and put her arm around Addy. "I'm so sorry. But this is what he wanted. You've got to do him proud and go out show the world that innocent people have been murdered to keep this technology hidden from them."

Addy nodded. The song went into the second verse and Addy knew time was running out. She slipped the vial from her yoga shirt, contemplating where it was supposed to be introduced into the fuel cell.

"One more thing," Nate said. "On the big screen, we're going to flaunt your magic formula. Perry told us that the whole world needed to see it. That was the only way everyone would know what was being kept from them. The only problem is that we don't have it."

Addy sprang into action. She ripped the clipboard from Claire's hand, took up the pen that was attached and began feverishly sketching it out.

"Here," she said, handing it back. "Get one of your graphics experts to tidy it up and flash the formula in the largest font you've got. Perry is not going to have died in vain." She ducked her head underneath the hood to locate the chamber for the catalyst.

The rhythmic beat and melodic tones of Zissy's next song began. A bead of sweat dribbled across Addy's temple and stung her eye. She shook off the droplets of sweat and continued her search, running her finger over a set of brightly-colored plastic caps. She popped one off and looked inside, then another. None of them looked like what she was expecting. *Where does the catalyst go?* she asked herself.

Suddenly, Addy froze. She could hear Claire arguing with someone. She craned her neck and peered over the fuel cell to see what was causing the commotion.

"We need to speak with your guest." A police officer wearing a forest green uniform, hands resting on his hips, was confronting Claire. From her vantage point, Addy couldn't tell if there were any other police in the vicinity. Reading the insignia on the officer's shoulder, she could tell he was from the local sheriff's office.

"That won't be possible," Claire sniped. "In less than five minutes, that car is going to be sitting on the fifty-yard line, and Addy is going to tell the world about a car that can run on water. Believe me, you don't want to be the person responsible for keeping that from happening."

"I've got a warrant for her arrest."

Addy swallowed as she watched Nate motion to his cameraman. A red light on the camera illuminated. From here on out, every word would be documented.

Addy shot up, banging her head on the hood. She grabbed it with her injured hand, doubling the agony, as she strode into the officer's personal space. "Trust me, you'll want to see this. Just give me five minutes, that's all I'm asking. Five minutes to show the world that this car, this very car sitting in front of you, is going to change everything. You, my friend, are part of history."

Gasoline is a thing of the past. Believe me, you don't want your name to be in every newscast as the officer who stopped the show, who rained on the Super Bowl. Just let me do my thing, and then I'll turn myself in."

Claire rushed forward, snatching a few papers from her clipboard. They were the documents Addy had obtained from her Freedom of Information Act request. Claire smashed them into the sheriff's chest. "Here, read these. They're government documents admitting they have a secret program to stop Addy's patents. How's it going to look if you're part of the government's conspiracy to stop this technology? Come on, give her a chance. Innocent until proven guilty—correct?"

Addy smiled. *This was Perry's doing. He must have given the papers to Claire.*

The officer looked back at his partner, who'd now joined the discussion, and scratched the back of his neck. He sauntered over to Hindy and kicked the front tire.

"This car? On water?"

"You got it. Imagine what it's going to be like."

A faint smile broke on his face and he shook his head. "This I've got to see. But I'm coming out on the field with you. Consider yourself in my custody."

"You can ride with me if you want," Addy offered.

He shook his head again. "That's okay, but don't do anything stupid. When you're finished, we're going to the station. I'm only doing my job."

"Deal," Addy said, holding out her good hand.

Addy had barely buried herself back under the hood when she felt another tap on her back. Nate was holding an oversized 49ers jersey. "I'm afraid this is all we have, but it's better than what you're wearing now."

She snatched it and threw it on over her yoga shirt, then dove back to her work, clueless that the jersey came nearly to her knees.

As Addy ducked her head beneath the hood, she noticed a plastic bag that was taped to the bottom. It contained a neatly folded piece of paper. She ripped the bag off, tugged out the paper and unfolded it on top of the fuel cell. It contained step-by-step instructions for how to load the catalyst, as well as the start-up protocol. She ran her finger down the steps, frantic because Zissy was now into her third song.

Following the instructions, Addy located a red handle and gave it a gentle tug. A hinged door opened, revealing a small compartment resembling the location in a dishwasher where the detergent is loaded. Addy hitched up her jersey and retracted the vial from her yoga shirt. Her hands were shaking as she twisted off the lid. She took a deep breath, then poured in the granules, careful not to spill any of them. Then she clapped the door shut.

For the next step, she twisted off a black cap and stuck her finger inside to confirm that the water holding tank of the fuel cell was indeed empty. Her finger came back dry and she held it up to the camera. Then she hurried and popped the trunk. Quinn's instructions told her to make sure the tank was completely full, and that he'd stored a gallon of distilled water in the trunk if she needed it.

As she rushed back to the front of the hood, she held up the water to the camera making sure the camera captured the large $H_2O$ label. Perhaps Quinn had intentionally let the water run low, just for this moment. She wondered how he was faring while she unscrewed the lid and poured in about half of the liquid until it reached the waterline. Then she twisted the cap back on.

Rushing around the front of the car, she read the next steps while she slipped into the driver's side seat. Unlike a traditional automobile, there was no ignition, just a series of switches and knobs. Following the protocol, Addy flipped a series of switches, then turned the starter knob. She fully expected to hear the fuel cell start humming, beginning the process of extracting the hydrogen from water. Instead, all she heard was the beating of the drum and the screaming Zissy fans.

She observed the sheriff take a step closer and lean his ear toward the motor. Claire shimmied forward too, hanging her hopes on any indication that the car had come to life. The camera lens didn't moved.

Addy jumped out and tucked her head beneath the hood, listening for any evidence that the fuel cell had come alive. She heard nothing. The stadium momentarily went silent as Zissy finished her ballad and the applause resumed. Zissy was ready to start her final number.

Addy smashed her fist on top of the fuel cell. She unrumpled the paper and revisited the steps. She'd followed them precisely.

What if something had happened to the catalyst? What if the landscaper wasn't really what he claimed to be? Maybe he had the real catalyst and all she had was dirt? What if a stray bullet had torn through the fuel cell?

The sheriff was now shaking his head, his arms folded over his large belly. "Can we help you with anything?" he asked.

Addy ignored him, but couldn't avoid Claire's concerned look. Claire tucked her chin beneath the clipboard.

She wished Quinn was there with her, walking her through the protocol.

"Anyone you can call?" Claire suggested.

Instinctively, Addy reached for her phone, but it was swallowed beneath her red and gold jersey. It was then she remembered that she had never turned on her phone. What if Quinn had tried to reach her? She hitched up her jersey and removed the phone that was wedged beneath her pants. She toggled the Wi-Fi switch and waited for a signal.

"What's the Wi-Fi password?" she demanded.

Claire waddled over and studied her screen. "SBsunday. The S and B are capitalized."

Addy tapped in the letters. Almost as soon as they were entered, her phone beeped and she saw a banner with Quinn's message. "Call me."

Realizing her phone wouldn't work, she spat out another order. "I need someone's phone. Now!"

Claire pulled hers from a purse that was hanging over her shoulder, and Addy hurriedly dialed his number, realizing every second counted.

She heard a click, indicating a connection had been made, but she didn't receive any kind of salutation. She pressed the phone to her ear, trying to listen over the roaring of the stadium.

"Quinn, is that you?"

"Addy, thank goodness you called." His voice was faint.

"Are you okay?" Addy pressed. "Where are you?"

"I'm fine," he said, sounding strange, "but I need to know about Hindy."

"She doesn't work," Addy blurted out. "Hindy, she doesn't work."

"Give it time," he said. "It takes several minutes for the reaction to build up enough hydrogen."

She heard a dull thud, followed by a groan. Then another, as if Quinn were being beaten. Another voice came through the phone's speaker.

"We've kept him alive so you can make a decision."

"Quinn," she screamed, realizing the phone had been snatched from his hand. "Put him back on. You can't hurt him."

"That's your decision. If you drive that car onto the field, his life is over. If you want him to live, you'll bring us the catalyst and call off this little charade."

"No, please don't hurt him," Addy pleaded. "Wilcox, I know it's you. I'll give you anything you want."

The officer stepped forward and leaned his ear toward her phone. She could smell his cheap cologne.

"Please," she said, holding back her tears. "I want to talk to Quinn."

"As you wish," Wilcox said.

Both Claire and the sheriff scooted closer. Addy hung her head, trying to secure some sense of privacy.

"Addy," Quinn said when he came on. "Don't listen to them. Show Hindy to the world. Push the red button. I'll be okay."

Addy heard another thud, a crunch, then the line went silent.

"That's what happens when people don't listen and cooperate," the voice interrupted. "Now, are you going to shut down the car and bring us the catalyst?"

Addy saw Claire step back, press her headset into her ear, and nod. Zissy's final song was well underway.

"The catalyst is already in the fuel cell," she said in a last-ditch effort to negotiate for Quinn's safety. "I can't get it out."

"Then bring us the car."

"They'll arrest me."

"Then I guess we don't have anything left to discuss."

Claire, sensing Quinn was now a hostage and that his life somehow depended on Addy's decision to stop the show, teetered over and put her arm around Addy. "I'm afraid it's time. I'm sorry, but I understand your decision. We're going to run the backup commercial."

Claire held her tighter. Somehow her human touch brought Addy back.

"No," Addy said. "Don't run the backup. This is what Quinn wants. I've got to honor his last request."

The sheriff snatched the phone and plugged it into his ear. It was too late. The call had ended.

Addy untangled herself from Claire's embrace. "Come on, we can't wait any longer. Let's get this show on the road."

Tears began to stream down her face as she slammed down the hood and bolted into the car. She poked the red button and immediately felt a slight tremor as the fuel cell hummed to life.

"It's running on water," she screamed over Zissy's blaring band. She wiped her watering eyes. "Just like Quinn promised. Just like he promised."

The cameraman moved closer, and the sheriff rested his hands on his hips.

"I'll be damned if I'm going to be the one to ruin this," he muttered.

Claire began yelping commands into her headset. A makeup artist appeared, poked her head through the window, and began dotting a pad on Addy's cheeks and above her injured eye.

She shifted the car into gear and gently pressed the accelerator. Hindy leapt forward, nearly sideswiping one of the stagehands.

"Sorry," she said through a half smile. "I wasn't expecting that."

A path within the tunnel instantly cleared, and Claire gestured her forward. Four cameramen jockeyed for position, and a few bystanders pulled out their phones to capture the historic event.

Zissy's final number was reaching its climax. Amid the screeching guitars and pounding drums, the fans clapped and sang. Addy heard an explosion as the fireworks display began.

*This is really going to happen*, Addy told herself.

She kept her foot steady on the accelerator, urging Hindy forward at a safe speed. She could now see fireworks exploding at the end of the tunnel. She'd managed to time her entrance just as Nate had orchestrated.

Addy was within twenty feet of exiting onto the track when four figures wearing black armor suddenly appeared, blocking her exit. Machine guns were leveled right at her windshield. One spoke into a megaphone.

"This is the Department of Homeland Security. Stop or we will be forced to shoot."

Addy didn't even pause to consider her situation. Nothing was going to stop her. She hit the accelerator. Hindy responded with increased speed. The gap between her and the federal agents was rapidly closing. Addy pressed harder and Hindy responded, threatening to mow over the black-clad agents.

Realizing Addy was refusing to obey their order, they stepped aside, just as Addy whizzed past them. As she did, she shot her hand out the window and pumped her fist.

The stadium lights were still dimmed, but the fireworks display provided enough illumination for Addy to find her way onto the outer track. With her window down, she could hear Zissy finishing the last words to her closing number. It was time to listen for the three loud explosions. According to Nate's plan, the stadium lights would then come back on and her commercial would go live.

She peeked into her rearview mirror. A police car was right on her tail. She couldn't tell if it was an escort, or one last attempt by law enforcement to stop her. It was rapidly closing in. Because she needed to time her position, going any faster was pointless. She looked again and saw another patrol car, this one with its lights flashing.

Zissy's song ended with a flurry of brilliantly colored flashes in the sky. Three loud pops shook the stadium.

Addy gauged her position. In the dim light it was difficult to tell if she was at midfield. As the stadium lights began ramping back up, Addy looked to her left. She was directly aligned with the center stage poised on the fifty-yard line. The dancers were already streaming off the field, exiting the field at both end zones. An army of stagehands was barreling out onto the field, some already dismantling the props.

But Zissy was still atop the stage, arms folded, chin up. Defiant.

Addy had forgotten that she was there to announce her

arrival. A man holding a tablet stepped onto the track and raised his hand, indicating that she needed to slow down until Zissy had made her introduction. When she did, the first patrol car crept up to her rear bumper. It flashed its lights and an officer jumped out. Instead of Zissy's voice over the public announcement system, she heard the patrol car's squawk box command her to get out of the car.

The hum of the crowd created by the fans chattering about the halftime performance was instantly silenced, riveting all eyes on Hindy and the flashing lights.

Addy knew she wasn't going to get out, and she wasn't going to halt. Instead, she gunned it. Zissy took this as her cue.

"Ladies and gentlemen, what you are seeing before you is the world's first car that can actually run on water. Give a hand to my good friend Addy, and her revolutionary new vehicle, Hindy."

Zissy began clapping and two spotlights illuminated Hindy. Addy kept her speed constant and shot her hand out the window, waving like a beauty queen in the Rose Parade. The spotlights shone into her eyes, making it impossible for her to see the large display screens at each end zone that that should be broadcasting the formula for Quinn's catalyst.

To Addy's surprise, Zissy kept with her impromptu monologue.

"Yes, you heard correctly. Addy is driving the first ever car to be fueled by pouring ordinary tap water into the tank. And what you see on these giant screens is the secret chemical that makes it all possible. But I won't steal her thunder. As soon as Addy finishes her lap, she is going to come right up here and explain how it all works."

Addy had gone the length of the field and was ready to make the turn at the far end zone. She eased the steering wheel counterclockwise, keeping an eye on the squad cars that were still tailing her. That was when she noticed a platoon of SWAT vehicles waiting to ambush her. One by one they screamed out of the tunnel and formed a barricade across the track, halting her progress. Armor-plated and constructed for battle, these war machines were poised to take her out.

Addy moved her foot from the accelerator to the brake. Soon Hindy would be motionless. In another eighty seconds, her window of opportunity would be over.

Once the crowd realized what was happening they jumped out of their seats and, with gusto, began booing the federal agents.

Zissy, microphone still in hand, voiced her frustration.

"Come on officers, that's not playing nice."

With state troopers behind and a Homeland Security team in front, Addy was boxed in. If she didn't make a move now, it would be all over.

Addy cranked the wheel hard and hit the accelerator, barely avoiding the lead SWAT truck. But now she was headed straight for the goal post. Hindy was now driving on turf. While all of the dancers were safely off the field, dozens of stagehands were still scurrying about dismantling the production equipment. Addy swerved left to avoid an electrician who was coiling a length of wire. Then a hard right and she shot through the goal posts.

The crowd was now fully engaged, clapping and chanting "Ad-DY, Ad-DY."

One of the SWAT cars followed, but wasn't nimble enough, and scraped the side of the goal post, causing it to tilt.

Zissy started laughing, as did half the fans.

Addy increased her speed, flying down the left hash mark like a wide receiver zipping toward the end zone. When she approached center field, she spied the microphone stand that was set up for her speech. She stomped on the brake, skidding along the slick grass. Even before Hindy came to a halt, Addy was out the door and perched in front of the microphone.

"Welcome to history in the making," she said, half out of breath. The entire stadium stilled. "Super Bowl Sunday is a day of celebration, so please join with me in celebrating a new way of life. You are all now a part of history, and none of us will ever be the same." Addy again paused and took a sweeping view of the stadium. All eyes were fixed on her. The cameraman edged closer.

"As you heard Zissy explain, this car is fueled by water," Addy said, presenting Hindy with a sweep of her broken hand. "Soon, none of us will ever need to go to a gas station, and there will be no further need for damaging oil exploration and extraction and pollution. Isn't that something we all want?"

Some of the spectators began to applaud, followed by more, and more, until it reached a crescendo. It felt like electricity had shot up out of the ground.

Addy turned to the jumbo screen and lifted her hand. "And I am here to give you the secret of how to convert water to hydrogen. It's right there for everyone to see. The inventor, who couldn't be here today, sent me to tell you that he is donating his technology to you, to the world. That means everyone is free to use it. There will be no patents, no license fees, just freedom for everyone to enjoy. So embrace the technology! Change the world!"

The standing spectators cheered their approval, whistling and stomping their feet.

Addy continued. "A lot of people tried to stop this day from happening." She cranked her head sideways, giving the SWAT team a death look. "But thank goodness they all failed.

"I know many of you have heard allegations that I stole this technology, or that I participated in the gruesome murder of a patent examiner. Nothing could be further from the truth. My law partner even sacrificed his life to get me here today.

"But I'm not here to point fingers or make accusations. I am here to ask you for your help. This technology needs to be part of everyday life, and I need you to help make it happen. We need production facilities, improved fuel cells, better operating software. What place in the world is better suited for doing this than right here in Silicon Valley? Here is where the world's most important technologies are born. You, of all people, right here in the heart of Silicon Valley, should understand."

The crowd exploded, bellowing their approval.

"I invite those industry leaders and innovators to come look at Hindy. See for yourselves what Hindy is all about. I'll be here to answer every question. I even have copies of the patent application that we've withdrawn from the Patent Office. So, as soon as the last second ticks off that game clock, please come be my guest."

Zissy, still on the stage observing events unfold, didn't want to wait for the end of the second half. She leapt down and rushed to Addy's side. "And I'm going to be your first customer," she said, then threw both arms around her and hugged her tight.

Neither said anything as the applause reached deafening levels.

Together, singer and patent attorney waved at the adoring crowd. Addy soaked in the moment, hoping she could always remember how she felt right now. It was something nobody could ever take from her.

Then, as quickly as it began, it was over. The cameras cut and Nate stepped forward and removed his headset. "Perfect," he said. "But now it's time to roll away the car and get ready for the second half. I have no idea what they're going to do about that goal post. It looks like the Leaning Tower of Pisa."

Zissy gave one final hug and wished her well. The porky sheriff who had threatened to arrest her stood watching, arms folded. Keeping her promise, Addy approached him, hands out. The sheriff shook his head.

A team of workers pushed Hindy off the field while Addy, escorted by the sheriff, headed for the staging area. She'd barely reached the track when the SWAT team swooped down on her, cuffing her hands behind her back, asserting their authority over the local sheriff, and taking her into custody.

# 39

MOLLY PEELE WAS side stepping past a row of spectators, desperately trying to reach the closest aisle. The stadium lights had just been raised and the Super Bowl crowd was abuzz with what they just witnessed. She fumbled with the latch on her purse as she squeezed herself past a large beer belly.

"Ain't no car that can run on water," he said, holding his beverage to the side so that Molly could squeeze past.

"I wouldn't be so sure of that." Molly couldn't help herself.

She wasn't a big football fan, but an event of this magnitude in her own backyard was too large to delegate to another lawyer. The tickets were free, but bordered on being nose bleeders. The Justice Department always sent a representative to the Super Bowl, not only because of the large amount of criminal activity that always surrounded these events—counterfeiting, bogus game tickets—but also the very real potential for terrorist activity.

Molly fumbled for her phone while she watched a small army of federal agents escort Addy from the field while the players began trotting on for the second half. The restless crowd began to boo, then started chanting: Ad-DY, Ad-DY.

Peele quickly dialed Jesse's number, held her phone to her ear and plugged her other ear with her finger.

"You won't believe what I just saw," she nearly yelled over the chant of the crowd.

"And you won't believe what I just did," Long replied.

As she skipped down the stairs, she explained how Addy had somehow managed to bring a car onto the playing field at the end of Zissy's halftime show and claim it was running on water. She'd even posted the formula for everyone to see. The worst part was that Homeland Security chased her across field and then arrested her in front of a stadium full of people who were convinced Addy was telling the truth.

"They looked like imbeciles," she ranted. "I think they've got her in custody. I'm running down to the field right now."

"Why is DHS there?"

"Probably the same reason I'm here. We've got a major worldwide event going on. Someone probably called in a tip and they reacted without thinking."

Peele reached the concourse and began looking for a staircase that would take her to the field level. She tried to weave her way against the onslaught of human traffic as fans pressed towards the concession stands. "What have you got?" she asked.

"Two dead and two wounded."

Peele froze and pushed the phone hard against her ear. "Say that again?"

"Shaun Ritter, aka the tattoo man, and Jerry Wilcox. They're both dead."

"Wait, tell me more. What went down?"

"Let's just say there was quite a shootout. Felt like the Wild West."

"Did you shoot them?"

"Only Wilcox. Addy got Ritter herself. Looks like he broke his neck when she flung him from her semi."

Recovering from her shock, Peele resumed her march. "What semi?"

"Looks like the one she used to get the hydrogen car to the stadium."

"I'll be damned," Peele muttered. "Who's injured?"

"Quinn Moon and one of the other terrorists."

"Quinn?"

"He was with Addy." Long explained how he'd received the tip of Addy's whereabouts and how he'd rushed to find her.

"When I arrived, Addy had already fled, but she left Quinn behind as a hostage. When I stormed in, a bullet shattered my windshield, barely missing my head. I ducked and drew my weapon. After another shot tore through my headrest, I raised up and shot her in the right shoulder."

"Are you okay?"

"I'm fine, just a cut on my forehead when I bumped it rushing to get out of my car."

"What about Quinn?"

"He's fortunate that I got to him in time. Wilcox was standing over him with a gun to his head. Wilcox's eyes were like saucers and he was foaming at the mouth. He was screaming at Quinn and kicking him in the ribs. I raised my weapon and told him to drop his gun. He said he was going to kill Quinn for stealing his invention and that he didn't care what happened to him."

"So you shot him."

"I didn't have a choice."

"Who is the woman?"

"Good chance she was the one who held Addy while Ritter punched her."

"Any others?"

"If there were, they escaped. We're casting a wide net right now, but we don't have any good descriptions."

"Is Quinn going to make it?"

"He's in bad shape. Ritter and Wilcox beat him up pretty good. He's on his way to UCSF Medical Center."

Peele noticed a security guard and told Long to hang tight. She flashed her badge at the security guard. "I need an escort down to the field."

# 40

ALTHOUGH HER HANDS were still in cuffs, that didn't stop Addy from barking at the DHS agents, insisting that she be taken to Quinn. The Santa Clara sheriff had his hand held out, trying to calm Addy while he attempted to explain to a group of federal agents why Addy was so upset.

As Peele entered the tunnel, she noticed at least two cameras rolling, while several bystanders had their mobile phones raised, capturing the historic moment. In a matter of minutes, this confrontation would be all over YouTube.

Peele pushed her way through the circle of agents. "Okay, everyone stand down. DOJ is taking over. She's in my custody."

"Somebody please help," Addy insisted. "Quinn, he's being held hostage. They'll kill him if you don't do something now."

"Everything is going to be okay," Peele said in a calm voice as she approached Addy. "Quinn is alive, and he's in route to the hospital. If you'll consent to remaining in my custody, I'll escort you to the Medical Center. Agent Jesse Long will probably beat us there. He has plenty of questions for you."

"Let's hurry," Addy sobbed.

Peele waved to one of the agents. "Can you please get these cuffs off?"

While the handcuffs were being removed, Addy remembered her offer to show Hindy after the game.

Addy rubbed her wrists and looked up to Peele. "What about Hindy? I promised to show everyone."

Peele glanced sideways to see if any cameras were still capturing their conversation. Then she looked over at the car that was now surrounded by a team of federal agents. "We've got a string of homicides we're investigating, and that car is a crucial piece of evidence. As much as I would love you to show the world what's under that hood, that car isn't going anywhere until we've completed our investigation."

"Okay, let's go. I've got to see him."

* * *

Addy rushed through the emergency room doors with Peele right on her heels.

"Jesse's already got us a private waiting room," Peele said.

The intake administrator stood when she saw the two women and directed them to room 207 on the second floor. The pair exited the elevator and turned left, then down a hall until they reached the waiting room.

Peele pushed open the door. Long was already standing, his shoulder resting on the back wall. He flipped off the television that was blaring coverage of the day's sensational events.

"I wish you hadn't done that," he said, tossing the remote onto the couch.

"I didn't come here for a lecture. I want to know about Quinn," Addy wished her voice wasn't wobbling.

"What's the latest?" Peele asked calmly.

"Quinn's still in surgery. The back of his skull has a small fracture, and he almost certainly has a concussion, but they think he's going to be okay. They are doing surgery for the gunshot wound on his shoulder. It may be tomorrow before you can see him."

Peele waited a few minutes, letting the news sink in.

"I want to stay here until I can speak to him. I'm not leaving,"

Addy announced.

Long glared at Peele, figuring the duty would fall on him.

"That's fine, but you can't be alone," Peele said. "We'll need an agent to stay with you."

"We might as well get comfortable," Long said. "We have a lot to go over. Let's start with me telling you that you have a right to have an attorney present."

Addy took a deep breath and pressed down her grief. "You forget what happened to my attorney," she said abruptly. "Let's get this over with so I can go see Quinn."

Peele led Addy to the couch and both women sat. Long paced back and forth with his arms folded, deep in thought. Finally he stopped and looked at Addy.

"I think you need to understand our predicament. We had this crazy inventor who was convinced Quinn stole his idea. He made such a stink that Peele had to formally investigate his claims. Right in the middle of our investigation, you come along, and your login credentials are used to access the Department of Energy's patent applications. We wanted to keep all of this out of the public eye until we could sort out the allegations. Not to mention there are certain political reasons that we've been asked to look into this. But now the cat is out of the bag and we can't put it back in."

Addy raised her eyebrows and looked steadily at Peele.

"Unfortunately, Long is right. Your stunt is going to put a lot of people on the hot seat, including me," Peele said. "How did you possibly think that public opinion could prove your innocence?"

"What about the fact that you were suppressing Quinn's patents?"

"Just to make sure they didn't contain stolen technology," Peele said.

"But they didn't."

"If you believe Quinn," Long added.

"What about the information from his patents that ended up with the Department of Energy?"

"That's what he claims," Long continued.

"I believe him, for some strange reason. Maybe I shouldn't, but I do. And you know what ultimately convinced me?"

Long shrugged.

"When Quinn jumped down from the semi and single-handedly took on those assholes."

Long raised his brows.

"You know who they are, don't you?" Addy probed.

"I shouldn't tell, but I suppose it will be on the news soon enough."

"Well?"

"The mastermind behind your attacks is a man named Jerry Wilcox. I've mentioned him before."

Addy remembered the name. He was the crazed inventor who claimed that Quinn stole his ideas while Quinn was working for HydroGen. Wilcox was the fourth assailant from of the black Suburban. She'd nearly struck him and the woman when she crashed her way out of the barricade.

"Where is he?" Addy said.

"Probably in the morgue."

"Are you sure?"

"You're looking at the agent who shot him."

"Wait, you're the one who saved Quinn?"

"Yes, I got there just in time. Your taxi driver happened to recognize you. And good thing I live close, otherwise I would have never made it in time."

"Well, I guess I should thank you for that," Addy conceded. "But you need to know that Quinn didn't steal his idea. Wilcox doesn't even have any patents. He couldn't make the technology work. That's why the patent office was looking at Quinn's patent applications—because Quinn was the one who figured it out."

"That will all be part of the investigation," Long said.

"And Wilcox went rogue when you couldn't stop him and decided to do it himself."

"Quinn didn't help his case when he hired you to hack into Wilcox's patents," Long reminded her.

"Sung-soo," she corrected him. "It was Sung-soo who used my login."

"You can see my dilemma. I have two inventors who claimed to have invented the same thing. And one of them thinks the other stole it. Add to all this a government who isn't ready for the next big thing. Oil is big business."

This time Peele glared at Long.

"And in the meantime, nobody gets the technology," Addy said.

"You see the issue."

"And now you can see why I revealed the secret to the biggest audience possible."

Peele put her hand on Addy's knee. "We're not getting anywhere with this. Why don't we all take a deep breath and relax for a bit?"

Addy wasn't ready to relax. "What about the other terrorists? The man with the tattoo? Did he kill Perry and Johnston?"

Long held up his hands. "Slow down a bit. I can tell you that his neck was broken. He won't hurt you again."

Addy remembered the image of the man flying through the air when she'd crashed the semi into the Suburban. "Serves him right. Did he kill Perry?"

"That's what we're going with right now. Wilcox may well have hired him and a team of terrorists to make sure you and Quinn didn't succeed."

"Well, they didn't manage it."

Partially satisfied with their explanations and completely exhausted, Addy allowed herself to fall back into the soft embrace of the couch. She could feel herself fading.

"Now maybe we can all work together," she said as her eyes closed.

# 41

ADDY SLEPT UNDISTURBED until morning, when the surgeon gently knocked on the door and Agent Long jumped out of his slumber and answered.

The surgeon was still in his teal green scrubs with surgical cap covering his head. Addy snapped to attention and began rubbing the sleep out of her eyes.

"Addy?" he said, holding out his hand. "I'm Dr. Scott." He took Addy's hand in his own, immediately noticing the swelling.

"Quinn, how is he?"

"This needs some attention," he said, gently rubbing his finger over the bump.

"Never mind that. Tell me about Quinn."

The doctor shook his head and grinned. "You're tough as nails. I'll give you an update, but then you're coming with me. We're giving that an X-ray."

"Fine," Addy said.

"It's all good news, considering." Dr. Scott folded his arms. "Quinn is conscious and in stable condition, but he's in no condition to be seen, so please don't ask. I'll personally let you know when I think he's okay to have visitors."

He confirmed that the skull fracture was not serious, but Quinn would be in pain for some time. His head was heavily bandaged, and he was suffering from severe headaches. As for his shoulder, the bullet had missed the joint, but had torn through muscle and ligaments. He should eventually have full use of his arm, but he'd need months of physical therapy.

"All in all, good news for what could easily have been a fatality."

She reached out and hugged the surgeon. "Thank you. Let's go look at my hand."

\* \* \*

The moment she saw Quinn, Addy rushed to his side, taking his hand in hers, ignoring that one was freshly plastered.

"Thanks for coming," Quinn whispered. "We've got to quit meeting in hospitals."

She rubbed his cheek. "This will be the last one."

"Tell me about the Super Bowl," he said, then closed his eyes.

Addy told him everything, from the wailing horn outside the stadium to the agents chasing her across the field. "Zissy was great. We couldn't have done it without her. And the formula was plastered right on the giant screen. You couldn't miss it. I told everyone that your invention was being dedicated to them, to the world. Our secret is out!"

Quinn's eyes cracked open and she swore she saw a hint of a twinkle. "Aren't you going to ask me about my day?" Quinn said.

"Are you sure you're up to it?"

"I've got to tell someone," he said through a slight smile. "I told you Wilcox was crazy. He kept demanding that I give him the catalyst—and the credit. When I refused to answer him, he kept cracking my skull and punching me in the stomach. Now I know how you must have felt."

Quinn paused and squeezed his eyes shut.

"That's enough. Get some rest," Addy demanded.

"I'm okay," he said. "I thought it was all over, but then Wilcox demanded I send you a message to see if I could stop you. I kept praying someone would find me. Then you called and bought me more time. When I told you to go ahead with the commercial, he started beating me again. Then he pulled out his gun and said it was all over. That's when Agent Long arrived."

"We got lucky. The taxi driver ratted on us. Turns out that saved your life."

"What happened to the others?"

Addy explained how the man with the tattoo was a hired gun and got what he deserved. "I think that's enough for now. You need to rest."

* * *

Addy returned the next day to find Quinn chatting with one of the nurses. A tray with scraps of scrambled eggs and toast was pushed off to the side of the bed.

"I forgot to ask you," he said when she entered, carrying an armful of flowers. "Have you heard anything from your stepmother?"

Addy sat beside him. "Oh yeah, I didn't tell you. We spoke this morning. She said she is so proud of me for what I did. I'm going to visit next week."

"That's fantastic," Quinn said, taking her cast in his hand. "My father—"

"I'm sorry," Addy said.

"No, it's all good. His plane is already in the air. I'm not sure what he's going to say, but at least he's coming. That's a start."

"I'm happy for you."

"Hopefully I'll be out of prison when he comes."

"Stop it," Addy said. "You can't be worrying about that, especially not until you get healthy."

"Can you blame me? And, you're forgetting that I still owe my investors a ton of money. I just gave away my invention."

Addy stood and rested her hands on her hips. "If you keep talking like that, I'm leaving. It's all going to work out. The Patent Office has already posted a notice on its web page officially halting the secret suppression program. There's so much chatter on the social media sites that the government would be crazy to prosecute you."

"Then what next?"

"Trust me."

# 42

ADDY'S BANDAGED HAND contrasted sharply with her black dress. Perry's graveside service was somber yet uplifting.

Right before the service began, Lynda and Addy's two stepsiblings, Billy and Cassandra, had sneaked into the back pew. Addy noticed them when she looked over her shoulder after Pingree had commented on the vast number of mourners in attendance. Lynda smiled and waved. Addy smiled and patted her chest, her heart full. She finally had a family.

Addy gave the closing remarks, reminding everyone how much Perry missed his wife after her passing, and revealing that he'd sacrificed all his assets to pay for the Super Bowl commercial.

If it weren't for Perry's patience and sacrifice, she reminded them, Hindy would never have made her maiden voyage.

Beneath a large oak tree, Addy, along with her former Wyckoff partners, tried to make sense of the previous week's events. Bob Pingree, Wyckoff's managing partner, fidgeted with the change in his pockets. His fleshy cheeks drooped, as did his bloodshot eyes. "Water to Gold," he repeated. "I still don't understand how you two got mixed up in this mess."

Addy had already explained it more times than she cared to count. But these were Perry's partners, and for him she would rehash the story one more time.

"It turns out that Quinn and WTG really did invent a technology that could efficiently extract hydrogen from water—and the catalyst was central to that technology. The problem was that Quinn began his career working for Jerry Wilcox who had his own program with the Department of Energy. When Quinn left, Jerry was convinced that Quinn stole his ideas."

"Sounds similar to the race to develop the atomic bomb during World War II," Pingree said. "But this time it was Korea versus the United States."

"In a way," Addy said. "The difference is that with the race to develop a hydrogen fuel cell, the US wanted to stall its development. In order to protect its heavy investment in fossil fuels, the DOE had tried to keep the technology hidden, at least for another decade, until the US investment in big oil had paid off."

"And that included trying to stop Quinn."

"Yes, and Wilcox added fuel to the fire. He ran to the Justice Department with his accusations. That was all the Justice Department needed to employ their resources to stop Quinn."

"What I can't believe," Pingree said, "was that the Patent Office actually had a program to suppress Quinn's patent applications. Our own government!"

"That's why Quinn hired me," Addy said.

"He picked the best. If anyone could get WTG's applications granted as patents, it would be you."

"But Quinn's strategy backfired. He didn't know that others at WTG felt entitled to spy on the US and troll for ideas in the DOE patent applications—using my login credentials."

"And that's what got you arrested."

Addy nodded.

"So what about this radical Muslim group we heard about?" Pingree asked.

"That was all Wilcox. He'd heard rumors that Quinn's catalyst was nearing perfection, and so Wilcox decided to take matters into his own hands. He hired a hitman, Shaun Ritter, who had taken the name of Azhar Nejem. It was the perfect solution to

Wilcox's problem. He counted on having US law enforcement and justice groups believe that a radical Muslim group would do anything to protect the oil economies of the Middle East."

"But it was really all a disgruntled American inventor," Pingree said.

"I'm afraid so. Wilcox was responsible for the death of both Examiner Johnston and Perry."

Pingree moved closer to put his arm around her and pull her close. "I'm so sorry. Is there anything we can do for you?"

She nodded. "Thanks, but I think I'm okay. They are going to drop all charges against me. The Justice Department was so embarrassed that the Patent Office had been suppressing WTG's technology that they decided to leave me alone rather than trying to explain what they had been doing to a judge. And it goes without saying that I couldn't possibly have murdered Johnston or Perry."

"You know you're always welcome to come back to Wyckoff," Pingree offered. "We need a partner to take over Perry's clients. He would have wanted that."

"I'll think about it," Addy said. "I'm going to need a few weeks off to rethink my life. I love being a lawyer, but something tells me I need to see this Hindy project through to the end."

"You could do both," Pingree said.

Addy smiled. The offer was tempting but unrealistic. Both were more than full-time jobs. "I'll let you know."

The group turned to remembering their happy times with Perry and Keri, trying to make it a day of celebration rather than mourning. Later, in small, murmuring groups, they got in their cars and drove away.

On the way to her own car, Addy noticed a familiar figure wearing a straight black dress lurking the shadows. Hesitantly, the woman emerged and walked toward Addy. It was Janice.

"I know you probably don't want to talk to me," Janice began, "but there are some things I need to tell you."

"This probably isn't the best place," Addy said.

"I understand, but I need to tell you this before I lose my nerve. I'm so sorry. I never meant any of this to happen."

"Well, it did," Addy said peering at Perry's casket, still perched above the freshly dug grave. "And you helped it."

"I admit that what I did was wrong, and I want to apologize. I let WTG suck me in, and that was wrong."

Addy was ready to stop her, but decided she wanted to hear Janice's story. She let her continue.

"When you and Quinn had the interview with Examiner Johnston, everyone at WTG freaked out when they learned that you'd been arrested. Sung-soo was bouncing around the office like a pinball machine, tearing apart the network like a tidal wave was ready to strike the office. I was scared about what was going to happen to me and my daughter. I was afraid I wasn't going to have enough money to take care of my baby. It was clear I was going to lose my job, and I was afraid that after your arrest there was no way any law firm in town would touch me.

"When I asked Sung-soo what was happening, he told me that I needed to speak with Jeyhu. Together, we called Korea, and Jeyhu told me I could either be fired or I could get a year's salary as a bonus if I would stay one more month and help them with a special project."

"Special project?"

"You were the only person outside of WTG who knew the technology. They were worried that you were going to do something vindictive. They wanted me to help them stop you."

Janice wiped away a tear.

"I had nowhere to turn. I was out of options. I was desperate."

Addy waited while Janice composed herself.

"I didn't realize Wyckoff had already decided to take me back until I was already committed. When I did get my job back, Jeyhu threatened me if I didn't follow through for WTG.

"I'm sorry I gave you a fake bank account to wire the money for the commercial. When Jeyhu discovered that Quinn was communicating with you, he feared Quinn was helping you with your plan. Jeyhu was doing everything he could to stop you."

"Did WTG send that laundry truck to the football stadium?"

For the first time Janice let a small smile lighten her expression. "It was all Jeyhu could think of. Nobody at WTG thought you'd get that far.

"I also want to remind you that I'm not all bad. I gave you the Freedom of Information papers because I hoped you could get the Patent Office to let Quinn's patents through."

*But only because WTG still owned the patents*, Addy thought.

"And I honestly didn't know WTG was hacking the PTO database until after you were arrested."

Addy had heard enough. "Well, thanks for the apology, but I need to get going. My family is waiting for me."

# Epilogue

"So tell us how you came up with the name for your new company," said Bryant Rose, the host of the *Today Show*.

"H?" Addy said with a grin.

She was seated next to Quinn in an elevated director's chair in front of her new nonprofit located in Mountain View. The morning California sun was just beginning to peek over the horizon. Today the doors officially opened for business.

"I love its simplicity. H is the periodic element for hydrogen, which is what our new nonprofit is all about."

"Well, your adventure to get you here was anything but simple," Bryant said. "Halftime at the Super Bowl will never be the same."

"I'm so thankful that Zissy offered to share the stage," Addy said. "Without her, I don't think we'd be here right now."

The camera panned back to Bryant. "Before we get to the question on everyone's mind, Quinn, tell us how you're feeling."

"Fine, probably better than an NFL linebacker after the Super Bowl," he said, rubbing the back of his head. "There won't be much tennis in my future, but at least I'm alive. Thank goodness Agent Long found me in time."

"We all know that you've both had some legal issues," Bryant said, moving along the interview. "Where do those stand?"

Quinn looked at Addy. "You're the lawyer. I think you should comment."

"After the dust settled, I think it was clear that I hadn't violated any laws. All charges against me have been dropped. As for Quinn, none were ever filed, and because of his generous donation—and the death of his main accuser—I think it is unlikely that the Justice Department would be interested in pursuing a case."

Bryant nodded in agreement. "Before we get to the matter at hand, I wanted to express my condolences for the death of your former partner."

"Perry was quite the man," Addy said. "He gave everything to make sure this technology became public. Thank you for remembering him."

Bryant paused for a brief moment of silence. "I guess that brings us to what we all want to know—tell us when we'll all be driving cars that run on water."

"Hopefully soon," Addy began. "The support for H, Incorporated, has been overwhelming. We have executives from all over the world who are lending their support, as well as scientists and engineers. We've raised enough money to develop three prototypes, and plan to build production lines as soon as the designs are finalized. Even the President has pledged his support."

Quinn reached out and put his hand on Addy's knee. "And I've got a surprise for you."

Addy's eyes twinkled with excitement.

"My former company, WTG, has been meeting with the Department of Energy, and they've finally reached an agreement. All of the intellectual property for both entities is going to be donated to H, and I personally want to invite anyone else who is working on other solutions to produce hydrogen to do the same. As Addy announced during the Super Bowl, we want to make this technology affordable for everyone, and get rid of all possible legal barriers."

Addy reached down and grabbed his hand. Her cast was now gone and she squeezed his fingers tight.

"Before you two get mushy on us," Bryant said. "We also have a special gift. Quinn, you've made quite the sacrifice in donating your technology, and you've inspired us here at the network to follow your example. So, we'd like to make a little donation. I'm not sure everyone knows, but Addy's former partner, Perry, gave nearly everything he owned before his untimely death to enable Addy to purchase her Super Bowl commercial. Well, we just didn't feel right about keeping that money."

Bryant waved, and an assistant trotted over and handed him an oversized check. "The network is donating all of it to H, and we're also going to do a special the day your first car comes off the production line. We also learned that there aren't many female patent attorneys. To help change that, we are setting up a scholarship fund in Perry's name to cover law school tuition for female engineers wanting to become patent attorneys."

Addy's mouth hung open and both hands flew up to cover her surprise. "I don't know what to say," she said when she recovered. "I'm so glad you didn't forget about Perry."

"Now, before we go," Bryant said, "we have one final surprise for both of you. Quinn, there's a vacant chair next to you for a reason. We have a special guest."

Addy looked to her right, just as the famous Super Bowl performer emerged. "Zissy!" she said, hopping down and throwing her arms around the singer. Quinn stood as well and kissed her cheek.

Zissy slid onto her chair and crossed her legs. "Look at all this," she said, opening her arms to encompass the new facility. "You did it!"

"And we have you to thank," Quinn said. "Sorry I missed your halftime performance."

Zissy shook her finger at him. "I think you're excused. And I also have a little present." Zissy reached down her blouse and emerged with a folded piece of paper. "I told Addy that when your cars start rolling off the line, I'm going to be your first customer. And here's a check for fifty thousand dollars as my deposit."

Addy opened the check and smiled. "I think I can make that happen."

Quinn placed his arm around her shoulder and pulled Addy tight.

"You two are looking very comfortable together," Bryant said. "Anything you want to share with us before we go?"

Addy and Quinn gazed into each other's eyes. "No," Addy responded. "That's the one thing we won't discuss."

# Acknowledgments

Over the past fifteen years that it took to write this book, there have been too many people to mention all of them by name. But I would like to thank T.J. Izzo, a long-time client and inventor of the double strap golf bag, for encouraging me to give the manuscript one more try and to use a patent attorney as the main character. That was the missing link that seemed to be eluding me. With that piece in place, I decided to discard all of my previous manuscripts and start from scratch. *Chasing Hindy* emerged a few months later.